P9-CJX-587

THE SEPOY MUTINY

Historical Fiction Published by McBooks Press

J. A. Ball
Nov. 2006

The Sepoy Mutiny

V. A. STUART

The Alexander Sheridan Adventures, No. 2

McBooks Press
Ithaca, New York

Published by McBooks Press 2001
Copyright © 1964 by V. A. Stuart
First published as *Mutiny in Meerat* in Great Britain
by Robert Hale Limited, London 1974

All rights reserved, including the right to reproduce this book or
any portion thereof in any form or by any means, electronic or
mechanical, without the written permission of the publisher.
Requests for such permissions should be addressed to
McBooks Press, 120 West State Street, Ithaca, NY 14850.

Cover painting: *Charge of the 16th Queen's Own Lancers at the Battle of Aliwal,
1846* by Harry Martens. Courtesy of Musée des Beaux Arts, Caen, France;
UK/Bridgeman Art Library.

Frontispiece: from *Gardiner's School Atlas of English History,* London, 1891.

Library of Congress Cataloging-in-Publication Data
Stuart, V.A.
    The Sepoy mutiny. / by V.A. Stuart.
        p. cm. — (Military Fiction Classics)
    ISBN 0-935526-99-4 (alk. paper)
    1. India—History—Sepoy Rebellion, 1857-1858—Fiction. 1. Great
Britain—History, Military—19th century—Fiction. 2. Great
Britain—History—Victoria, 1837-1901—Fiction.   I. Title
PR6063.A38 S4 2001
823'.914—dc21   2001045239

Distributed to the book trade by
LPC Group, 1436 West Randolph, Chicago, IL 60607
800-626-4330.

Additional copies of this book may be ordered
from any bookstore or directly from
McBooks Press, 120 West State Street, Ithaca, NY 14850.
Please include $3.50 postage and handling with mail orders.
New York State residents must add sales tax.
All McBooks Press publications can also be ordered by calling
toll-free 1-888-BOOKS11 (1-888-266-5711).
Please call to request a free catalog.

Visit the McBooks Press website at www.mcbooks.com.

Printed in the United States of America

9 8 7 6 5 4 3 2 1

PROLOGUE

➻➻➻ • ⇜⇜⇜

THE INDIAN LEADER spoke aloud, but Alex Sheridan had heard such words before, always whispered, passed in secret from man to man—not intended for English ears.

"I tell you truly, Sheridan Sahib, the days of the Company are numbered. Is it not written that John Company will endure for only one hundred years after Plassey, due to fall next month? It is the will of Allah, that all the *feringhi* shall be ground into dust. None shall escape from the vengeful swords of the True Believers—men, women, even little children, all will die! *In'sha Illah.* . . ." Carried away by his own eloquence, the Moulvi talked on, his voice raised, careless of who might hear him.

"The times change," he went on. "Now it is our turn. We shall throw off the shackles of servitude and all Hind will follow our example, religious differences forgotten. When the hour comes, we shall kill for the Faith—we shall restore our king. You British are too few to stand in our way. No man can know the exact hour of his death. But I will tell you this, Sheridan Sahib—you will be dead within a few hours of the dawn of *that* day!"

For a *Glossary of Indian Terms* see page 227, and for *Historical Notes* on the Mutiny, see page 230.

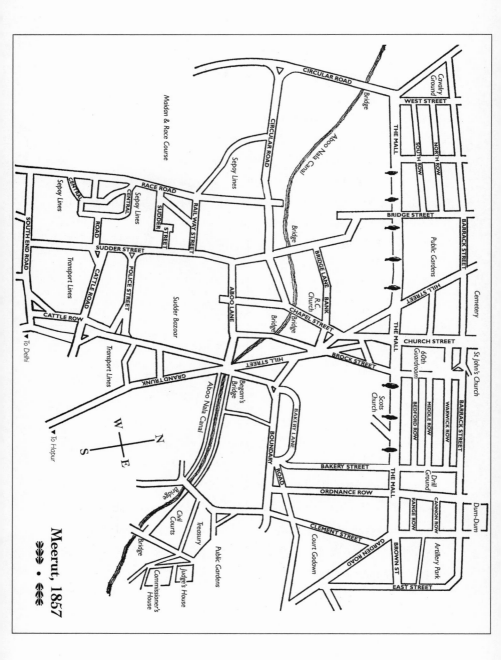

Meerut, 1857

CHAPTER ONE

➤➤➤ • ⋘⋘⋘

"SAHIB!" A hand grasped his shoulder, shaking it gently, and Alex Sheridan sat up, taut nerves jerking him to instant wakefulness. Then, remembering where he was, he let himself relax. "Is it time, Partap Singh?"

"It wants an hour to dawn, Sahib," his Sikh orderly told him in a sibilant whisper. "There is tea, as you commanded, awaiting you and shaving water also in the *ghusl-khana.*"

He withdrew as silently as he had entered the bedroom and Alex rose, careful not to disturb his wife, still sleeping peacefully in the bed beside his own. Anxious to let her sleep for as long as possible and thus postpone—for her, at least—the agony of parting, he picked up the oil lamp his orderly had brought for him to dress by and carried it into the adjoining bathroom. He gulped down two cups of milkless tea as he shaved, finding the task as irksome and difficult with his left hand as he always did, yet persisting with it—again as he always did—obstinately determined to overcome the disability which had resulted from the loss of his right arm at the elbow.

He had lost the arm two and a half years ago, in the Crimea, when a Cossack sabre had all but severed it in the shambles which had followed the Light Cavalry Brigade's charge at Balaclava. He bared his teeth in a mirthless smile, mocking his image in the mirror propped up in front of him.

Who was he to complain of the loss of an arm, when over two hundred and forty of the six hundred men who had charged the Russian guns with him had failed to return from what had since been called "The Valley of Death," he asked himself grimly.

For God's sake, he was one of the fortunate few! In any case, he had learned to do most things with his left hand now and with reasonable efficiency—he could ride a horse, write a fair letter, fire a pistol, dress himself. Shaving was the only task that caused him the slightest trouble and Emmy, bless her, aware of his difficulty, often performed it for him. No doubt she would reproach him, when she wakened, for not having called her so that she might do so today but . . . Alex swore softly, feeling the blade nick his cheek.

There was a muffled sound from the room he had left and he heard Emmy call his name. Her voice held an underlying note of fear as if, glimpsing his empty bed, she sought to reassure herself that he was still there. Before he could call out to stop her, she came running to him in her bare feet, without waiting to don a dressing gown over her thin muslin nightdress.

"Oh, Alex! I thought, I was afraid—"

"That I would attempt to slip away without bidding you farewell?" he accused, setting down the bloodied razor.

She clung to him, hiding her face against his chest.

"Well, yes. To spare me the pain of watching you go."

He caught her to him hungrily, conscious of the swelling contours of her slim body as it pressed against his own. The child they both wanted so much was not due for another two months and he wondered how long it would be before he saw his firstborn. Certainly he would not be with her when her time came; if that which he feared happened and the Bengal army rose up in open mutiny, it might well be six months or a year before he could hope to make the journey to Calcutta to join her. But it was best that she should go there; she would be safe in Calcutta with her sister and brother-in-law.

As if guessing his thoughts, Emmy raised her small, elfin face to his and asked, her tone flat and devoid of hope, "I suppose it is no use begging you to change your mind at this late hour?"

Alex shook his head. "Darling, I dare not—for your sake and the child's. You *must* go. Harry's appointment to the Bodyguard will come through in a few days and *he'll* have to go . . . I want you to travel with him, with Anne to look after you. It's a devilishly trying journey at the best of times, as you very well know, but at least with them, you'll travel in more comfort than I'd be able to provide. The steamer will take you to Benares and it will only be by *dak* from there to the railhead. You—"

"I know, I know," she interrupted, with weary impatience. "We've been through it all so many times. I know it is the sensible thing to do—but when was I ever sensible, Alex?"

"Very seldom," he agreed, laughing. "You have never grown up, my love, and I doubt if you ever will! Not that I would have you any different." He smiled down at her tenderly and then spun her around, sending her from him with a playful but admonitory tap on her rounded, thinly clad rump. "Back to bed with you now and let me finish shaving. It's bad for that child of yours to stand here without a wrap or slippers. There's tea still left in the pot—I'll carry the tray in for you."

Emmy did not respond to his attempt at jocularity, but she obediently went back to bed, carrying the tea-tray herself. When, booted and spurred but still in his shirtsleeves, Alex rejoined her, he saw with concern that the tea stood untouched and that she was weeping silently, her head buried in her two outstretched hands and her shoulders shaking.

"Oh, come now, darling, this isn't like you." He went to her, smoothing the ruffled dark hair which cascaded over her face.

"You mustn't take it so hard. We've been parted before and I've always come back to you. I shan't stay away an instant longer than I must, believe me, dearest, because this time it will not only be you I'll be coming back to, it will be the child—*our* child—as well, Emmy. Don't you realize that I—"

She cut him short. "I think I almost hate the child," she told him fiercely. "It is on the child's account that I must leave you. If there had been no child you—"

"Darling, I should still have jumped at the chance of your going to Calcutta with Anne and Harry," Alex answered gravely. "This is a serious situation and, when it comes to a head—as I fear it must—it will be dangerous. I shudder to think *how* dangerous for those who cannot defend themselves."

"But you would have let me stay if you had still been in Adjodhabad," Emmy persisted, her tear-bright eyes reproaching him.

Perhaps he would, Alex thought, because in Adjodhabad he would have been in a position to take effective action to avert the danger. As district commissioner, he would have had the power to compel even men as blind and pig-headed as old Colonel Chalmers to disarm his recalcitrant sowars before the plots they were hatching had had time to come to fruition. But it had, of course, been on this account that he had been relieved of his post; "Bay" Chalmers had influence in high places and he had used it, in order to save his beloved regiment from what he conceived to be the ultimate dishonor. Even when offered proof that his men were intriguing with the *fakirs* who visited them secretly, Colonel Chalmers had refused to listen . . . and there were others like him. There were far too many others, in the Army of Bengal, for any attempt to be made to avert disaster until it was too late. He smothered a sigh as Emmy went on,

"Other women aren't being sent away. The wives here in Cawnpore are remaining with their husbands—even those who are pregnant and it's the same in Lucknow and most of the other stations, I've been told. Very few have gone or are thinking of going and, naturally, they are keeping their children with them. They're not afraid or—"

"More's the pity," Alex said, with genuine regret. "Because if the sepoys rise, they may impede their husbands more than they will help them. No fighting man can give of his best when there are women and children to be considered—that has been proved, time and again."

"Perhaps so, but"—Emmy remained unconvinced—"you cannot be sure that the sepoys *will* rise."

"Every scrap of evidence points to it, Emmy."

"I know that some of the regiments are disaffected," she conceded. "But only a few and surely they can be disbanded and sent back to their villages, like the 19th were? And if, as they say he has, Lord Canning has ordered those wretched greased cartridges to be withdrawn, what reason can the sepoys have to mutiny?"

"Reasons for revolt are still not lacking," Alex told her. "In any case, the cartridges were more a means to an end than a reason—an excuse to stir up trouble, their importance deliberately exaggerated by . . ." he broke off, reluctant to tell her too much, and reached for his jacket. "Time's marching on, my love."

"But, Alex . . ." Emmy caught at his arm. "Every officer I've spoken to here has assured me that his men are loyal, and General Wheeler says that it is wrong to show mistrust or to—"

"I heard what General Wheeler said," Alex put in, an edge to his voice. "The general has a Hindu wife and a misguided trust in the friendship of the Nana Sahib. I spent most of the evening listening to his views and I can only tell you that I wish to heaven

I could share his confidence. Alas, I cannot. The Nana has no love for us—he's bitterly resentful because the Company refused him a pension when his adoptive father died."

"Why did they refuse him?"

"Probably to save money, darling." Alex spoke dryly. "The official reason is because Baji Rao had no legitimate son to succeed him. The Nana—his real name is Dundoo Punth—was adopted, and the Company lawyers decreed that he had no right to the pension which Baji Rao enjoyed or to the title of Peishwa."

"But he *is* a maharajah, is he not?" Emmy questioned uncertainly. "They speak of him as such."

Alex shrugged. Thinking to distract her from the grief of parting, he went into details. "Oh, he calls himself the Maharajah of Bithur but he has no legitimate claim to that title either, although he did inherit his adoptive father's personal fortune—which was considerable—and the palace of Bithur. Rumor has it that he's now heavily in debt and in the hands of the money-lenders. Small wonder, considering the state in which he lives, with his own army and some fifteen thousand retainers to support! And he entertains the garrison right royally, I'm told, giving dinners and hunting parties and picnics, as well as presents of silks and jewels to the officers' ladies. The general is a frequent guest at the palace and, as I said, trusts him implicitly."

"But surely he's trying to be friendly," Emmy defended. "Yet you condemn him for it. Would you rather he exhibited hostility towards the garrison?"

"Yes, in his case, I think I would. The Nana is a Mahratta, you see, and—"

"What difference does that make?"

Alex completed the buttoning of his stable-jacket and came to sit on the edge of the bed. "All the Mahrattas, as Sir Henry

Lawrence once said, are adept at deceit, my love. It's part of their character and they are most to be feared when—like the Greeks—they come bearing gifts and professing friendship. Yet General Wheeler told me, quite seriously, last night that if his native regiments *do* give trouble, he intends to appeal to the Nana Sahib for aid. He intends to guard the Magazine and the Treasury with men of the Nana's bodyguard and, if he deems it necessary, to confide the British women and children to his care at Bithur! If that is not an act of madness, then I do not know what is—as well let a pack of wolves into a sheepfold as place such an opportunity in the Nana's reach!"

"Not everyone thinks as you do, Alex," his wife said, a catch in her voice. "You know what they called you in Adjodhabad, do you not?"

"I could hardly help knowing, when I was called a fearmonger to my face!" Alex answered harshly. "I had hoped, though, that they might have spared *you* their opinion of me." Seeing the pain in Emmy's dark eyes, he took her hand in his and asked gently, "Which of them told you?"

She looked down at their two linked hands, avoiding his gaze. "Most of the wives, at some time or other . . . and Colonel Chalmers lectured me once concerning your—your attitude to the tired and trusted sowars of his regiment. I suppose he hoped that I might try to change your attitude."

"But you didn't try, did you?"

"Since you never discussed it with me," Emmy said, with a hint of bitterness, "I couldn't, could I?"

"Darling, I wanted to spare you," Alex began and was startled when she rounded on him, in a rare flash of temper.

"When did I ever ask you to spare me? We are husband and wife, Alex, and I . . . I love you! My place is by your side, not hundreds of miles away in Calcutta. Please, Alex, if you love me, don't send me away. I beg you to let me stay."

"But I cannot take you with me to Meerut," Alex protested, dismayed. "In your condition, my love, it is out of the question. For God's sake, it's two hundred and fifty miles and I shall be traveling light and fast, without tents or baggage camels. You—"

She silenced his protests, a finger pressed against his mouth. "I'm not asking to go with you to Meerut; I know that isn't possible. But it is by no means certain that you will have to go there, is it?"

Alex stared at her. "Not certain? My darling, I've been ordered to rejoin my regiment in Meerut—you know that. I *have* to go!"

"Your orders could be changed or revoked, could they not?"

"Of course they could, Emmy, if circumstances required it. You don't need me to tell you that."

"No," she acknowledged. "Alex, you intend to call on Sir Henry Lawrence in Lucknow on your way, do you not?"

"I told you I did—at his invitation. I imagine he wishes me to make my report on Adjodhabad to him in person and I shall welcome the opportunity because I—"

"Because," Emmy interrupted quickly, "you hope that he may offer to reinstate you in Adjodhabad or, failing that, perhaps, that he may give you another district in Oudh." It was more a statement of fact than a question and Alex reddened guiltily. He had been careful to make no mention of the reason for his visit to Sir Henry, to her or to anyone else, and he wondered how she had guessed the truth.

"What makes you think so?" he evaded.

"Oh, Alex my dearest, I know you! You cannot bear to leave a task unfinished and you feel a responsibility for the people in Adjodhabad in spite of everything that happened, in spite of what

they did to you. But why didn't you tell me? Were you afraid"
—her tone was accusing—"that I'd refuse to be packed off to
Calcutta if I knew that there was any chance of your staying in
Oudh?"

"Yes, I suppose I was," he confessed reluctantly. "And it is only
a faint chance, Emmy. Sir Henry may have no desire to avail himself of my services in Adjodhabad or anywhere else. I was not a
conspicuous success in the political service, was I? Sir Henry may
consider me fit only for regimental soldiering."

"He has sent for you, has he not?" Emmy countered. "And it
was Mr Jackson who had you relieved, not Sir Henry Lawrence.
Oh, please, Alex"—her eyes pleaded with him, suddenly filled
with hope, "if you are reinstated, won't you take me with you?"

Alex shook his head and saw the newly kindled hope in her
eyes fade into despair. "I'm sorry, darling, I dare not take the risk.
If there were no alternative, I should have to but Harry has offered
an alternative and—"

"And there is the child," she finished for him, her lower lip
trembling. "Well, if you will not take me with you, could I not
stay here, where at least I should be nearer you?"

"Stay in Cawnpore—under the Nana Sahib's protection?" Alex
recoiled in horror. "No! In God's name, no, Emmy—that is quite
out of the question."

"Then in Lucknow—Doctor and Mrs Fayrer would offer me
hospitality, I am sure, if you asked them, or the Polehamptons.
And there are British troops in Lucknow, a whole regiment of
them. Alex, I beg you!"

He almost weakened—it went against the grain to refuse her
anything—but finally he repeated his headshake, unable to trust
himself to speak. If the nightmare fears which had haunted him
for so long became reality, there would be few places in Oudh

where any white woman would be safe, for Oudh, he knew, would be the center of the revolt—if, indeed, it were not the cause of the outbreak. The sepoys of Oudh, scattered throughout the length and breadth of Northern India and laboring under a bitter sense of injustice since the annexation of their ancient kingdom, were the ones from whom the spirit of sedition had sprung. It was they who plotted betrayal, they who whispered of treason to their less volatile comrades and it seemed logical, therefore, that when the blow fell, it would fall first in Oudh.

Emmy expelled her breath in a quick, unhappy sigh and Alex braced himself but, to his heartfelt relief, she did not argue. "At least," she said tonelessly, "send me a message, after you have seen Sir Henry, so that I shall know whether or not you will be returning to Adjodhabad."

"Of course I will, darling." He rose, to stand looking down at her uneasily, puzzled by her unexpected capitulation. Emmy, for all her youth, had a mind of her own and more than her fair share of courage and determination; she was a dutiful and devoted wife but she did not always obey him if she considered it in his best interests not to do so. Remembering how she had braved the perils of the filthy, cholera-infested wards of the barracks hospital at Scutari—and the wrath of the formidable Dr Menzies—in order to nurse him when, more dead than alive, he had been brought back from Balaclava, he said sternly, "Emmy, I want you to promise me that, when Harry's orders come through, you will go with him to Calcutta. There's to be no delay, whatever may be the result of my interview with Sir Henry. Come, my love— I've a long ride ahead of me and it's time I left."

Emmy met his gaze stonily. "Don't you trust me?"

He sighed. "Darling, I dare not . . . for I know you too, don't forget. And it *is* for the best, believe me it is. I shall have no peace of mind until I know that you are safe in Calcutta, so please— give me your word that you'll go."

She bowed her head, valiantly fighting against her tears. "If it means so much to you, Alex, then you have my word. I'll leave when Harry's orders come. It will break my heart but if it is what you truly wish—"

"It is, dearest Emmy, although it breaks my heart too." He bent, drawing her to him, his mouth seeking hers, and felt her arms go round his neck. "I want this parting as little as you do," he told her huskily, freeing himself at last. "But for the sake of the child you carry, for the sake of our son, my love, we have to endure it. God bless you and keep you, Emmy, until we meet again."

"And you, Alex, and you . . ." her voice was choked with sobs. "Promise that you—that you will come back to me, darling, wherever I am and . . . however long it may be."

"I promise." Alex straightened, his throat tight. He tucked the bedclothes about her and, pausing only to take his pistol from the drawer in which he had placed it, made for the curtained door-way. "*Au revoir*, my love."

"Good-bye, Alex." Her voice was a faint whisper of sound, barely audible above the rhythmic creak of the *punkah* as it swung to and fro above his head. He closed the curtain behind him, willing himself not to look back. Outside, in the shadow of the pillared veranda, his small escort waited—Partap Singh, his orderly, and the two *syces*, squatting in the dust beside the laden baggage ponies.

His white-bearded bearer, Mohammed Bux, raised the hurri-cane lantern he was holding to light him on his way and salaamed respectfully. Alex laid his hand briefly on the old servant's bowed shoulder and said, in Hindustani, "I leave the memsahib in your care. Guard her well, Mohammed Bux."

"Ji-han, huzoor. Khuda hafiz!"

"As salaam aleikum!" Alex responded and, assisted by one of the *syces,* swung himself into the saddle of his powerful, seventeen-hand black Arabian mount, Sultan. The first pale light of dawn was tinging the eastern sky as he led the way out of the compound at a brisk trot and headed in the direction of the river along a road of hardbaked earth. Soon the rows of white-painted bungalows occupied by the British officers of the garrison were left behind and he glimpsed the lights of the native city in the distance, its teeming population of some sixty thousand already waking to life. A number, early risers, were like himself making for the river, most of them devout Hindus, preparing to perform their ritual ablutions in the sacred waters of the Ganges before the day's toil began.

"Sahib—" Partap Singh offered a low-voiced warning. "See who comes!"

Alex followed the direction of his orderly's pointing finger. There was a *doolie* approaching, borne at a rapid jog-trot by four bearers, and evidently coming from the native lines on the southeast side of the city. As it descended to the bridge of boats leading to the Lucknow road he saw and recognized its occupant with a swiftly suppressed gasp of dismay. So someone—heaven knew who—had released Ahmad Ullah, the Moulvi of Fyzabad, from prison, he thought and, touching Sultan with his spurs, he cantered over, just as the curtains of the *doolie* were hurriedly drawn across. The Moulvi was a noted troublemaker and, for several months prior to his arrest, he had traveled from city to city, preaching holy war against the infidel British and sowing sedition in the minds of those citizens and *zamindars* of Oudh who were followers of the Prophet.

Since Cawnpore was predominantly Hindu, it seemed logical to suppose that Ahmad Ullah's visit had been to the lines of the 2nd Native Cavalry and Alex glanced about him for some evidence of this, finding it in the presence of half a dozen sowars, in white undress uniform, who were hovering watchfully on the edge of a crowd of Hindu bathers on the *ghaut* fifty yards below him.

"Salaam, Moulvi Sahib!" he greeted, reining in beside the litter. "I had not expected to see you at liberty again so soon." His tone was deliberately curt but he used the polite Urdu form of address and the curtain was drawn back.

"*Salaam O aleikum!*" Ahmad Ullah responded smoothly. "And I had not expected to see you, Sheridan Sahib. Indeed, I had heard . . ." he coughed, as if to cover a simulated embarrassment, the dark, intelligent eyes gleaming with malice, "I had heard a rumor, no doubt false, that you had ceased to hold the reins of government in Adjodhabad." He barked a command and the litter bearers halted to enable him to alight. He stood, a tall, commanding figure in his flowing white robes and immaculately wound green turban, fingering the *tulwar* at his side, his beetling dark brows raised in mute and faintly insolent question.

"You heard truly," Alex acknowledged, hard put to it to hide the intense dislike he felt for this glib-tongued rabble-rouser, whose activities in his district the previous year had caused him so many sleepless nights and futile, wasted journeys. Ahmad Ullah was not a native of Bengal—he hailed from Arcot, in the Madras Presidency—and, until the annexation, had been one of a legion of hangers-on at the court of Wajid Ali, the corrupt old King of Oudh.

A penniless teacher of religion, dependent on the king's erratic bounty, he had wielded little influence until the widespread resentment of landowners, soldiers and peasants alike, which had followed the annexation, had given him the opportunity to indulge his fanatical hatred of British rule and of the men who sought to enforce it in Oudh. Ironically, it had been Mr Coverley Jackson—Sir Henry Lawrence's predecessor as chief commissioner—who had brought him to prominence. Jackson, while he had spared no effort to humiliate the deposed king and his senior officials, had given patronage and promotion to many of inferior rank, on the grounds that all who had previously held power under the king had abused it. Ahmad Ullah had been among the chosen and, for a time, Jackson had given ear to him, until even he had to realize that his confidence in his protégé was being abused. He . . .

"Even in prison, news reached me." The Moulvi's voice broke into his thoughts and Alex roused himself. "Accurate news in your case, since you confirm it. And, while I have been here in Cawnpore I heard another rumor concerning you, Sheridan Sahib. A rumor that interested me."

"What interests *me,*" Alex countered, "is how you contrived to obtain your freedom, Ahmad Ullah."

"If you have come, thinking to apprehend a fugitive from justice, you are wasting your time, Sahib." The dark, hawk-like face lit with a triumphant smile. "No charges could be proved against me. They were, of course, absurd charges, quite without foundation. I have been guilty of no crime—unless to preach the Faith, which is my calling, can be held against me . . . and surely it cannot? So . . ." he shrugged. "Your much-vaunted British justice for once lived up to its reputation, and the magistrate ordered my immediate release."

"I see. And where do you go now?"

The Moulvi's smile widened into mockery. "Like yourself, I go on a journey . . . but humbly, not on a fine charger such as yours." So smiling, he laid a slim, long-fingered hand on Sultan's neck and the big horse, startled, jerked his head back, snorting and attempting to rear. The cavalry sowars moved closer, the movement protective, though prompted by curiosity. They were evidently an unofficial escort, sent to ensure that Ahmad Ullah went on his way unmolested but Alex, calming the restive Sultan, affected not to notice them. It would do no harm to find out what he could, he decided—the Moulvi's destination, if nothing else—so that he could pass the information on to Sir Henry Lawrence. The man was clever and as cunning as a snake but he was vain and, given a little judicious encouragement, he would probably be unable to resist the temptation to boast of his achievements or even to offer a subtle insult to a British officer in front of an audience that would applaud his temerity.

"And what rumor have you heard concerning me, Moulvi Sahib?" he asked, when the sowars were within earshot.

The Moulvi eyed him speculatively. "It is said that, now you no longer govern in Adjodhabad, you will return to the *rissala*— to the 3rd Light Cavalry in Meerut."

"That is also true," Alex admitted.

"You go to command the regiment, no doubt? With honor and promotion?" The suggestion was provocative; Ahmad Ullah knew his rank and was well aware that the command of a regiment was not given to a mere captain—certainly not to one who had recently left his well-paid civil post under something of a cloud.

Alex let it pass, refusing to be provoked, and answered lightly, "No, not to command, Moulvi Sahib. And as to promotion, why . . . I have not yet sufficient grey hairs to merit a step in rank!"

"True," the Moulvi agreed. He glanced at the sowars and, satisfied that they were listening avidly, went on, his tone derisive, "The Company's regiments are all commanded by old men. Greybeards, who sleep through the heat of the day, dreaming of past glories and long forgotten battles, in ignorance of what is going on around them now. They will have a rude awakening when the Company's *raj* comes to an end and the soldiers they command desert them."

"How so?" Alex exclaimed, in well-simulated disbelief. "These are wild words, Ahmad Ullah. They have no more substance than the air a man belches when his stomach is full!" He added, fixing a stern gaze on the sowars, "The soldiers of John Company will not betray their salt. They have grievances, perhaps, and they have listened to too many words like yours but they will remain true to their oath of service, you will see."

"*I* will see?" Angered, the Moulvi turned on him. "It is you who will see! I tell you truly, Sheridan Sahib, the days of the Company are numbered. Is it not written that John Company will endure only for one hundred years after Plassey and is not the hundredth anniversary of Plassey due to fall next month? It is the will of Allah that all the *feringhi* shall be ground into the dust. None shall escape from the vengeful swords of the true believers—men, women, even little children, all will die! *In'sha Illah . . .*" carried away by his own eloquence, he talked on, his voice raised, careless of who might hear him.

The sowars listened open mouthed. They were too well trained, too much in awe both of himself and the Moulvi to applaud openly but their approval was evident and Alex, registering the fact that Ahmad Ullah had now said more than enough to invite arrest, knew that it would be worth his life to attempt to apprehend him. Here on the tree-grown *ghaut,* out of sight and sound of the British cantonment, he and Partap Singh were virtually alone in a crowd which, being mainly Hindu, would endeavour to close its eyes to whatever he did or whatever was done to him, but which could be provoked into hostility against him all too easily. The two *syces,* of course, would fly in terror at the first hint of trouble and the sowars, although they might be reluctant to lay hands on him, for fear of the consequences, would undoubtedly do so if their Moulvi appeared to be in danger, counting on the crowd's silence to protect them, if—days later— his body were found in the river.

He sighed, glancing at Partap Singh to see the same thoughts mirrored on his orderly's anxious face. Only a few months ago, he reflected wryly, he would unhesitatingly have ordered any sol- dier in the Company's uniform to place Ahmad Ullah under arrest for seditious utterances, confident that his order would be obeyed without a murmur from the watching crowd.

"The times change, Sahib," Ahmad Ullah observed, as if he had spoken his thoughts aloud. "Now it is our turn. We shall throw off the shackles of servitude and all Hind will follow our example, religious differences forgotten. When the hour comes, we shall kill for the Faith—we shall restore our king and you British are too few to stand in our way, for you are not the great warriors that once you were. Too many of you left your bones in the Crimea. That was where you"—he gestured to Alex's empty sleeve—"lost your right arm, was it not? Your *sword arm!*"

Alex said nothing and, emboldened by his silence, two or three of the sowars smiled behind their hands and one, a young man with a scarred face, spat in the dust, his mouth curving into an insolent grin as he started to move away. He could not let the incident pass, Alex decided, and he called them to attention, his voice cutting through the thin veneer of their complacency like a whiplash. His was the voice of an authority they were accustomed to respect and they obeyed him instantly.

"Escort the Moulvi Sahib to his *doolie,*" he bade them. "And see him across the bridge. He journeys to Lucknow, does he not?"

The Moulvi eyed him angrily, looking for a moment as if he intended to hold his ground. Then, evidently thinking better of it, he spun around and strode across to his waiting litter. Turning when he reached it, he raised his clasped hands to his forehead in mock obeisance and called back softly, "Yes, I too journey to Lucknow . . . perhaps we may meet again while you are there, Sheridan Sahib. But you would be well advised not to continue on to Meerut—hasten rather to Calcutta with your memsahib and from thence take ship to your homeland, if you value your life. Give the Lord Lawrence Sahib this advice also, when you have audience with him. He is a good man and I would not have *his* blood on my hands when the hour strikes." With a contemptuous jerk of the head, he motioned the sowars to stand aside and settled himself on the cushioned seat of his *doolie.*

"Wait!" Alex kneed his horse across the intervening space. "When strikes the hour, Ahmad Ullah? On the anniversary of Plassey, perhaps, as I have heard—or is that also vainglorious boasting, intended only to seduce the Company's soldiers from their duty?"

The Moulvi, his good humor apparently restored, met his gaze with an enigmatic smile, ignoring the challenge. "No man can know the exact hour of his death," he returned. "But I will tell you this, Sheridan Sahib—you will be dead within a few hours of the dawn of *that* day, and any of the *sahib-log* who are not dead will be in mortal terror, seeking in vain for a hiding place!" He drew the curtain across, as the *doolie*-bearers took up their poles and, at a word from him, they set off down the slope towards the bridge of boats spanning the river.

Alex nodded to Partap Singh, put Sultan into a canter and, with his orderly and the two baggage animals at his heels, swept past the *doolie* to cross the bridge some fifty yards ahead of it. The sky overhead was tinged with pink by the time he reached the opposite bank. Lucknow lay just over forty miles to the north-east and he set a brisk pace along the flat, dusty road, anxious to cover as many miles as he could before the sun rose to its full height and compelled him to call a halt until the heat became once more endurable.

He thought of Emmy as he rode, the pain of their parting still fresh in his mind. She, at least, would be safe in Calcutta, he told himself, sustained by this hope—whatever happened in Oudh or elsewhere in Northern India, she and her child would surely be safe. Then, recalling the Moulvi's threatening words, he shivered, conscious of a hideous presentiment of what was to come.

He had heard such words before, of course, but always they had been whispered, vague warnings and promises, passed in secret from man to man and not intended for his ears. He had read them in letters smuggled into the native lines, when he had sought evidence with which to convince old Colonel Chalmers of the danger of sedition among the sowars of his regiment; and he had discerned the echo of those same words in the mysterious *chappaties* passed from village to village under cover of darkness, with the cryptic message which had accompanied each batch but . . . Alex drew in his breath sharply. Never, until today, had he heard the threat of an uprising openly and fearlessly expressed, as the Moulvi of Fyzabad had expressed it, and if he had ever doubted the truth, he could no longer do so.

But how many others would believe it? How many of the grey-beards—who, as the Moulvi had mockingly claimed, commanded the Company's regiments and garrisons—how many of *them* would take the threat seriously or act in time and with sufficient vigor to stave off the consequences of their own blindness? A few, no doubt, of the caliber of Sir Henry Lawrence and his brother John, chief commissioner of the Punjab, and the men they had worked with and trained—Edwardes, Chamberlain and Nicholson—and some of the younger regimental officers, whose urgent pleas for decisive action had, like his own, gone unheeded. But they would have to carry the deadweight of the others, the Chalmers and the General Wheelers, who could not bring themselves to question the loyalty of regiments they had first led into battle forty or fifty years ago. . . . It was there that the awful danger lay. To shake their trust in the sepoys who were, even now, plotting to murder them, would take time and there was so little time left.

Indeed, if the Moulvi of Fyzabad were to be believed, there were only a few short weeks, for had he not hinted that the signal for a general uprising might come *before* the anniversary of Plassey on the twenty-third of June? Had he not implied that it would all be over when that day dawned?

"*Aista,* Sahib," Partap Singh warned, gesturing to where the road ahead was blocked by a long line of straggling bullock carts, most of whose drivers—after the habit of such men—had been lulled to sleep by the swaying of their slow, ponderous vehicles.

Alex drew rein, turning in his saddle to look back across the flat expanse of cultivated land to Cawnpore. The sun rose in a blaze of glory and the scene spread out before him was one of tranquil beauty, at once familiar and reassuring. Most of the city was shrouded in shadow, the labyrinth of narrow streets, the

crowded dwelling places and the teeming thousands who inhab-
ited them hidden from view, but here a tall white temple on the
skyline took on the colour of the sunrise and there, above a fringe
of trees, the dome of a mosque was turned to molten bronze as
a ray of sunlight reached slowly out to touch it.

Sounds of returning life reached him, borne on the soft morning breeze. Temple bells set up a musical clangor, the voice of the
muezzin, muted by distance, called the faithful to prayer. The
clear, shrill notes of a British bugle sounded Assembly, the call
taken up and echoed by others in cantonments and native lines.
Alex was turning away when suddenly, almost as if the bugle call
had been a signal, a great flock of vultures rose on flapping wings
from walls and trees and from the burning *ghauts* beside the river,
to hover, like harbingers of doom, above the huddled rooftops of
the newly awakened city, their bodies ominous black specks against
the blood-red brilliance of the eastern sky.

There were so many of them that he could not suppress an
involuntary shudder.

"A-jao!" he bade Partap Singh thickly and, choking in the
dust which hung in the wake of the plodding bullock carts, forced
an impatient way past the strung-out line and continued on his
journey to Lucknow, driven by a sense of urgency that would
brook no delay.

From the concealment of a clump of trees by the roadside, their
horses tethered nearby, a group of well-armed riders watched
him pass.

They were cavalrymen of the now disbanded army of the King
of Oudh, most of whom had been forced, since the termination
of their royal employment, to eke out a precarious living as robbers and freebooters. This group, however, under the command

of a wealthy *talukdar,* were in the service of the Moulvi of Fyzabad and it needed only a word from their leader to silence the murmur that went up when they glimpsed the two laden baggage ponies, cantering past their hiding place at the heels of a sahib on a black horse.

"I could have picked the sahib off with ease," one of the men said regretfully, fingering his matchlock. "That is a fine horse he rides, better than this jade of mine. And doubtless his baggage contains much of value."

"We are not here to rob sahibs," the *talukdar* reminded him harshly. "Thou art a fool, Ismail Khan! Have patience, for when the time comes, thou shalt have thy choice of fine horses and plunder beyond thy dreams. Only wait for the word."

"I grow weary waiting, *huzoor,*" the soldier grumbled and one or two of his companions nodded agreement.

"Rapacious curs! Mindless sons of misbegotten bitches!" Their leader cursed them roundly. "Canst thou not understand that all will be lost, unless we strike as one man throughout the length and breadth of Hind? To rise prematurely, in small, isolated groups, is to invite failure and defeat. The Company is weaker than of yore but it still has many white soldiers to fight in its defense. Not until *every* Indian *paltan* has given its promise to join us can we be certain of victory. The time is not yet, there are still preparations to be made—but it will not be long in coming. And no doubt Ahmad Ullah, the Wise One, will bring us good news of his visit to the *rissala* in Cawnpore."

The grumbling ceased and when, twenty minutes later, the *doolie* of Ahmad Ullah was seen approaching along the straight, dust-shrouded road, the men's excitement mounted. The weary bearers set down their burden with relief and the Moulvi emerged, mopping his brow, to be surrounded by eager questioners.

"Yes, yes, my brothers, the men of the Second *Rissala* are with us," he answered. "They have taken the oath. So, too, have the sepoys of the 1st and the 56th *Paltans,* but those of the 53rd still waver. They—!"

"They are dogs of Hindus!" Ismail Khan exclaimed wrathfully. "What else is to be expected of them?"

"They are of Hind," the Moulvi said reprovingly. "United with us in the struggle against the Company. Religious differences must be forgotten until victory is won. After that . . ." he smiled, looking from one to another of the fierce bearded faces pressing about him. "It will be as Allah wills, my brothers! Remember that this is the Year of the Prophecy, the last of the Hundred Years of Subjection, when it is written that we, the Faithful, shall over- throw the infidel tyrants and restore to Hind the great and powerful Empire of the Moguls. What matters it if, for a time, our allies are not True Believers? What matters it even should one, who calls himself the Peishwa, seek to regain his throne as reward for aiding us? We need his aid against the common foe."

The men eyed him doubtfully but their leader, spitting his contempt for such addle-pated fools, endorsed his words.

"My horse," the Moulvi ordered, washing his hands of them. "I go now to Lucknow, to speak with the sowars of the 7th Irreg- ulars." He hesitated, frowning. "Saw you a sahib ride past some distance ahead of me? A sahib with an empty sleeve, riding a black horse?"

There was an eager chorus of assent and Ismail Khan volun- teered, "I had my rifle sighted on his back, Wise One, but the Lord Akbar forbade me to fire."

"The Lord Akbar is right—we want no trouble yet and I have told the Company soldiers that they must continue to obey all the orders of their officers. But"—again the Moulvi hesitated and then, evidently reaching a decision, laid a hand on Ismail Khan's shoulder—"the sahib of whom I speak is Sheridan Sahib, he who lately governed in Adjodhabad. He is a danger to our cause, for he is not blind, like so many—he watches and listens and takes heed. Go thou after him to Lucknow, Ismail, whither he goes to seek audience with the Lord Lawrence Sahib. If Lawrence Sahib should send him back to Adjodhabad, let him go, for he can do little there to harm our cause—all the *paltans* are with us. But if he leaves for Meerut, as his orders from the Company require, then see to it that he never reaches his destination. Dost thou understand?"

"I understand, Moulvi Sahib." Ismail Khan darted a triumphant glance at his leader but then his face fell. "How shall I know the destination of the sahib? It is not easy for a man such as myself to learn these things. The servants will not talk and—"

"Take service with him, fool," the *talukdar* advised. "He has but three men—a dog of a Sikh and two *syces.* If one of them should be found with his throat cut or a knife in his back, Sheridan Sahib will seek another in his place."

Ismail bowed his head. "May I keep his horse when the deed is done, *huzoor?* The fine black horse he rides?"

The *talukdar* laughed. "The horse shall be thine, grasping one, and mayest thou have joy of it! Now go and do what thou hast been charged to do." He was engaged in low-voiced conversation with the Moulvi as Ismail Khan swung himself into the saddle of the bony country-bred he despised and set off at a shambling canter in pursuit of his quarry.

"Can he be trusted?" the Moulvi asked uncertainly. "Matters advance in Meerut, I am told."

"Thy trust is better reposed in him than in any treacherous

Mahratta, be he or be he not the Peishwa," the *talukdar* answered, with a hint of sullenness. "Besides, he desires the horse."

"Good." The Moulvi nodded, satisfied. "Thy fears concerning the Nana are groundless, brother. True, he is a Mahratta but he occupies a privileged position—all the officers of the garrison are his friends and the old general confides in him and seeks his advice. It is even said that he will call upon the Bithur bodyguard, under Tantia Topi, to take over the Treasury and Magazine guards, should his own sepoys prove unreliable!" He threw back his head and laughed, with cynical amusement. "The general grows soft in the head with his great age and plays into our hands, Akbar Mohammed! But so also does the Nana. He thinks to vacillate, keeping a foot in both camps lest all we have planned should come to naught but, when the time comes, he will have no choice save to throw in his lot with us."

"How so, Wise One?" Akbar Mohammed enquired, eyeing him with new respect.

"Oh, come! Has he not one of us at his right hand?"

"Azimullah? Meanest thou Azimullah Khan?"

"Who else, brother?" The Moulvi laughed again, softly this time. "Azimullah is the Nana's chief adviser but the advice he gives to his master comes from *me!*" He mounted his horse, still chuckling to himself and, accompanied by the Oudh cavalrymen, set off in the direction of Lucknow by a cross-country route which avoided the road.

CHAPTER TWO
➤➤➤ • ⫷⫷⫷

ALEX reached Lucknow just before nightfall. He was expected and a room had been prepared for him at the Residency, to which Captain Thomas Wilson, Sir Henry's aide, escorted him.

They exchanged news as Alex washed the stains of travel from his person. "The situation here might be worse," Wilson told him. "In Oudh itself, Sir Henry has wrought a minor miracle. In a few weeks, he has made friends with some of the most influential of the *talukdars* and done more than anyone believed possible to alleviate the discontent, not merely by devising conciliatory measures but also by making the chief sufferers believe that he feels deeply for their sufferings. Given time, I am convinced that his wise counsel would prevail, because he's winning the same trust here that he enjoyed in the Punjab. But he fears that he will not be given time."

"The sepoys?" Alex suggested wryly.

The aide-de-camp inclined his head. "The sepoys," he confirmed. "They seem to be too deeply infected by the taint of disloyalty to be reached by any cure and they are constantly being inflamed by religious leaders, who tell them that it is the Company's irrevocable intention to convert them forcibly to Christianity. The high-caste Hindus are especially ready to believe these lies—small wonder, I suppose, when one realizes what loss of caste can mean to a Brahmin and how easy it is to lose caste."

"Yes." Alex toweled himself briskly. "I saw a fire just after I crossed the Dilkusha Bridge. One of the bungalows was well alight but it was being dealt with very efficiently by servants and some men of the 32nd."

"Doctor Wells' bungalow," Thomas Wilson supplied. "And do you know why? Young Wells is surgeon to the 48th and a couple of days ago, feeling unwell, he went to the hospital for some medicine. He's not been out here long and, quite forgetting that he'd be polluting it in the eyes of his Hindu patients, he put the bottle to his lips and swallowed a draught. There was a shocking outcry and, even when the colonel had the bottle smashed in their presence, the sepoys weren't satisfied." He spread his hands helplessly. "And so it goes on—trifling incidents are constantly being magnified out of all proportion to their importance, and this business over the cartridges is the most pernicious of the lot! You know, I imagine that Sir Henry is taking steps to provision and defend the Residency, in case the worst comes to the worst?"

"I had heard he was, yes." Alex looked a question and the aide-de-camp sighed. "Oh, being Sir Henry, of course he's doing all in his power to avoid trouble. He's called a *durbar* in the Residency garden on the twelfth, to be attended by fifty native officers and men from each of the sepoy regiments, and he intends to appeal to their loyalty and good sense . . . always supposing they've got any!"

"He might succeed. They hold him in great esteem."

"And so they should!" Wilson said vehemently. "He's working himself to death in his efforts to find a solution to their problems—problems that were never of his making and many of which have arisen because his advice was ignored. He really *cares,* you know." He rose as Alex, his toilet completed, reached for the mess jacket which had been laid out for him and with a quick, "Here, let me," assisted him to don it. "Well, if you're ready, we'll go and look for him, shall we? Er—how long is it since you've seen him?"

Alex stared at him, puzzled by the question. "Not since he left Ajmeer. But—"

"He's aged almost out of recognition," Lawrence's aide-de-camp warned. "I think by ten years since he came here. He's lost without his wife, of course—I don't think a day passes that he doesn't tell me how little his life means to him, now that she has gone. And his domestic arrangements are chaotic at times, without a woman's hand to smoothe them over. He's always inviting dozens of people to dine and then forgetting to tell either George Cooper or myself that he's done so. This evening we're to be a party of nineteen or twenty, I'm not sure which, and Sir Henry informed me an hour ago! However"—he smiled, his good-looking young face losing its habitual gravity for a moment—"the ladies of the garrison are very good. They send their *khansamas* over with food from their own tables and so we manage."

Alex was conscious of a feeling of keen disappointment at this final item of news. With the limited time at his disposal, he had hoped for the opportunity of an hour or so in private with his old chief, but this, he thought glumly, would hardly be possible if Sir Henry were occupied in playing host to a large party of dinner guests.

Sensing his chagrin, Thomas Wilson said consolingly, "He didn't forget that he was expecting *you,* Sheridan, and I know he wants to talk to you. The guests won't stay very late, so I'm sure that he'll make time for you before he retires. He'll probably invite you to smoke a cigar on the roof with him, when the others have gone."

They found Sir Henry Lawrence in the drawing room, which was already crowded with ladies and gentlemen in evening dress, all of whom seemed in good spirits. Among them, Alex recognized Doctor and Mrs Fayrer; the financial commissioner, Mr Martin Gubbins; Colonel Inglis, commanding officer of Lucknow's only European regiment, the 32nd Queen's; the chief engineer, Major Anderson with his attractive wife, and the commissioner of the Lucknow Division, Major Bankes. He responded automatically to those who greeted him but he had eyes only for Sir Henry and, in spite of young Wilson's warning, was profoundly shocked, when his host shook him warmly by the hand, to see the change a few short weeks had wrought in him.

Never robust, Lawrence now looked alarmingly frail, his tall body thin to the point of emaciation. Haggard and careworn, his wasted cheeks were deeply lined, and his eyes, beneath their massive, craggy brows, had sunk far into his head, bloodshot and fever-bright, as if he had been for too long without sufficient sleep. His thinning hair and the small, untidy chin-beard he wore had both turned from grey to white, making him appear much older than his 53 years—an impression enhanced by the careless shabbiness of his ill-fitting evening suit, which hung on him as though it had been tailored, a long time ago, for someone else.

He could still radiate much of his old charm, however, and over dinner—a badly cooked and somewhat muddled meal—he set himself to put his guests' fears at rest and to inspire them, instead, with his own confidence and faith in the future. Talk was inevitably of the signs and symptoms of impending trouble but Sir Henry, always a brilliant conversationalist, while neither evading nor making light of the issue, contrived to introduce a note of optimism and soon smiling faces surrounded him and laughter rang out across the long, candlelit table.

"Our preparations are well advanced," he reminded his listeners. "And they are being made without the knowledge of the sepoys whose loyalty, until the last, I shall do all that is humanly possible to ensure. I shall not provoke them, and—unless I receive clear proof that they intend to break out in open mutiny—I shall neither disarm nor disband their regiments, thus offering them no excuse for betrayal. If, despite every endeavour, a situation should develop when we must defend ourselves against them, then trusting in God's infinite mercy, we shall do so. All the women, the children and the sick will be moved into the Residency, in which provisions for up to a three months' siege have been stored. We have an adequate store of arms and ammunition—including cannon—a good supply of drinking water and medical necessities, and work on fortified positions is fast approaching completion. We also have a well-trained Queen's regiment, under Colonel Inglis, to man our defenses. So until reinforcements are sent to us—which surely will be only a matter of weeks—I am satisfied that we can more than hold our own with, perhaps, some slight discomfort for you ladies, but without serious danger to our lives."

Murmurs of approval and relief greeted his brief speech, although one or two of the officers, Alex noticed, were frowning and the financial commissioner, Martin Gubbins, looked as if he were about to challenge at least one of the chief commissioner's statements. He was a clever, forceful man, who held strong opinions and who had frequently engaged in acrimonious differences with Lawrence's predecessor, Mr Coverley Jackson. But when Sir Henry turned the warmth of his smile on him, Gubbins shrugged and remained silent. The conversation, adroitly steered into less controversial channels by their host, became general and, when the ladies rose to leave the gentlemen to their port, the mood of the whole party was one of mutual goodwill and considerable cheerfulness.

"We must not linger for too long, gentlemen," Sir Henry

announced, as the port decanter began its round. "Miss Arbuth-not has promised to sing for us and that is a pleasure I'm looking forward to—the young lady has a glorious voice."

Martin Gubbins gave vent to an audible sigh. "I appreciate the efforts you are making to put the ladies in good heart, Sir Henry," he said impatiently. "You succeeded most admirably this evening. But we are men and we should face up to the ugly truth . . . which is that there's not a single one of the sepoy regiments in this garrison we dare trust. The 7th Irregulars are talking quite openly of murdering their officers—the only thing they haven't said is when! And the rest are almost as bad. The officers who are required to sleep in the lines are taking their lives in their hands night after night, and they're too far away for help to reach them in time if they need it. Come to that, of course, so are we, with your regiment billeted a mile and a half away. Damn it, we're at the mercy of the native guard this very minute!"

"The 13th Native Infantry have shown no sign of disaffection to my knowledge," Sir Henry answered mildly. "I prefer to complete my preparations quietly, and offer no provocation which might precipitate a mutiny."

"Suppose we're attacked without warning? We could quite easily be and—"

"No, Martin," the chief commissioner asserted, with calm conviction. "We shall be given ample warning—I've made sure of that. Come now, my dear fellow"—he pushed a silver cigar box across the table—"light one of these and let us try to relax and enjoy ourselves. I can arrange a table of whist, if you would prefer that to listening to Miss Arbuthnot."

There were nods and murmurs of agreement but Martin Gubbins refused to be placated. "I cannot relax and I most certainly cannot enjoy myself with disaster staring me in the face," he protested. "More especially when there is a means by which the danger could be averted—a simple, perfectly straightforward solution to our problem, if only I could persuade you to agree to it, Sir Henry."

"And what is your solution, sir?" one of the Native Infantry officers asked, before Sir Henry could intervene.

"Why, to disarm every sepoy regiment in the garrison or, better still, disband the lot of them and send the men back to their villages! We've got a British regiment and enough artillery to enable us to do it, haven't we?" Gubbins glared at Colonel Inglis. "That's if your regiment is here for our protection which, at times, I take leave to doubt." His tone was deliberately offensive and Alex, seated opposite Colonel Inglis, saw him flush angrily.

"I assure you it is, sir," he began stiffly. "But if you doubt my word, then I—"

"Gentlemen!" Sir Henry did not raise his voice. "Have done, I beg you. You know quite well, Martin, that the colonel is acting in accordance with the policy I have advocated. It is not one I advocate from choice, believe me."

"Then in God's name, sir, why adhere to it?" Gubbins demanded aggressively.

"Because," Sir Henry told him, still in the same quiet, courteous tone, "as you may have forgotten, I am chief commissioner not merely for Lucknow but for the whole of Oudh, in which capacity I am responsible for every district and out-station throughout the area. In none of these are there British troops— only a handful of civil and military officers, with their wives and families. *They* cannot disarm the native troops in their garrisons— their very lives depend on keeping their men pacified. It is my considered view that were news to reach these isolated stations that, here in Lucknow, we had disbanded our native regiments, nothing is more certain than that every sepoy in the Province would rise in open and murderous revolt. The alternative, which is to bring in the officers and their families, is at once impossible and unthinkable at the present time. I have no force available to send out to guard their retreat—unless I denude Lucknow. In any event, my dear Martin, to recall them from their posts now would be to abandon Oudh to anarchy and chaos, which none of us would survive."

A shocked silence followed this stark and realistic assessment of the situation. The officers glanced at one another through the smoke of their cigars and then away, none able to challenge the unpleasant conclusions Lawrence had drawn, but all finding them unpalatable. Even Martin Gubbins appeared deflated and, after a few moments' hesitation, he mumbled an apology.

Sir Henry accepted it graciously. "I think," he said, "that it may well be necessary to disarm the 7th Irregulars. To do so may serve as a warning to the others—I hope it will." He turned to Alex and added unexpectedly, "Captain Sheridan has this day come from Cawnpore. Tell us, my dear boy, what Sir Hugh Wheeler has decided to do? He is, of course—like those in the out-stations—in no position to disarm his sepoy regiments, for he is heavily outnumbered. He has, I think, fewer than two hundred European soldiers in his garrison, of whom a number are invalids."

Alex nodded in tight-lipped confirmation. "He has also a large number of women and children, sir. But he told me that he has sent urgently for reinforcements and that he expects them to reach him fairly soon."

"He has an excellent defensive position in the Cawnpore magazine," Major Bankes pointed out. "Better by far than any building we have here. Nearly three acres, enclosed by strong walls, with the river guarding one front, a good well and, of course, a more than adequate supply of guns and munitions. If he provisions the magazine and removes his entire white garrison—including the women and children—within its walls, he should be able to hold out indefinitely should the need arise."

Alex hesitated. General Wheeler had talked of building an entrenchment on the open plain, outside the city and on its southeast side, where he would be close to the road by which his expected reinforcements would come. But his senior officers had, almost without exception, urged him to reconsider, most of them subscribing to the view just expressed by Major Bankes—if it came to a siege, the magazine would be the best place in which to make a stand.

"When I parted with the general last night, sir," he said, "no decision had been reached, except that . . ."

Meeting Sir Henry's gaze and being given an almost imperceptible headshake, he broke off but Martin Gubbins finished the sentence for him. "Except that, in the event of trouble from the sepoys, Wheeler intends to call upon his trusted friend the Nana Sahib for aid—isn't that what he's decided? Come, Sheridan, you're not always so careful what you say!"

Alex reddened, as Colonel Inglis had done, affronted by the financial commissioner's hectoring tone but before he could reply to the taunt, Sir Henry got to his feet.

"Let us join the ladies," he suggested firmly. "We have already kept them waiting far too long for their evening's entertainment."

It was a little after midnight when his guests departed and, as his A. D. C. had predicted, Alex was invited to smoke a final cigar with him on the roof of the Residency. There, leaning against the Italian balustrade which surrounded it and looking out over the moonlit city, Sir Henry listened in pensive silence to his report.

"Things are worse in Adjodhabad since you left, Alex," his old chief told him sadly. "From what I hear Colonel Chalmers' Irregular Horse are indulging in arson almost nightly. Like the 7th, they ought to be disarmed but . . ." He sighed despondently. "You told Tom Wilson that you encountered the Moulvi of Fyzabad on your way here, I believe. Did you speak to him?"

"Yes, I did, sir, at some length." Alex repeated the gist of their conversation and saw a glint of anger in his host's tired eyes.

"And he told you he was coming here? That is a pity; he's a dangerous agitator—I would as soon harbor a man-eating tiger! But I fear it's no use attempting to arrest him . . . disarming the 7th would cause less provocation than putting that man in jail, as matters stand at present. We shall simply have to do our best to counter his lies. My *durbar* may help in that direction, although I dare entertain no serious hope that it will." Sir Henry started to pace slowly up and down. "I suppose," he said, reverting to Martin Gubbins' earlier remarks at dinner, "Mr Gubbins was right concerning Sir Hugh Wheeler? He *does* continue to place his trust in the Nana? And he is still determined to call on the Bithur troops to guard his magazine, instead of provisioning it for defense by the garrison?"

"That was the impression I received, sir," Alex confessed. He described General Wheeler's projected entrenchment. "His officers are against the plan and, as I said at table, the general has not yet reached a decision."

"I have urged him repeatedly not to rely on the Nana," Sir Henry said. "And so, even more forcibly, has Mr Gubbins! I did not want to add fuel to the flames of his indignation this evening, Alex, that was why I stopped you in mid-sentence. But I admit that I am anxious. Wheeler is not under my command, so I cannot order him to reject the Nana's overtures. Neither can I insist that he should make use of the magazine as a citadel, although I would consider it infinitely safer than hastily constructed earthworks on flat ground, exposed to the full heat of the sun, with—what? A few brick barrack blocks, thatched with straw, affording the only shelter for upwards of five hundred Europeans, many of them women! Dear heaven! Let us pray that he never has to resort to it, that's all I can say. If reinforcements reach him within the next few weeks, all should be well. You say he's confident that they will?"

"He appeared to be, sir. He said they had been promised."

"H'm. And you have left your wife there, have you not?"

"Temporarily, sir, that's all," Alex said. "She is to leave for Calcutta in a day or two, with her sister, who is the wife of young Harry Stirling. He has been appointed to the Governor-General's Bodyguard and is awaiting orders to proceed to Calcutta. I felt it wiser, in view of Emmy's condition—the baby is due in a couple of months, sir—to persuade her to go with the Stirlings. She was exceedingly reluctant, of course, but as I told you in my letter, I am ordered to Meerut and—"

"Ah, yes!" Sir Henry crushed out his cigar and came to lean once more on the balustrade, staring with furrowed brows to where, behind the imposing bulk of the Machi Bhawan, the River Gumti flowed placidly beneath the two bridges which spanned it on either side of the palace wall. In the distance, from the Mariaon Cantonments, three miles north of the river, a thin, flame-tinged cloud of smoke rose skywards, to be followed swiftly by a second and a third. "Arson," the chief commissioner observed wearily. "I shall have to consider moving a detachment of the 32nd Foot into the Machi Bhawan, I suppose, to discourage such demonstrations here." He sighed. "Where were we, Alex?"

"I told you that I have been ordered to Meerut, sir."

"And you would like me to have those orders revoked, I imagine. You would like me to send you back to Adjodhabad—from whence, needless to say, *I* should never have removed you! Is that right, Alex?"

"I hoped it might be for some such reason that you sent for me, sir," Alex answered truthfully. "But if there is any other way in which you require me to serve you, I am yours to command."

Sir Henry's lined face relaxed in a smile of singular warmth and affection. "Thank you, my dear boy—that's what I expected you to say. Perhaps, had you been permitted to remain in charge at Adjodhabad, you might have saved something from the wreckage but now, I fear, there would be little you could do. Your friend Colonel Chalmers has had the bit between his teeth for too long! Adjodhabad is one of the isolated stations of which we spoke at dinner, where every European is in danger now. I'll send you back, if you wish, but I should in all probability be sending you to your death . . . and I could make better use of you here." He laid a thin hand on Alex's braided sleeve. "As a cavalry commander, I should count myself fortunate to have the services of a veteran of Balaclava, Alex."

"I'd be honored to serve under you, sir," Alex assured him eagerly. "But—"

"You are wondering *what* cavalry I shall have for you to command, no doubt," Sir Henry put in ruefully. "Well, it will have to be a scratch force, composed of civilian volunteers, unemployed officers and those native officers and men whose loyalty is beyond question . . . and I do not propose to begin recruiting them yet, for various reasons. Mainly because I believe we have a little time still—a few weeks, at worst."

His own view coincided with this and Alex nodded. "Do you

think that they will wait for the anniversary of Plassey, sir?" he asked. "For a general uprising, I mean?"

Sir Henry Lawrence resumed his slow, measured pacing. "I think that is the plan. The reports I have had from spies seem to confirm it but there are signs—too numerous to be discounted—that there may be spontaneous outbreaks before then. Where provocation is offered, I'm convinced that we must expect trouble." He went into detail and then said, his smile returning, "I have every confidence that the Sikhs will support us, and my brother—who is in a better position to judge—has assured me that they will. There's no love lost between those who fought in the *Khalsa* Army and the high-caste Hindu sepoys, who have treated them so arrogantly during the time they have garrisoned the Punjab." Again he gave details, to which Alex listened with rising spirits, never for a moment doubting the validity of his reasoning. No one knew the Punjab better than Henry Lawrence, who had been its first chief commissioner, and no one—not even his brother John, who was its present ruler—had a more profound knowledge of the Sikh character.

"It would be ironic, sir," Alex suggested, when the tired old voice lapsed into silence, "if we were to find ourselves recruiting an army from the Punjab for the purpose of putting down a mutiny in that of Bengal!"

"Ironic, perhaps, but a strong probability nonetheless," Sir Henry asserted. "Indeed, it may well be that the Punjab will save India for us. I think that . . ." he broke off, as a fit of coughing seized him and Alex was shocked to see, when the spasm passed, that the handkerchief he had been holding to his lips was heavily stained with blood. "You did not know?" his old chief asked gently, meeting his alarmed gaze.

"No, sir. I thought you looked ill but—"

"I am sick unto death, my dear Alex. But I hope that, by God's mercy, I may live long enough to see an end to this terrible threat which is hanging over our heads."

"Amen to that, sir," Alex said, a catch in his voice and his heart suddenly heavy.

"I am tired," Henry Lawrence confessed. "Were it not for the present crisis I should ask nothing more of my Maker than to be allowed to join my beloved Honoria. But as it is . . ." he passed a hand through his sparse white locks. "There is much to be done before I can find the eternal rest I long for. Don't mention the state of my health to anyone, Alex. Those who have a right to know have been informed, of course."

"I shall say nothing, sir," Alex assured him. He was profoundly shocked and hard put to hide his distress. From their first meeting, soon after his arrival in India eleven years before, he had loved and revered this one man above all others, seeing in him all that was best and noblest in those chosen to rule in the Company's name. By his humanity and understanding, Henry Lawrence had tamed the newly conquered Punjab and won the trust of the defeated Sikhs. . . . But now, when the qualities he possessed were so sorely needed to temper justice with mercy in Oudh, it seemed a cruel fate was about to deprive this land of his guiding hand. Without his influence, revolt would be brought nearer, because control would pass into the hands of men like Martin Gubbins who, seeing the danger, could conceive only one way to counter it.

Sensing his distress, Sir Henry said, smiling, "I'm not dead yet, my dear boy. This battered hulk will keep afloat for a while longer —please God until we have weathered the storm. But I am forgetting the reason for which I sent for you. . . . I want you to go to Meerut, Alex."

Taken by surprise, Alex stared at him. "Of course, sir, if you wish me to but I thought you said—"

"That I wanted you to command my makeshift cavalry? I do, but the time for that is not yet. We have a few weeks and I propose to make the best use of them that I can. Don't worry, I'll apply for you, by the electric telegraph if necessary. But Delhi is the key to the whole complex plot which is being hatched against us."

"Delhi, sir?" Alex echoed, still puzzled.

"Bear with me and I'll explain," Sir Henry bade him, with a return to his normal quietly decisive manner. "Let a mutiny succeed in Delhi, Alex, and it will be the signal for an uprising all over the country, from the Afghan border to Calcutta. If it should fail, on the other hand, I am of the firm opinion that the planned insurrection will fizzle out everywhere else like a damp squib. I think it was some fourteen years ago that I published an article in the *Calcutta Review,* pointing out with what ease a hostile force could seize Delhi . . . although, when I wrote it, I was imagining the Sikhs in the role of aggressors, not our own Bengal sepoys!" His tone was wry. "I can even quote to you from memory the grim forecast I made. 'Does any sane man doubt,' I asked my readers, 'that 24 hours would swell the hundreds of rebels into thousands and that, in a week, every ploughshare in Delhi would be turned into a sword?' Alas, I believe those words to be true now and the danger never greater. I also believe that the mutiny will begin there because, as you know, the Delhi garrison contains no British troops."

Alex inclined his head, aware of the strange anomaly by means of which the last Mogul Emperor, the eighty-year-old Shah Mohammed Bahadur—although, in fact, a pensioned puppet—had been permitted to retain the outward trappings of his lost sovereignty. Under a treaty concluded with his father, the Company paid him a princely salary, allowed him to occupy the palace of his ancestors within the walls of Delhi's Red Fort and, for political reasons, maintained the carefully fostered pretense that he was still the ruler of India's Muslim millions. Although the army's largest arsenal was situated in Delhi, it was guarded by native troops. They were stationed in cantonments built on a two-mile-long stretch of high, rocky ground, known as the Ridge, on the northwestern side of the city and outside its walls. Under the terms of the treaty, no European regiments could be included in the Delhi garrison, lest their alien presence offend the old king or destroy the already fading illusion that he ruled in fact, as well as in name. The nearest British troops were in Meerut, 38 miles away and these, Alex knew, included the 60th Rifles—a fine regiment, over a thousand strong—and six hundred men of the Carabineers, the 6th Dragoon Guards, both Crimean regiments, which . . .

"General Hewitt has over two thousand British troops under his command in Meerut, Alex," Sir Henry said, as if reading his thoughts. "And his command includes Delhi. . . . I am not the governor-general and I have no more power to issue instructions to him than I have to General Wheeler. I wish, between ourselves, that I had! In the light of my firmly held conviction that what happens in Delhi must affect us all, I would give a great deal to be able to talk to General Hewitt—indeed, if God were to give me a pair of wings at this moment, I would use them in order to transport myself to Meerut. And once there"—he sighed—"I would exercise all the eloquence I possess in an effort to persuade the general to send some of those two thousand British soldiers to Delhi—on any excuse! And, if I failed to persuade him, I should endeavour to convince Brigadier-General

Graves that it would be in his best interests, as station commander in Delhi, to request that a battery of horse artillery and a
strong detachment of Her Majesty's 60th Rifles should be posted
there, at least until this trouble is over." He paused, eyeing Alex
keenly, the craggy white brows lifted in mute question. "I have
no wings and I cannot go myself, but I have you! Alex, my dear
boy, do you understand what I am asking of you?"

Alex met the question in the anxious grey eyes, conscious of
a sick sensation in the pit of his stomach, as the enormity of the
task he was being asked to undertake slowly became clear to him.
He had met Major-General William Hewitt some years ago in
Peshawar and had formed no very favourable impression of the
obese, indolent old man, whose lack of initiative had led to his
being relieved of his previous command. The Moulvi's scornful
description of the Company's grey-beards fitted Hewitt all too
aptly, he reflected; of the two, Brigadier Graves was the more
likely to chance his arms if he considered the situation sufficiently
serious to demand it. But even he might hesitate to break the
terms of the treaty on his own responsibility; it would be a different matter were Sir Henry Lawrence to advise such a course
in person or perhaps by letter. In that case . . . Alex frowned.

"Am I to take it, sir," he asked diffidently, "that you require
more of me than simply to carry a despatch to General Hewitt?"

"A great deal more, Alex. *I* have no authority to issue written advice to military commanders beyond my own boundaries.
Indeed, some of those within my boundaries are not above dis-
regarding my attempts to guide them." Sir Henry sighed
resignedly. "I have requested Lord Canning to grant me plenary
military powers and I've no doubt he'll accede to my request but,
even when he does, my authority will still be limited to Oudh.
I'd put my case to him but there isn't time and, in any event, I

cannot absent myself from here. So I can only ask you to be my unofficial advocate . . . and I ask because the matter *is* of such importance."

It was impossible to refuse. "I'll go to Meerut gladly, sir. But I have neither your powers of persuasion nor your influence, so do not, I beg of you, place too much reliance on me. I mean, sir, for one of my rank to presume to suggest a course of action to a general officer commanding a division would be . . ." suddenly lost for words, Alex broke off. He added unhappily, "General Hewitt would listen to you, of course, but he may refuse even to give me a hearing. From what I know of him, sir, he's not keen to take action on his own responsibility."

"So I have heard," Henry Lawrence agreed. "But he has the power to act—Delhi is under his command—and desperate situations call for desperate remedies, do they not? You can only do your best to persuade him of the extreme gravity of the situation, and I know I can rely on you to do that, Alex. I intend also to arm you with written proof that the King of Delhi has been approached by certain of the plotters, and that both he and his son, Abu Bakr, recently received the Nana of Bithur in audience."

"The Nana, sir?" Alex stared at him. "Then he *is* in it!"

"I believe that he is in it up to here!" Sir Henry gestured to his throat. "But he is cautious, like all Mahrattas. He waits to see what success the conspirators achieve before openly throwing in his lot with them. And old Bahadur Shah also waits, for he is afraid lest his pension should be taken from him. Besides, he is very old and he has everything to lose. For his sons, however, it is a different matter—they are aware that his pension and his title will die with him. Theirs are the letters I shall give you and, if the evidence of conspiracy they contain fails to convince General Hewitt, it may jolt Brigadier-General Graves. My secretary,

George Cooper, has them ready for you—copies, of course, for I dare not part with the originals in case Lord Canning requires to see them. I shall be sending him copies also, as soon as I can find a reliable courier. But you'll be ready to leave in the morning, I trust?"

It took an effort to hide his misgivings but Alex made it. "Yes, of course, sir, I'll be ready."

"Then you had better allow George to brief you now. He will give you chapter and verse and explain how I came by the letters." Sir Henry put an arm round his shoulders as they descended from the rooftop together. Reaching the door of his office, he halted and held out his hand. "May God go with you, my dear boy! My gratitude is yours, whatever may be the result of your efforts but I shall pray for your success, and sleep a little easier in the hope of it. And"—he smiled—"if the plenary military powers I have asked for are accorded to me, I will give you a step in rank to enable you to talk on more equal terms with General Hewitt. Notice of it will come by the electric telegraph, with your secondment to the Lucknow force."

An anxiously hovering aide-de-camp bore him off to sleep for what remained of the night and Alex sought out his secretary who, as Sir Henry had promised, had the letters he was to take with him already tied up in a neat package, waiting to be collected.

"Study them at your leisure, Captain Sheridan," George Cooper advised. "You read Persian, I believe, but anyway I've included a translation and a note which confirms their authenticity. As you will see from the note, they were brought to Sir Henry—at considerable risk to himself—by a *subedar* of the King of Delhi's own bodyguard. I don't know for what purpose my chief wishes you to have them but you'll take good care of them, won't you? They are dangerous documents and if even these copies were to fall into the wrong hands, I don't like to think what the consequences might be." Receiving Alex's assurance, he got to his feet, stifling a yawn. "I'm tired," he confessed. "Sir Henry keeps late hours . . . but you must be even more weary than I am. You had an early start, did you not?"

"And I am due for another," Alex said ruefully, placing the package in his breast pocket. "I ride for Meerut at dawn."

"Meerut? Sir Henry did not tell me your destination. Some rather disquieting news came in from Meerut by *dak* this evening. I haven't passed it on to him yet, thinking to let him have an undisturbed night." Cooper hunted among the papers on his desk. "Yes, here it is." He read through the report, frowning. "Apparently the C.O. of the 3rd Light Cavalry, Colonel Carmichael Smyth, ordered a parade of a picked body of 90 of his sowars and 85 of them refused to accept the Lee-Enfield cartridges. General Hewitt convened a court of inquiry and, based on its findings, the eighty-five men are to be tried by court martial on a charge of mutiny . . . *that* will bring matters to a head, will it not? Although one doesn't know whether it's a good thing or not— to grasp the nettle, I mean. Certainly Sir Henry won't like it. He's very much opposed to provocation in any form just now. He's convinced that it could lead to a full-scale sepoy rebellion, as he probably told you. Indeed, you heard him at dinner."

"Yes," Alex said thoughtfully, "I did." The news was, as Cooper had said, disquieting, but there was little to be gained by discussing it now. Recalling his promise to let Emmy know the result of his interview, he arranged for the forwarding of a letter to her next day and went to his own room to pen a few hasty and deliberately uninformative lines. The brief missive addressed and sealed, he entrusted it to the house servant who had lighted him to his room and instructed the man to have him called at dawn. This done, he undressed and flung himself thankfully onto his bed but he had hardly fallen asleep when he was awakened by Partap Singh calling him urgently by name.

"Oh, for pity's sake!" He sat up irritably, swearing under his breath. No light entered the room through the window opposite and, with the taste of wine and cigar smoke stale in his mouth, he was in no mood to consider his orderly's feelings. "I sent an order that I was to be called at dawn. Was it not given to you?"

"Yes, Sahib, it was. Unhappily—"

"Unhappily it is not yet dawn!" Alex accused. He rubbed the sleep from his eyes and saw then that Partap Singh's bearded face was set in anxious lines. Relenting, he asked, "Is there something wrong? Tell me what it is."

"One of the Sahib's *syces* . . ." the orderly began. "I think, Sahib, that you should see for yourself. The man is dead and his fellow, as might be expected, has run away, lest he be apprehended for the deed."

"You mean that one of them *killed* the other?" Alex held out his hand for his shirt. It seemed unlikely; his two *syces* were brothers—quiet, inoffensive men, who did their work well and had been in his employ for almost two years.

"I do not know, Sahib." Woodenly, Partap Singh assisted him to dress. "I know only that when I went to rouse them, so that they might prepare our horses for the journey, I found the fellow who is named Ram Dass lying dead. The other, Lal Dass, was nowhere to be seen. The horses have not been harmed and nothing has been stolen from the baggage packs, so it would seem not to be the work of *budmashes.*"

"I see." Fully awake now, Alex accompanied him across a

moonlit courtyard to the Residency stables. A little group of *syces* and grass-cutters had gathered round one of the stalls, chattering excitedly amongst themselves but they lapsed into silence at the sound of his approach and, standing aside to permit him to pass, eyed him apprehensively as he did so. Like Lal Dass, they were ready to vanish into the darkness in an instant if they scented trouble or feared that they might be blamed for what had occurred. Wisely, he said nothing. With Partap Singh a tall, martial figure at his back, he entered the stall and Sultan, who was tethered there, whinnied in recognition, straining at his head-rope as if he, too, were anxious to take flight.

Alex soothed the frightened animal and, motioning to Partap Singh to bring his lantern nearer, dropped to his knees beside the crumpled body, which lay face downwards on a heap of blood-soaked straw. It needed only a glance to tell him that the unfortunate man was dead and the cause of death became apparent when he turned the body over—the *syce*'s throat was slit from ear to ear. The onlookers exclaimed in horror when they saw it and pressed closer but he ignored them. The body was warm to his touch; this, and the crimson stream that still oozed sluggishly from the hideously gaping wound, suggested that whoever had taken the life of Ram Dass could only have done so a short time ago . . . an hour, perhaps, certainly not much more. Could it have been the brother, as Partap Singh appeared to think?

Bending lower, Alex studied the dead man's thin, pock-marked face, shocked by the expression of abject terror that lingered in the wide-open, staring eyes and drawn-back lips. He had seen death in all its forms on the battlefield and in the cholera-infested camps of the Crimea but seldom had he seen such fear in any human face before, living or dead. A brother, even if he had suddenly gone out of his mind and run amok, would surely not have inspired so great a degree of fear. Ram Dass, bound by the ties of kinship, would have sought to reason with him and restrain him from violence. As a last resort, he would have defended himself but there was no indication to suggest that he had. The straw on which he lay was scarcely disturbed; his clothing, though bloodstained, was not torn and there were no cuts or slashes on his skinny arms. Clearly he must have lain paralyzed with terror, like a sheep awaiting the slaughterer's knife, too scared to attempt to ward off the blow that had killed him.

A stranger then but who . . . and why? Unless robbery had been the motive. But according to Partap Singh nothing had been taken. What reason could anyone have to murder a humble, defenseless *syce?* Anyone, that was to say, except his brother, whose reasons could have been legion. Still only half-convinced, Alex got to his feet. Glancing at the circle of dark faces clustered round the stall, he asked of no one in particular, "Was anything heard? This man had a brother, who has vanished—did any of you witness a quarrel between them or hear voices raised in anger?"

Heads were shaken in mute denial. Nothing had been seen or heard, a white-bearded *chowkidar* asserted, finding his tongue at last. No voice had been raised, until the Sahib's orderly had found the body and roused the sleepers with news of his discovery.

"But you did not sleep—you are a watchman," Alex reminded him. "Saw you no stranger, no *budmash* without lawful business here?"

"I was wakeful, Sahib," the old chowkidar assured him. "But I saw nothing untoward. My post"—he pointed with the stout staff that was the badge of his trade—"is yonder, on the other side of the stable compound. I saw no one enter or leave."

But Lal Dass could have made his escape by the rear of the

stables, Alex reflected. He had only to cross a smaller compound, clamber over a low wall and he could swiftly lose himself in the narrow, twisting streets of the native city, where it would be useless to search for him. The killer, if he were *not* Lal Dass, could, of course, have entered and departed by the same route without anyone being the wiser. These stables were used by visitors to the Residency and no particular check was kept on the occupants; if the *chowkidar* and the other *syces* denied all knowledge of what had happened here during the hours of darkness, there was nothing more that he could do. He could not delay his own departure for any longer than it took to replace his two lost *syces*. Already daylight must be fast approaching, and he had a very long journey ahead of him. He would leave a chit in George Cooper's office, he decided, and then start on his way, depending on the secretary to report the matter to the civil authorities if he saw fit to do so.

He said, turning to Partap Singh, "Engage two men, if you can find any here, in place of the two we have lost. We must start at first light, even if we have to lead the baggage animals ourselves. There'll probably be men in the first village we come to, if there aren't any here."

"*Ji-han,* Sahib," the orderly acknowledged. He hesitated and then asked, "Are we to return to Adjodhabad, Sahib?"

Alex shook his head. "No, we go to Meerut. I shall be ready in half an hour, Partap Singh, so do the best you can." He stepped out of the box and Sultan whinnied again, pawing nervously at the straw beneath his feet, nostrils distended in sudden fear. There was a movement in the little crowd of watchers and a tall, powerfully built man in a knee-length *achkan* of military cut thrust an arrogant way through their ranks.

"The horse is frightened, Sahib," the newcomer volunteered.

"Doubtless the stench of blood disturbs him. If the Sahib desires, I will walk him in the courtyard until he quiets down."

Partap Singh bristled indignantly at the suggestion but Alex nodded, a warning hand on his orderly's arm. The tall man's presence puzzled him; he was obviously not a *syce* or a servant—dress and manner precluded either calling—and, although he wore no weapons, he looked like a soldier. One of the deposed king's recently disbanded Oudh cavalry troopers, perhaps, or one of the many small landowners, whose land had been taken from them under Coverley Jackson's harsh administration. As if sensing the unvoiced question, the man gave him a dignified salaam.

"My name is Ismail Khan and I came here seeking employment, Sahib. My own horse is tethered yonder." He waved a hand towards the dark inner recesses of the stable. "I arrived only at nightfall, and with no roof over my head, I was given permission by the head *syce* to sleep in this building." He untied Sultan's head-rope and, handling the big horse with practiced skill, led him out into the courtyard, the crowd parting to let him pass.

Alex followed him, still a trifle puzzled. The man's story sounded plausible enough but he decided to ask a few more questions, in order to set his lingering doubts at rest. Ismail Khan was capable of inspiring the terror he had seen in the dead face of the unhappy Ram Dass, but why should a man of his type descend to murder, without apparent motive or gain?

"Come," he bade Partap Singh, "and bring the lantern with you." The orderly beside him, he went out into the shadowed courtyard and waited, seemingly without impatience, until Ismail Khan led Sultan back to him. The horse was calm now, the sweat drying on his glossy neck.

"This is a fine animal, Sahib," the tall man said, with genuine admiration. He halted, gentling the horse's muzzle with strong fingers and, by the light of the lantern, Alex subjected his hands and clothing to a searching scrutiny. Both were clean but there was, he saw, a long, curved dagger at the man's waist, half-hidden by the folds of his cummerbund.

"You carry a knife, Ismail Khan," he stated bluntly.

"*Ji,* Sahib." Without hesitation, Ismail Khan took the weapon from his belt, unsheathed the blade and offered it for inspection. The finely tempered steel glittered in the lantern-light, innocent of stains. "See for yourself," he invited. "It has not been used."

There would, of course, have been time for him to wipe and polish the blade, ample time, but to rid his hands and clothing of any telltale signs of guilt would have taken much longer and, indeed, could not easily have been done without attracting the attention of someone in the stable. Yet no one had reported it. Alex returned the dagger, his suspicions largely allayed.

"What manner of employment do you seek?" he asked curiously.

"Any employment, Sahib. I have a wife and children who cry out to me for food. I must provide for them by what means I can. The Company"—a gleam of anger flared in the deep-set eyes—"demands that I pay tax on my poor plot of land, but I have no money even to buy seed to plant there."

"Did not the king tax you more heavily?" Alex countered. "And did you not, in addition, have to give *baksheesh* to his agents?"

"True, Sahib," Ismail Khan shrugged his powerful shoulders disdainfully, "but the king gave me employment and I lived well when I was in his service. Now it is ended and those who served in the old *rissala,* as I did, are beggars living from hand to mouth."

So his guess had been right, Alex thought. He had placed the fellow correctly. Like many of his kind, the annexation had left him bitter and vengeful, feeling himself, perhaps with reason, the victim of injustice. A number of the ex-king's soldiers had enlisted in the Company's regiments, unwilling or unable to follow any other calling and presumably it was for this reason that Ismail Khan had come to Lucknow.

"Sahib," Partap Singh reminded him, "it will soon be light and if I am to find *syces* and prepare for the journey, as you commanded, there is not much time."

He was right, Alex realized. He felt in his pocket for some coins. "Give these to the head *syce* for the funeral rites, Partap Singh, and ask him if he can recommend two good men. Say I will pay them well and give them money for the return journey also." He was turning away when Ismail Khan said unexpectedly, "Sahib, I will come with you."

"You? But you are not a *syce*."

"No, but I seek employment. I will serve you well, Sahib, and ask no more than you would pay a *syce*. You go to Meerut?"

"'Yes," Alex confirmed, "I go to Meerut." He frowned. It had not occurred to him to offer such menial employment to one of the ex-king's sowars and his suspicions were momentarily rekindled, until the man added, in explanation, "I have a wealthy relative in Meerut, Sahib, who will make a place for me in his household, so it would suit me well to accompany you. And I will work, you need have no fear on that account."

Partap Singh said nothing, his expression carefully blank but when Alex invited his opinion, he answered with an indifferent shrug. "It is as you see fit, Sahib. If this man is willing to work, let him do so. It will leave me only one other to find."

Half an hour later, they were on the road, heading north-westward towards Sitapur and Bareilly.

CHAPTER THREE

≫≫≫ • ≪≪≪

FROM the time the sun rose, the day became one of fierce, searing heat and what little breeze there was served only to raise the dust in dense, choking clouds from which there was no escape. Alex set a steady pace but well before midday the baggage horses had begun to flag and even the normally resilient Sultan moved listlessly, ears back and neck extended, showing the whites of his eyes as he loped reluctantly along the flat, dun-coloured ribbon of road.

There was a storm brewing somewhere in the distant hills, which manifested its presence by the low mutter of thunder at intervals and, although it was still a long way off, it brought out hordes of vicious black flies to add to the discomfort of horse and rider alike. Anxious though he was to get as far as possible on his way before calling a halt, Alex knew that, with a seven- to eight-day journey ahead of him, he dared not risk knocking up his horses at this early stage. He was looking about him for a suitable stopping place when Ismail Khan spurred his jaded animal to a level with Sultan's shoulder and, ignoring a reproving glare from Partap Singh, waved a hand in the direction of a village about a quarter of a mile ahead.

"Sahib," he shouted, "I know this place well. There is a *dak* bungalow just beyond the village. Would it not be best to wait there until evening and continue on our way when the horses have been watered and rested?"

The suggestion was a sensible one, in view of the threatened storm and, after a few moment's thought, Alex gave his assent to it. They had covered only 25 of the 40 or so miles he had set as their daily target and a prolonged halt now—while it would enable the horses to recoup their strength—would mean riding through part of the night. In the present unsettled state of the country, no night journey was free of risk but . . . he hunched his shoulders and rode on. It was a chance he would have to take and he decided that it was justified.

Although the vile assassin's cult of *thuggee* had been suppressed, the Indian roads still had their quota of lawless robber bands, particularly in Oudh, where many of the dispossessed had lately joined their ranks to prey relentlessly on defenseless or unwary wayfarers. For this reason, the majority of travelers chose to suffer the heat and discomfort of daytime journeys rather than venture abroad after dark, when the danger of a hold-up was greatest. His own small party, however, was well armed and well mounted and thus less likely to invite the attention of any roving predators they might encounter than a party consisting of a few stout, slow-moving merchants, from whom little or no resistence might be expected.

Reaching the *dak* bungalow ten minutes later, Alex dismounted with relief, pleased now that he had agreed to halt there. The rest house itself—like the thousands of others situated at regular intervals along the road—was cheerless and sparsely furnished, intended for the use of travelers who required no more than food and a temporary roof over their heads. But it was well shaded by trees, and a stream ran through the neatly tended garden. Two more than usually efficient servants served him tea when he entered, with the promise of a meal as soon as he was ready to eat it. He asked for bath-water, which was brought at once, and stripping off his sweat-drenched clothes he soaked himself gratefully in a tub of mammoth size until the *khitmatgar* came to tell him that his meal was ready.

Clad in a clean shirt and trousers, he fell to with a keen appetite, finding the stewed chicken better cooked than his dinner of the previous evening. The vegetables served with it were fresher than those on Sir Henry Lawrence's table. Pancakes and cheese followed the first course and the meal was rounded off with a bowl of mangoes, still warm from the sun, and a pot of strong, fragrant-smelling coffee. Alex was feeling refreshed and comfortably replete when, the coffee pot empty, he instructed the *khitmatgar* to call him at four and stretched himself full length on the *charpoy* that had been prepared for him in one of the darkened bedrooms.

He ought, he knew, to study the letters Sir Henry had entrusted to him but the desire for sleep was suddenly overwhelming. He had had very little sleep during the past week and there would be time enough to read the letters before he arrived at his destination, he told himself, letting his heavy eyelids fall. It was only Thursday, for heaven's sake. The earliest he could hope to be in Meerut was Friday, which would be May 8th, and then only if those damned baggage horses stood the pace, which they might well fail to do.

Voices and the thud of hooves roused him briefly; he heard the *khitmatgar* ushering someone into the room next to his own—evidently more travelers had decided to break their journey at the rest house, Indians judging by the voices. He heard the *khitmatgar* addressing one of the newcomers obsequiously as *"Bunnia sahib"* and then the crash of thunder overhead drowned the voices and Alex drifted back to sleep, dimly conscious of a sense of relief because the storm had not caught him on the road.

Partap Singh followed the *khitmatgar* into the room with his tea and he sat up, the mists of sleep clearing swiftly from his brain.

"Is the storm over?" he asked, reaching for the teacup. Partap Singh put it into his hand.

"Yes, Sahib, it is over. It has cooled the air."

"Good! Then we will ride through the night. I want to . . ." he broke off, noticing the glum expression on his orderly's bearded face. "Is something wrong, Partap Singh?"

"The *Poorbeah,* he who calls himself Ismail Khan—he has gone, Sahib, without a word."

"Gone?" Alex stared at him. "When did he go?"

"I do not know, Sahib. He did his work, he and the other new *syce,* but it being Ramadan and he a Muslim, he did not eat with the rest of us. I did not see him go but when I went to order the horses prepared, he was not anywhere to be found."

"Well, he probably has friends, or relatives in the village." Alex drained his tea and swung his legs to the floor. "Did you tell him at what hour we should depart from here?"

The orderly nodded, avoiding his gaze, his own fixed miserably on the slowly moving *punkah* above their heads. "Sahib, that is not all."

"*What* is not all? What else is there?"

"The man has not gone alone, Sahib. He has taken the Sahib's horse."

Alex swore, loudly and angrily. He had owned the big black Arab since his return from the Crimea and, apart from having paid a high price for the animal, he had become deeply attached to him, riding no other.

"Perdition take the infernal fellow! How could he have taken the horse? Did you not hear or see him?"

Partap Singh shook his turbaned head shamefacedly. "I slept,

Sahib. He it was who was guarding the horses. He offered and I
. . . Sahib, the blame is mine. I did not trust the dog. He had that
in his eyes which made me doubt him. I should not have permitted him to remain alone with our horses but I was weary. And
he had been engaged for that purpose, he was the *syce* I told
myself, and so I left him."

Alex controlled his anger. "It was not your fault, Partap Singh.
Rather it was mine, for I engaged him."

"Shall I go to the village, to see if any trace of him can be
found?" the orderly offered.

"No, the villagers will tell you nothing." Alex got to his feet.
"He is known there, he told me that. They are probably all hand
in glove with him. But I shall have to procure another horse, I
suppose." Partap Singh assisted him to don his boots.

"The man left his own horse, Sahib, together with the Sahib's
saddle," he said doubtfully, "Shall I . . .?"

"Yes, saddle the brute for me," Alex ordered resignedly. "I shall
have to make do with it. All right, off you go, Partap Singh. I'll
be with you as soon as I have settled with the *khitmatgar.*" The
orderly gathered up his discarded clothing, made a neat package
of bedding-roll and saddle-bag and went out noiselessly. Alex
completed the buttoning of his jacket and strode into the adjoining dining room, calling for the *khitmatgar.*

The man came running, a second tea-tray in his hands. "If the
Sahib will wait for one moment," he begged. "I have just to take
this but"—he nodded in the direction of the table—"the *chitti* is
there, Sahib, with all accounted for, if you will permit me to take
the *Bunnia* Sahib his tea." He parted the door curtain of a bedroom next to the one Alex had occupied and vanished behind it,
only to reappear a few moments later, his return heralded by the
clatter of breaking china as the tray fell from his shaking grasp.

"Sahib!" He was gibbering with fright, his words tumbling over each other and barely comprehensible. "Come look, I beg you! Something terrible has befallen the *Bunnia,* he . . . I fear he is dead, Sahib! Murdered as he slept!"

With a sense of unpleasant foreboding, Alex went into the room. It was dark, as his own had been, the shutters closed, and he flung them open to admit the afternoon sunlight. He knew, almost without looking, what he would see and his gaze traveled reluctantly to the opposite side of the room. The plump, dark-skinned body of his unknown neighbor, naked save for a loincloth, lay spread-eagled across the bed, limp and motionless. He approached it and saw, as he had guessed he would, that the wide-open, staring eyes held the same look of frozen terror that had been in the eyes of Ram Dass earlier that day. This time, however, the killer had left proof of his identity—if proof were needed—in the hilt of the dagger which protruded from the dead man's smooth, hairless chest. Alex looked at it and, leaving it where it was, pulled the sheet up so that it covered the *Bunnia*'s face. He returned, grim and tight-lipped, to where the *khitmatgar* waited.

"Bring me pen and paper," he bade the shivering servant. "And then call my orderly, the Sikh, Partap Singh."

The man obeyed and, seating himself at the table, Alex started to write. When Partap Singh came breathlessly in response to the summons, he told him in a few brusque, explicit words what had happened and sent him to the *Bunnia*'s room to see for himself. The *khitmatgar,* joined now by two of the dead man's servants, stood apprehensively at his elbow, watching as he wrote but making no attempt to interrupt him, all of them seemingly struck dumb. Partap Singh came from the bedroom, his eyes blazing and Alex put down his pen and asked quietly, "What did you see?"

"I saw the knife of the evil one, Sahib—he who calls himself Ismail Khan—thrust deep into the heart of the poor merchant. But I think, Sahib, that it was meant for you." From some instinct of caution, Partap Singh spoke in his native Punjabi, instead of the Hindustani he had learnt to use during his service in the Bengal army, and the servants looked at him blankly.

"Tell them the name," Alex said, "and then append your mark to this report I have written." The orderly did so; Alex signed and sealed the sheet of paper and addressed it to the district magistrate. Then, rising, he gave it to the *khitmatgar.* "Send one of the *Bunnia*'s servants with this to the *Kotwal* Sahib at once. It contains the name and a description of the killer and of the horse he was riding."

"His horse, Sahib?" the *khitmatgar* echoed. "But surely the horse—"

"He has stolen *my* horse," Alex told him curtly, offering no other explanation. That Partap Singh was right he did not doubt. The knife had been intended for him but, in the dim light of the shuttered bedroom, Ismail Khan had mistaken his victim. And presumably, in the belief that he had left Sultan's owner for dead, he had taken the horse and fled.

"Is the man a *dacoit,* Sahib?" one of the others ventured.

"He may be, I do not know. But he killed your master, I have no doubt of that and, if and when he is apprehended, I can identify him. I have told the *Kotwal* Sahib this and that I am on my way to Meerut. When I return, I shall seek for him. . . . I cannot, alas, delay my journey to do so now." Alex counted out the amount of his bill, gave it to the still ashen-faced *khitmatgar* with a generous addition and, motioning Partap Singh to follow him, went out to where the horses were waiting. A ragged boy was, he saw, assisting his sole remaining *syce* and Partap Singh said apologetically, "The *chokra* is willing to ride with us, until we can find a man. I engaged him, subject to your approval, Sahib."

The boy salaamed and, as Alex walked over to the raw-boned country-bred that had belonged to Ismail Khan, he knelt, offering a thin brown hand to give him a leg-up into the saddle. The animal snapped at him ill-temperedly but he did not move. "I can manage by myself," Alex assured him. "What is your name, *chokra?*"

"Sukh Lal, Sahib." The boy smiled. "I can ride, Sahib, and I should like to serve you."

"Have you the permission of your father to leave your village?"

"I have no father, Sahib, and no work here, save when travelers come and then I help with their horses, for which sometimes they pay me a few *pice*. I am fifteen and," the smile faded, "I am hungry, Sahib. But do not worry, I will earn my keep."

The last assertion was probably true, Alex thought pityingly, although he was certainly not fifteen. "Very well," he said. "I will employ you. But only until we are able to find a man."

The boy grinned cheekily. "You will find no man to work better than I, Sahib, you will see. I shall be with you in Meerut. And I," he darted a sidelong glance at Partap Singh, "*I* will not permit the Sahib's horses to be stolen!"

He made good his boast during the next week, cheerfully doing the work of two men. It was a weary but uneventful journey, the relentless heat compelling them to travel for the most part during the hours of darkness and in the early morning and to find what rest they could by day. They encountered no footpads or *dacoit* bands and, once the Oudh border was left behind, the risk of any such encounter appreciably lessened, but there was more traffic on the road and long trains of crawling bullock carts and grunting, overloaded camels constantly impeded their progress, even at night.

Alex, stiff and saddle-sore, regretted the loss of the splendid Sultan with each mile he traveled. The hard-mouthed, evil-tempered animal Ismail Khan had abandoned was an uncomfortable ride, badly mannered and responsive only to the spur. There were times when he was tempted to accept Partap Singh's offer to exchange mounts, if only in order to afford relief to his aching arm and leg muscles for a few hours. But he persisted obstinately, unwilling to be beaten, and the thin brown horse, partly as a result of better feeding and the care Sukh Lal lavished on him, began to improve and become more tractable.

Alex had half-expected Ismail Khan to come in pursuit of him. It would not have been difficult for the man to learn of the mistake he had made, particularly if he had friends in the village near the *dak* bungalow, where the inhabitants would no doubt still be agog over the death of the ill-fated *Bunnia*. But when two days had passed with neither sight nor sound of a pursuer, he decided—almost regretfully—that this was the end of the matter, at least until he returned to Oudh.

He had at first suspected an ulterior motive behind the murderous attack, but Ismail Khan, it seemed, had only wanted Sultan. No doubt he had cast covetous eyes on the horse when he had been in the Residency stables, and had wantonly killed two men in order to get what he wanted. Now that he had done so, it was evidently of no importance to him whether the owner of the horse were dead or alive. Had it been, he must surely have made some attempt to rectify his error. Instead, he had vanished, and Sultan with him, like any common thief . . . which, Alex told himself wryly, at least cleared the ex-sowar of complicity in some more sinister plot, aimed to prevent him from reaching Meerut with the letters Sir Henry Lawrence had charged him to deliver. Although these, heaven knew, would have provided motive enough for half a dozen hired assassins to follow his trail. George Cooper had not exaggerated when he had described them as dangerous documents, for they were that and more.

At the first of their day-long halts, he had done as the secretary had advised and read the letters, both in the original and in translation. When he had recovered from his initial horror and dismay at the treachery they revealed, he resolved to take every precaution he could against a second attack or attempt at robbery. The plotters would undoubtedly have their spies and informers in Lucknow, as they had elsewhere and it would need only a whisper from some innocent-seeming clerk in George Cooper's office, perhaps, or a hint from a house-servant with keen ears, to alert them to the danger and betray the real purpose for which Sir Henry had sent him to Meerut. Ismail Khan might have been careless and only out for his own gain, but there would be plenty of others on whom the plotters could call if they thought it expedient to relieve him of the package he was carrying.

Alex worried over this possibility for a while, keeping a vigilant lookout when he was on the road, and sleeping with the precious package under his pillow. But no one attempted to molest him, and his anxiety gradually faded as day followed day in monotonous succession, with little to trouble his small party save the heat and dust of their seemingly endless journey. But even this came to an end at last; by dint of leaving two hours earlier than usual and covering the final twenty miles at a brisker pace than he had dared to set before, Meerut was sighted just before sunset on the evening of Friday, May 8th. They entered cantonments, on the north side of the city, and it was not quite dark when they halted outside the Orderly Room of the 3rd Light Cavalry and Alex slid thankfully from his horse.

The acting adjutant, a dark-haired lieutenant named Melville Clark was, somewhat to his surprise, still working in the inner office. "You've chosen a bad moment to join us, sir," he observed grimly, after Alex had introduced himself and Partap Singh had been directed to the vacant quarter which had been prepared for his occupation. "The regiment is, I regret to say, in disgrace, and General Hewitt has decided to complete the sorry story of its humiliation at a parade of the entire garrison tomorrow morning. That's why I'm still here . . . I have to post the order for the parade in Regimental Orders."

He sounded bitter and dispirited and Alex offered sympathetically, "For a native regiment to be disbanded is no longer a unique disgrace. It will happen to many others, I fear."

"We are not to be disbanded," Melville Clark corrected.

"But your sowars have refused to accept the Lee-Enfield cartridges, have they not?"

The adjutant nodded, tight-lipped. "Eighty-five of them refused to accept the *old* cartridges, the type they've been in the habit of using for years. The colonel returned from leave in Simla and had our skirmishers paraded—to test their reaction, he said— and five took the accursed cartridges. Five! The rest have all been convicted of mutiny by a district court martial, consisting of Indian officers of this and the Delhi garrison, half of them Muslims and the other half Hindu. The sentences are harsh—ten years deportation with hard labor for all except a dozen of the younger men, whose sentences have been halved. Perhaps they deserve it, I don't know—their own countrymen awarded the sentences. But," he sighed, in angry frustration, "the general is determined to make an example of them. A public example, in the hope that it may act as a deterrent to the other native regiments."

This was what Sir Henry Lawrence had been dreading, Alex remembered uneasily, and his heart sank as Lieutenant Clark went on, "They are to be paraded, under the guns of the Royal Artillery, marched in front of their comrades, stripped of their uniforms and then fettered, Captain Sheridan! That's the general's decision and he will not go back on it. What he can hope to achieve by such a spectacle God only knows! And if that sounds as mutinous as refusing those damned cartridges, I can only beg your indulgence."

"You do not think it will act as a deterrent to the other regiments, then?"

The adjutant shook his head emphatically. "No, sir, I do not. Do you?"

"To be honest," Alex answered, "I doubt it. But I haven't been with a regiment for three years, so I am not in a position to judge."

Melville Clark controlled himself with an almost visible effort. "Mutiny has to be punished, I realize that," he said bleakly. "But these are good men, the best we have, believe me, sir. If they are to spend ten years in the Andaman Islands like common criminals, that is enough, in my opinion. They should not be degraded in front of their comrades. This is a fine regiment, as you do not need me to tell you, and I've been proud to serve in it. But I would rather see it disbanded than have to stand by and watch it publicly dishonored, as General Hewitt has commanded that it shall be tomorrow morning. I . . . I . . ." he shrugged helplessly and Alex saw that there were tears in his eyes. "The 19th Native Infantry refused their cartridges but at least General Hearsey permitted them to end their service with dignity—He even thanked them for their past loyalty and valor before sending them back to their villages, did he not?"

"Yes, I believe he did," Alex answered. The valiant old Sir John Hearsey had behaved, as always, with firmness and courage but with an understanding of the sepoy mentality and the problems which faced them, and the men of the 19th Native Infantry, their arms obediently piled, had cheered him before departing for their homes. Even from the 34th—to which the now infamous Mungal Pandy had belonged—he had exacted no harsh penalties, such as General Hewitt apparently planned for the unfortunate 3rd Light Cavalry. He had tempered justice with mercy, although his own life had been in danger when Mungal Pandy had run amok; Pandy had been hanged, but the 34th had also been permitted to end their service with what young Clark described as "dignity." But Hewitt, of course, wasn't Hearsey. Alex got to his feet. "Is there any possibility of my being able to call on General Hewitt this evening?" he asked. "I'd make my request through the colonel, naturally, if you would be so kind as to inform him that I have arrived and ask him to receive me. It won't take me long to remove the stains of travel from my person and change, so perhaps after dinner, you—"

"I'm sorry, sir," the young adjutant put in. "The colonel will receive no one tonight and he won't be dining in mess. None of us will, it's . . . well, I suppose it is the only way in which we can show our feelings. I'll arrange for a meal to be sent over to your quarters, of course, and you will be able to report to the colonel on parade tomorrow, and see him when it's over. But as to calling on General Hewitt tonight, frankly, sir, I would not advise it. The general is . . . that is to say, he—"

"I am acquainted with him," Alex said flatly. "But my business is of some urgency. I'm acting as courier for Sir Henry Lawrence in Lucknow and it is just possible that the documents I have to show him may cause him to think again about the parade tomorrow. I cannot promise that it will but I believe there's a chance of it."

Lieutenant Clark brightened perceptibly. "In that case," he responded, "I'll brave the C.O.'s wrath on your behalf, sir. I'll send a *chitti* round to his bungalow now and, if he consents to receive you, I will pick you up later this evening and we'll call on him together. Say about nine or nine-thirty, so as to give you time for a bath and a meal?"

"Thank you, my dear chap," Alex acknowledged. "I'm obliged to you."

The boy was as good as his word. He reappeared soon after nine with the news that Colonel Carmichael Smyth had agreed to his request. "He isn't too pleased, I'm afraid," Clark added apologetically. "But he told me to bring you over. It's not far; we can stroll along now, if you're ready, sir."

Alex nodded and fell into step beside him. The senior married officers' bungalows were situated on the north side of the lines, with the garrison church and the European barracks beyond, in which the 60th Rifles and 6th Dragoon Guards were quartered. A wide ditch and the wilderness of the Sudder Bazaar, which extended southwards in the direction of the native city, separated the queen's regiments from the Company's two miles of narrow alleyways, flanked by flat-roofed houses, in which a variety of merchants and peddlers plied their trade, and where the Street of the Harlots was a nightly rendezvous for the soldiers of the garrison.

It was, Alex thought, looking with narrowed eyes at the moon-lit scene before him, a curious decision on the part of whoever had planned the original layout of the station, to have permitted this maze of dark and crowded streets to form a barrier between the European and native lines. Although no doubt, like so many of India's other anomalies it had happened gradually and no one had noticed or worried about the potential danger the bazaar represented, until now. And now it was too late. *He* had never thought about such matters, when he had been here as a young officer years ago, he recalled, and let a sigh escape him.

Following the direction of his gaze, Melville Clark observed, "The bazaar is a rabbit warren of a place, as they all are, of course. I fancy quite a few of the *fakirs* and so-called holy men, who have been visiting our fellows in order to stir up their religious scruples, have taken refuge there when we've tried to hunt them out. They're the ones who are doing the harm; the sepoys are like children, they believe these infernal troublemakers and they are genuinely afraid that we're out to destroy their religion, so that we can convert them to our own. It's absurd though, isn't it, sir, when you think that these priests are trying to stir up revolt in Meerut, which is the one station in the whole of northern India where the queen's regiments are almost equal in strength to the Company's? The Carabineers are admittedly only six hundred strong and most of them are recruits, only just drafted out here, who are still under instruction in the riding school, on partly trained horses. Yet for all that," his voice had an angry edge to it, "I don't imagine that old swine Hewitt would have been quite so keen to make a public example of our wretched, misguided sowars if he'd been commanding in Allahabad or Bareilly, do you, sir?"

Or in Cawnpore, Alex told himself, where Sir Hugh Wheeler's handful of British gunners, pensioners and invalids were outnumbered by something like fifteen to one. He thought, with a pang, of Emmy and then banished the thought and the fear that came with it. Emmy would be on her way to Calcutta by now—on her way or preparing to go; he need have no more anxiety on her account. And once she was safely delivered of her child . . .

"*Do* you, sir?" Clark prompted.

"No." Recalling the question his companion had asked, Alex shook his head. "Probably not, since you invite my opinion. Speaking of opinions, though, I wouldn't, if I were you, air your opinion of General Hewitt *too* freely. To say the least, it's unwise, however strongly you may feel concerning tomorrow's parade. The general is in command and, for all you or I know, he may have received orders from a higher authority to inflict the punishment you so deplore precisely *because* Meerut is the only station with parity in numbers, and it could not be carried out with impunity anywhere else. Don't misunderstand me, Clark. I've come from an out-station with an entirely native garrison and I'm as convinced as you are that excessive harshness will precipitate trouble, rather than prevent it, particularly in the out-stations of Oudh. But a good many others hold the opposite view. Almost as many, indeed," the memory of Colonel Chalmers returned fleetingly, "refuse to admit that any danger of mutiny exists at all! Official policy may have changed. If it has, then General Hewitt may have been left with no choice in the matter. Had you thought of that?"

"No, I had not," the adjutant admitted but his tone was unrepentant as he went on, "I don't believe General Hewitt has received orders from a higher authority, honestly, sir. From the outset he's talked of punishing our men with the utmost rigor of military law and I know, from one of his A.D.C.s that every detail of tomorrow's ghastly procedure was drawn up according to his instructions. I have the order, under his signature, on my desk! And as to my opinion of him, it's an opinion most of us hold and

I . . . well, I was under the impression that you shared it. The man's a—"

"Lieutenant Clark!" Alex turned to look at him, suddenly suspicious. "Have you been drinking?" he demanded sternly.

The boy flushed. "Hugh Gough and I shared a bottle of port in our quarters. We were trying to drown our sorrows. But I'm not drunk, sir. Damn it, I wish I were!" He shrugged angrily and pointed to the bungalow they were approaching. "That's the colonel's quarters, sir. Will you permit me to speak frankly before we go in?"

"In *vino veritas?*" Alex suggested, again feeling a good deal of sympathy for him. He was very young, poor little devil, hurt and angry to the point of recklessness; it might be as well, for his sake, to let him speak his mind before he had to face his commanding officer. Colonel Carmichael Smyth was a cold, austere individual, he remembered, ambitious and a stickler for discipline, who would be unlikely to welcome either confidences or complaints from a junior officer, whose attempt to drown his sorrows had succeeded only in loosening his tongue.

A *chowkidar* with a lantern came shambling towards the gate of the bungalow and Alex halted, the scent of roses wafted to him from the garden beyond. "Wait," he bade the breathless old servant and turned enquiringly to Melville Clark. "What do you want to tell me?" he invited.

"About the General—I wanted to warn you, really, because you haven't seen him for some time, have you?"

"Not for a couple of years, no. Has he changed?"

"I imagine you'll think so," the adjutant said. "He weighs over twenty stone and can no longer sit a horse, so he comes on parade and makes his inspections in a buggy, into which his A.D.C.s have to lift him. He suffers from gout and by eight o'clock in the evening he's got through a bottle of whisky and is incapable of standing up unaided. By *this* time he's simply incapable—which was why I advised you not to try and see him until tomorrow morning. You'd do better to seek an interview with the station commander, Brigadier-General Wilson. Believe me, sir, you'll get nowhere with General Hewitt, however urgent your despatches are. But if there's anything in them which *might* cause this parade to be called off or postponed, General Wilson would listen. He's about the only man who could persuade General Hewitt of the necessity to call it off."

"I see." Alex was careful not to commit himself. Colonel Carmichael Smyth was now his commanding officer also; it would rest with him to decide to whom the Delhi letters and Sir Henry Lawrence's advice should be delivered. "Thank you, my dear fellow," he said. "I'm grateful for your advice and for all you've told me. Shall we go in?"

Clark stood aside to let him pass. "I think," he volunteered, with unexpected good sense, "that I'll take my leave, if you don't mind, sir. I *have* had rather a large dose of Dutch courage and I might be tempted to talk out of turn. But if you need me for anything, please don't hesitate to send for me."

Alex repeated his thanks, with genuine gratitude, and followed the salaaming *chowkidar* down a long paved path to the bungalow. A bearer admitted him, and Colonel Smyth after a five minute delay received him on the rear veranda. They had served together in the Sikh War of 1849 but, although they had known each other well, the colonel's greeting was noticeably lacking in enthusiasm.

"I have a guest," he said. "So I cannot spare you more than a few minutes, Sheridan. But young Clark insisted that your business was urgent. He'll have told you, of course, about the regrettable turn of events here and tomorrow's parade?"

"Yes, sir, he told me, and I'm extremely sorry. Indeed I—"

"Eighty-five mutineers, who have betrayed their salt and disgraced a fine regiment, are to be dealt with as they deserve," Colonel Smyth interrupted, his tone harsh.

"You *approve* of the punishment, sir?" Unable to keep the astonishment from his voice, Alex stared at him.

"God damn it, of course I do! This epidemic of mutiny has to be stamped out—and I agree with the general. Mild measures won't do; an example has to be made. Naturally I regret that my regiment has had to be singled out but I concur fully with the decision of the court martial." He waved Alex to a chair, the gesture impatient.

A decanter of whisky and glasses stood on the table behind him, and he had a glass in his hand but he pointedly did not offer his visitor a drink. The omission was calculated to give the impression that he was not in the habit of entertaining those of inferior rank to his own, unless by invitation.

"Well?" he demanded. "What *is* your urgent business, Captain Sheridan?"

The colonel, at least, had not changed, Alex thought wryly, as he explained the reason for his visit with the brevity clearly expected of him. He was older and a trifle grayer, but just as thin and ramrod-stiff. His manner was just as distant and as icily formal as it had always been. In the Punjab, they had been on Christian name terms, with only one step in rank between them but this was forgotten now, although Carmichael Smyth's lieutenant-colonelcy was a brevet, earned in the Punjab after the war. He was an efficient and courageous soldier and a splendid all-around sportsman, stoic and possessed of an iron will—qualities which should have appealed strongly to the fierce Muslim horsemen he commanded—yet he had never been popular with either his sowars or his brother officers. They respected and admired but certainly did not like him and he had, for this reason, taken refuge behind a self-imposed barrier of arrogant aloofness. The barrier was more apparent now, Alex decided—probably because he took less trouble to hide it than he had in the old days. With advancing years, he appeared to have abandoned the efforts he had once made to court the liking of his fellows and even, in his own case, deliberately to offend and antagonize, as if he were determined to sever all links with the past—perhaps because he feared that advantage might be taken of them.

"May I see these letters?" the colonel asked, after listening, with ill-concealed disbelief, to Alex's account of his interview with Sir Henry Lawrence.

"Yes, of course, sir. They're here. Sir Henry has retained the originals—these are copies, with a translation which—"

"Copies, dammit?" The interruption was scornful. "Then they're of no value, they don't offer proof."

"Sir Henry has signed a statement which guarantees their authenticity," Alex pointed out patiently. "He has sent a similar set of copies to the governor-general, I understand."

"So Lord Canning's being brought into it," the colonel observed, sounding less skeptical. "In that case, I suppose I'd better read them." He shuffled through the translations and read in silence, brows furrowed, his expression changing to one of shocked dismay as the full implication of what he was reading slowly sank in. "God in heaven!" he exclaimed, staring down at the flimsy sheets as if stunned. "These are—these are . . . did *you* read these nauseous documents? Did Sir Henry Lawrence take you into his confidence?"

"Yes, sir, he did. And I was as shocked as you are. Don't you think, sir, that General Hewitt should be shown them at once?" Alex rose to his feet, anxious to lose no more time. "Sir Henry felt that the general might feel justified in sending a detachment of British troops to Delhi, in view of the threat these letters contain. Perhaps if we were to call on the station commander now and request his permission to—"

Again Carmichael Smyth cut him short, but this time without any deliberate intention of giving offense. "General Wilson is here. He dined here, as my guest. I'll have a word with him, show him these papers and let *him* decide what's best to be done. Certainly the matter is urgent and I'm grateful to you for bringing it to my attention, Alex." In his agitation, he failed to notice the lapse. "Er . . . wait here, will you? And help yourself to a peg, if you feel like one. I'll call for you, when you're needed."

He went inside and Alex obediently waited, hearing the subdued hum of voices coming from the lamplit drawing room to his left. The conference with the station commander lasted for over half an hour and he was left, cooling his heels in ever increasing frustration, awaiting a summons that did not come. If young Melville Clark had not exaggerated, General Hewitt would by this time have retired with his second bottle of whisky, he thought anxiously and his second-in-command might well be reluctant to disturb him, still more so to admit a newly arrived junior officer to his presence. In fact he . . . the handsome grandfather clock in the hall of the bungalow chimed the half-hour and, to his relief, he heard footsteps. Rising, he stiffened to attention as Colonel Carmichael Smyth came towards him, a tall, gaunt-featured officer with a goatee beard at his side.

"This is Captain Sheridan, sir," the colonel said. "As I mentioned, he brought the letters from Lucknow and he has seen Sir

Henry Lawrence quite recently, so if you would care to ask him for any details I may have omitted, I am sure that he will gladly place himself at your service."

General Archdale Wilson acknowledged the introduction courteously. He asked a few questions, seeming worried and undecided, tugging at the scant white hairs of his small, carefully trimmed beard as he listened to Alex's replies.

"H'm . . . I don't know what we ought to do," he confessed. "The matter's urgent, I realize, but we can't do a great deal tonight, can we? To whom were you instructed to deliver these letters, Captain Sheridan?"

"To General Hewitt, sir," Alex told him. He added, forestalling another string of questions, "Sir Henry Lawrence instructed me to tell the general that, in his considered view, Delhi is likely to become the focal point of any revolt which may break out. In these circumstances, sir, and in view of the evidence contained in the letters, he believes that the general would be fully justified in reinforcing the Delhi garrison with a detachment of British troops from here."

"The general could not possibly send troops to Delhi on his own responsibility," Wilson objected in horrified tones. "British troops—good heavens, there's the treaty to be considered! To break that would require authority from the commander-in-chief who, as you probably know, is in Simla."

"Could not the necessary authority be obtained by means of the electric telegraph, sir?" Alex persisted.

"Yes, I suppose it could," the station commander conceded uncertainly. "If General Hewitt conceives it advisable to send troops to Delhi. He may not. The Delhi station commander hasn't asked for them, has he? And the King of Delhi—"

"The King of Delhi's sons are deeply involved in the plot, sir,"

Alex reminded him, keeping a tight rein on his temper. "As the letters prove."

"That is true, they are. But all the same . . ." the brigadier-general continued to tug agitatedly at his beard. "We have our own crisis here, you know, Sheridan. I doubt if the general will feel inclined to weaken the Meerut garrison in the circumstances. It could lead to serious trouble. At the punishment parade tomorrow—why, good heavens, it could be touch and go!"

"Is there no possibility that the parade could be canceled or postponed, sir?"

"Canceled—postponed! Of course it can't. The general wouldn't hear of it. In any case, unless General Graves asks for help, I don't see . . . tell me, has *he* been shown these letters?"

Alex was compelled to shake his head. "No, not yet, sir. I was instructed to bring them first to General Hewitt, since Delhi is under his command. But Sir Henry Lawrence was anxious that General Graves should see them and he suggested that, with the general's permission, I should take them to Delhi when he had perused them."

"Wait, my young friend!" Wilson put in eagerly. "That is the answer, is it not?" He appealed to Colonel Smyth. "I will have these letters sent to General Graves at once. He is in a much better position than we are to assess the possible danger and to decide whether or not the Delhi garrison should be reinforced. He has a perfectly adequate native force under his command—quite sufficient to deal with a palace intrigue which, in any event, comes more within the civil commissioner's province than his. He has not reported that any of his regiments are disaffected, rather the reverse, in fact. It is we in Meerut who have an incipient mutiny on our hands . . . one which may require every British soldier we have to contain, don't you agree?" For a moment, he looked almost happy, the burden of responsibility lifted from his shoulders but, meeting Colonel Smyth's reproachful gaze, his thin, angular face reverted to its accustomed expression of careworn melancholy. "I didn't mean to imply that you could not restore discipline in your regiment, my dear George. Quite the contrary. I have every confidence in you, believe me."

"But, sir," Alex besought him, before the colonel could reply, "surely you will show General Hewitt these letters or at least inform him of their contents before sending them to Delhi? Sir Henry Lawrence charged me to deliver them in person, sir, so that I could make his views known to the general and point out, unofficially of course, that as a precautionary measure he——"

"That will do, Sheridan," Colonel Smyth said coldly. "The matter is out of your hands now. You have done all that is required of you and you may safely leave General Wilson and myself to deal with the letters as we see fit." He added, with biting sarcasm, when Alex attempted to protest, "For God's sake, man, you are not a jumped-up political officer now! You are serving under my command and I'll thank you to remember it. When the general officer commanding this division needs you to point out precautionary measures at the instigation of a civilian, I'm sure he'll let you know."

It was his dismissal and, with the awareness that he had failed in his mission, Alex felt a wave of bitterness sweep over him. He picked up his forage cap, stony-faced, controlling himself withdifficulty. General Hewitt might be senile, incompetent, even drunk, but authority was vested in him; he was the only one who had the power to take decisive action and he was about to be bypassed and, it seemed, deliberately kept in ignorance of the danger Henry Lawrence had foreseen with such clear, cool certainty.

*"Let a mutiny succeed in Delhi and it will be the signal for an upris-
ing all over the country, from the Afghan border to Calcutta . . ."*
Lawrence had said, he remembered, hearing the tired old voice
as if it were coming from beside him. *"If, on the other hand, it
should fail there, I am of the firm opinion that the planned insurrection
will fizzle out everywhere else like a damp squib . . ."*

"I think I'm right, George." Archdale Wilson's voice also
sounded tired, with a lingering note of doubt in it, as if he still
sought reassurance. "I'll send a courier to Delhi with these infernal things and Harry Graves can decide, after consultation with
Commissioner Fraser, whether they're to be taken seriously. Come
to that, he can refer the matter to the commander-in-chief if he
considers it advisable to break the treaty. It's not really up to us,
is it? Frankly I don't much relish the idea of facing the Old Man
with a problem like this, when he's got so much on his mind
with tomorrow's unhappy affair. He'd probably only shelve it.
Perhaps when the punishment parade is safely over, I . . . dammit,
you understand how I feel, do you not?"

"I understand perfectly, sir," the colonel responded promptly.
"You've reached the right decision, I'm sure. There's nothing to
be gained by disturbing General Hewitt tonight. And you are the
station commander, after all. How about a nightcap, before you
go?" He turned, reaching for the decanter and, realizing that Alex
was still within earshot, said with an abrupt change of tone, "All
right, Sheridan, no need for you to wait. You'll be on tomorrow's
parade, of course. I want all my officers present and, even if there
hasn't been time to post you to a troop, you had better be there."

"Certainly, sir." He might have been addressing a newly joined
cornet, Alex thought, anger catching at his throat, but he forced
himself to speak quietly and with the correct degree of respect-
ful formality. There was one last card he could play; judging by

General Wilson's anxiety to rid himself of the letters, the colonel must have forgotten to tell him of the possibility that Lord Canning was, by now, aware of their existence. He added, still respectfully, "If you will allow me, sir, I should like to mention one point to General Wilson—it's a point which may have been overlooked, although I did inform you of it."

For a moment it seemed as if his new commanding officer was about to refuse his request; the colonel reddened with annoyance and his mouth tightened ominously.

"In God's name, Sheridan, I've told you to go, haven't I?" he exploded wrathfully. "You are taking too much upon yourself. Dammit, you—" General Wilson laid a restraining hand on his arm.

"Let us hear what he has to say, George," he suggested and summoned a smile. "Well, Captain Sheridan? You are undoubtedly a very conscientious young man and, since Sir Henry Lawrence appears to have reposed his confidence in you, what point do you think we may have overlooked?"

Alex faced him squarely. "The fact that copies of these letters have been sent to the governor-general, sir. Sir Henry felt that their importance demanded that they should be brought to his attention without delay and he intended to despatch them to Calcutta as soon as a suitable courier could be found to deliver them to his lordship."

The effect of his announcement on both his listeners exceeded his expectations. It was evident, from Colonel Smyth's barely suppressed fury, that he had omitted to pass on this information to his superior, and from the exclamation of alarm to which the station commander gave vent, it was equally evident that he considered the omission a serious one. He controlled himself admirably, however, and said flatly, "Thank you, Captain Sheridan.

This does place a different complexion on the matter, most certainly, and I'm obliged to you for mentioning it." He exchanged an anxious glance with Colonel Smyth. "We shall *have* to show them to him, George. Even at the risk of . . ." he broke off, mopping at his brow.

"Tonight, sir?" Smyth's hard blue eyes held a steely glint, more calculating than angry. He poured two liberal measures of whisky into his own glass and the general's and gestured in the direction of the room they had left. "Let's go inside, shall we?" He took a sip of his whisky and added, frowning, "We cannot cancel the parade, so I hardly think—"

"I entirely agree with you. Tomorrow morning will be time enough," Archdale Wilson decided. "After the parade. We'll wait until after the parade."

Alex drew himself up, recognizing that there was nothing more he could do. When they had gone, he left the bungalow and made his way through the sweet-smelling garden to the road, stepping quietly past the old *chowkidar* who was dozing, his lantern at his feet, by the gate. To his surprise, he found Melville Clark waiting for him when he reached his own quarters. Like the *chowkidar* he, too, had fallen asleep, sitting bolt upright in one of the high-backed cane chairs with which the room was furnished, but he roused himself as soon as Alex entered.

"I brought this, sir," he said and held up a bottle. "Gough discovered he had one left and I thought you might need it. I'm afraid it's only mess port but perhaps it'll be better than nothing. At least we can drink a toast in it, if there's anything to celebrate. I hardly like to ask but . . . how did you get on, sir?"

Alex sank wearily into the chair at the foot of his bed. "Not as well as I had hoped," he answered honestly. "But, I suppose, better than I might have done, all things considered. I'm grateful for your kindly thought," he gestured to the bottle. "I'm as dry as a bone, having talked myself hoarse. To no avail, I regret to say, so far as the parade is concerned."

Clark's smile faded. "It's still to be held?"

"Yes, it's still to be held . . . and General Hewitt will not be shown my despatches until it's over. On the credit side, though, General Wilson has seen them. He was there, with the C.O."

"He wants this damned parade, you know—the colonel," Clark said bitterly. "He has to prove he's right. Those 85 sowars defied him. They refused to listen to him when he pleaded with them to accept the cartridges. He *wants* them to have to eat dirt." He poured the port, his hands so unsteady that he splashed it over the tops of both glasses. "To what or whom can we drink then? Obviously not to a regiment that is about to die of its own shame, condemned by its own commanding officer. Oh, well, what the devil," his young voice was harsh with disillusionment. "Let's drink to John Company, which offers us the chance of fame and fortune, with a soldier's glorious death as an alternative! How's that for an inspiring toast, Captain Sheridan? May I give you the Honorable Company, sir?"

"Unless it, too, is dying," Alex said softly, thinking of the letters he had brought from Lucknow. He had spoken more to himself than to his companion and when Clark asked, startled, "*What* was that, sir?" he shook his head.

"It was nothing, my dear chap, nothing of consequence. I'm tired and that makes me pessimistic." He raised his glass in his left hand, looked down wryly at his empty right sleeve and then drank the toast with a smile. "To the Company! Long may it prosper and continue to command the loyalty of all who serve it!"

"Hear, hear," the adjutant echoed. He topped up their glasses.

"This is capital stuff for drowning one's sorrows. Another toast, sir? It's your turn to propose one."

"I'm going to bed," Alex told him. "And I think you should too, old son, because you'll need all your wits about you tomorrow." Clark stared at him incredulously.

"Me, need my wits? For pity's sake, what for? I don't want to see it happen, I want to blind myself to what's going on, don't you understand? That's the only way I'll be able to stomach the sight of my men being treated like felons, sir, truly it is."

"Don't be a selfish, idiotic young fool!" Alex reproved him sharply. "Eighty-five sowars are only part of the regiment. The rest of them will be looking to their officers to stand by them, to give them the courage to remain true to their salt. It will be the very devil of an ordeal for them and they'll be afraid, tempted to kick over the traces if ever men were, when their pride is trampled in the dust and they've nothing left in its place. Less than nothing, if the officers they know and trust desert them."

"I hadn't thought of it like that, sir," the boy admitted. "You're right, of course, I . . . I'll go and sober up, sir."

"Wait a minute," Alex said quietly. "I'll give you a final toast, if you wish. To the 3rd Light Cavalry, for all that it has been and all, please God, that it may be again!"

"Amen to that," Melville Clark responded huskily. He gulped down the contents of his glass, and then, letting the glass fall to shatter at his feet, he stammered a slightly slurred good night and left the room. He was, Alex saw, weeping unashamedly.

CHAPTER FOUR

⇛ • ⇚

BUGLES sounded reveille long before dawn, and in the brick-built European barracks and the Native Lines bordering the racecourse, sleepy-eyed soldiers and yawning sepoys answered the call with varying degrees of reluctance. In bungalows and bachelor quarters, lights flickered to life, officers buckled on their swords, donned helmets and shakos and called for their horses and, still in darkness, cantered off to join their regiments. Also in darkness, the first of several gun teams of the Bengal Horse Artillery limbered up and trotted smartly down Cannon Row from their park in East Street, a nine-pounder thudding behind them.

Soon the tramp of marching feet woke echoes in the still sleeping Sudder Bazaar, as the Meerut garrison of four thousand men started to converge, as ordered, on the Rifles' drill square, between Barrack Street and The Mall. It was a sultry dawn, with low-lying storm clouds and a hot wind to stir the dust on the freshly watered parade ground. An occasional growl of distant thunder drowned the shouted commands as regiment after regiment marched up and wheeled into its allotted position, to form three sides of a hollow square.

Facing each other were the two Queen's Regiments, the 60th Rifles in dark green, the 6th Dragoon Guards in scarlet and blue, pale sunlight glinting on their plumed brass helmets, as they kneed their still awkwardly recalcitrant Cape horses into a close-packed line. The third side of the square was formed by the Indian regiments, the sepoys of the 11th and 20th Native Infantry making a bright splash of colour in their red coatees, with white crossbelts and collars. Last to arrive and line up beside them, dismounted, were the sowars of the 3rd Light Cavalry, their French grey and silver uniforms dusty from unaccustomed foot drill and the long march from the racecourse to The Mall. The brown faces beneath the light dragoon shakos were glum and apprehensive as, under the stern eye of their colonel, they took up their dressing and shuffled, with booted feet, into line with the 11th.

Behind the square, two batteries of artillery were drawn up, backed up by a solid phalanx of blue-clad British gunners, each gun double-shotted with grape and the portfires lighted. The Indian troops had paraded with their arms, but no ammunition had been issued to them and their apprehension grew when they realized that they were trapped between the guns to their rear and the formidable ranks of close on a thousand riflemen, facing them with loaded Lee-Pritchetts. Not a man moved, however, and they came obediently to attention when a carriage, fashioned of wood with a basketwork frame and drawn by two ponies, made its appearance on the edge of the parade ground.

Positioned between the front rank of B Troop and the little knot of prisoners standing under guard and in miserable isolation, Alex watched the approach of the pony carriage with oddly conflicting emotions. This, then, he thought, was the buggy Lieutenant Clark had described—the equipage which did duty for the charger General Hewitt could no longer contrive to mount. The carriage came briskly towards the center of the square, escorted by two A.D.C.s on matching chestnuts. Little could be seen of its occupant, save the waving plumes of his cocked hat and it was not until the general was assisted to alight that Alex was able to get a clear view of him and he was hard put to it, despite Clark's warning, to suppress a horrified gasp.

The white-haired, tottering figure climbing unsteadily up the steps of the saluting base was a caricature of the man he had once been, so grossly obese that his uniform frock coat could scarcely be buttoned and was open at the throat, so shapeless that only his straining sword belt hinted at the position of his waist. At first it seemed as if he were too ill to be fully aware of his surroundings; he stood, looking vaguely about him, his heavily jowled face devoid of expression. Then, recovering himself, he nodded in the direction of the prisoners. To the roll of drums, a staff officer stepped forward, saluted and proceeded to read out the sentences in English, pausing occasionally to enable his words to be repeated in Hindustani by an interpreter, who was posted in front of the Indian regiments.

A visible tremor ran through the sepoys' ranks as they listened. The prisoners, discipline momentarily forgotten with the realization that there was to be no last-minute reprieve, turned to look at each other in ashen-faced disbelief. The price to be exacted from them was high and now they must fare it. No longer would they be proud soldiers, swaggering in the Company's uniform, fighting its battles. They were to be transported to a penal colony in the Andaman Islands where, pensions forfeited and honor lost, most of them would labor in felons' chains for ten long, weary years, while their families starved.

An old *daffadar,* wearing the medals for Ghuznee and the Sutlej campaign, started to weep; another dropped to his knees, praying wordlessly, but they were given no time in which to protest or plead for mercy. In response to a shouted order, two heavily laden ammunition carts, drawn by artillery troop horses, moved towards them and a detachment of British soldiers—armorers and smiths of the Horse Artillery—marched out from behind the silent ranks of the Rifles.

The old *daffadar* was the first to have his uniform stripped from him. A slash from behind rent the blue-grey cloth; medals and crested silver buttons were ripped off, to fall and be trampled underfoot, as the smiths moved on, spurs jingling, to the next in line, leaving the old *daffadar* to kneel, in his scant white loincloth, and remove his boots.

Alex felt sick with pity as he watched. Mutiny had to be punished, it was true, but not like this, not with thousands looking on. There was worse to come, he saw, as the blue-uniformed artillerymen crossed to the ammunition carts and returned, carrying leg-irons and lengths of chain over their shoulders.

One by one, the prisoners submitted to having fetters hammered about their bare ankles, the chains attached to them, riveted to necks and arms. None offered any resistance but, as the sun rose higher and the slow, humiliating work went on, their spirit broke and a chorus of voices pleaded humbly for forgiveness. Their appeals were addressed to the colonel but Carmichael Smyth sat his horse in silence, seemingly deaf to the frantic cries. After a while the pleas turned to curses and several of the men hurled their discarded boots in his direction but he continued to ignore them.

"The Government has imprisoned us without fault, Colonel Sahib!" the old *daffadar* screamed, struggling to hold himself upright in his chains. "We are not mutineers! What we did, we had to do, for our Faith! Show us mercy, *huzoor!* Did we not serve you well, I and others like me, for twenty years?"

His appeal, like all the rest, went unanswered. The colonel sat immobile, gazing stonily to his front and at last the prisoners were marched off in a shambling line, stumbling frequently as the heavy shackles impeded them. A few, bolder than their fellows, raised a defiant cry of *"Deen, deen!* For the Faith! Remember us!" as they came within earshot of the general but he, too, turned a deaf ear to them. Before they were out of sight, he descended from his wooden platform, leaning on the arm of an A.D.C., clambered awkwardly into the waiting buggy and was driven off, leaving General Wilson to dismiss the parade.

The Indian regiments marched off in turn, led by the 20th, the two British regiments standing firm until Colonel Carmichael Smyth gave the order for the Light Cavalry to follow them. Aware that the men behind him were weeping, Alex called them to attention again and made them dress ranks before permitting them to move off. Like the other troop officers, he was on foot and, while the dressing was in progress, he walked across to where he had seen the old *daffadar's* medals fall and, bending swiftly, picked them up. B Troop, under his temporary command, wheeled past the unlimbered guns and back on to the wide, tree-shaded Mall. He trudged in front of them and kept them marching to attention with their heads held high until they turned out of Bridge Street, into Circular Road, and the gaping watchers in the cantonment bungalows were left behind. The children had meant no harm, of course—they could not distinguish one regiment from another—but some of the Muslim servants had called out abuse and he had seen the men flinch.

He said to the native officer at his elbow, "B Troop may march at ease, *Rissaldar* Sahib. Before you dismiss the men to their quarters, tell them that they did well."

The *rissaldar* shouted the order. Falling into step with Alex again, the man, who was also wearing a Sutlej medal, remarked diffidently, "The Captain Sahib did a wise thing. It was well to remind these men that they are still soldiers, for they came close to forgetting it out there this morning, with so many to witness their shame."

"It need not be their shame, *Rissaldar-ji,*" Alex told him. "These are good men. If they stay true to their salt and obey the Company's *hukum,* today's shame can be wiped out. Make this clear to them also, before you dismiss the troop." He thought of Colonel Chalmers' Irregulars, remembering how they had run riot, looting and burning in the Civil Lines at Adjodhabad, and yet had incurred no punishment, because their commander had refused to believe in their guilt. *"Budmashes from the bazaar,"* Chalmers had insisted obstinately, when he had demanded redress. *"My men are well in hand. I will not insult them by making unfounded charges against them."* He sighed irritably. There had to be a happy medium, damn it—a line drawn between Colonel Chalmers' attitude and that of Carmichael Smyth, when it came to dealing with disaffection and mutiny. Old Chalmers' complacency had invited contempt, because his sowars imagined that he was afraid of them; they had interpreted his efforts to protect them from the consequences of their misdeeds, not as trust but as proof that he was seeking to buy their loyalty. They gave it, derisively, and continued to plot behind his back. Alex glanced at the line of dark faces at his own back and repeated his sigh.

What had Colonel Smyth achieved by forcing the issue? What emotions had his icy rejection of the mutineers' pleas for mercy and forgiveness aroused in these men, out there on the parade ground, under the threat of the double-shotted guns? Fear, perhaps, but also hatred, mingled with despair; they had been shown the price of mutiny, clearly and unequivocally—but would that ensure their loyalty? The faces were sullen and unhappy; they slouched along now, kicking up the dust, cowed and vulnerable, robbed of their pride, their eyes on the ground, looking like a rabble, many not even in step. For God's sake, how could these men be expected to forget what had been done to them? General Hearsey's way was better, surely. They should be disbanded now and permitted to return to their homes.

"Sahib," the grey-haired *rissaldar* ventured, as if guessing his thoughts, "there is one way in which hope might be restored."

Alex turned to look at him, checking his stride. The man's face was set in grave lines, his eyes anxious but they met his searching scrutiny without flinching. "Well, *rissalar-ji,*" he invited. "How might hope be restored?"

"If a new trial could be granted to those who are condemned —a good advocate hired, Sahib, to plead for them in mitigation. They are truly contrite. If the sentences could be reduced, perhaps, to a dishonorable discharge for each of them, with forfeiture of pension, would that not be punishment enough?"

It was a chance, Alex told himself—a slim one, heaven knew, but still a chance, if Colonel Smyth could be persuaded to consider such a possibility.

"They are not felons, Sahib," the *rissaldar* went on earnestly. "Many have served the Company for twenty years. *Daffadar* Ghulam Rasul—he whose medals the Sahib plucked from the dust—won his promotion for bravery at Sobraon, yet he is fettered just like the others, his past service counting for nothing."

"Are you asking me to intercede with the Colonel Sahib?" Alex questioned, frowning.

"The Colonel Sahib would not listen," the native officer answered sadly. "He turned his face away when they cried out to him and they cursed him, they flung their boots at the feet of his horse. The Colonel Sahib is a hard man—he will not forgive them for that."

"Then what is left, *Rissaldar* Sahib?"

"If the Captain Sahib would speak to the men, if he would hear their pleas. They are confined in the jail now, no longer in the hospital. Later today, I am given to understand, their troop officers will visit them to pay them off. Perhaps, Sahib, a petition . . . a humble confession of their fault and—"

"A petition to whom?" Alex interrupted, thinking despondently of General Hewitt. There was a possibility that he might be summoned to the general's presence, in order to supply him with any further information he required concerning the letters he had brought from Lucknow, although it seemed unlikely. Colonel Smyth would see to that. In any case, would General Hewitt consider a petition from the men he had so recently and publicly condemned?

"To the commander-in-chief, Sahib, in Simla," the old *rissaldar* said, lowering his voice. "That is the only chance left for them."

They were in sight of the long rows of thatched white huts that marked the native cavalry lines now and ahead of them, Alex saw, A Troop was forming up, preparatory to being dismissed. The colonel had led them off the Rifles' parade ground but had not ridden back with them—presumably as a sign of his disapproval— and the only mounted officer was the acting adjutant, Melville Clark. He hesitated, brows again furrowed.

"I will visit the men, *Rissaldar* Sahib," he promised. "Although I can hold out little hope that such a petition would be permitted to leave here—or that it would be heeded if it were. But I will talk to the other officers and see if anything can be done."

Over a gloomy *tiffin* in the mess, he discussed the *rissaldar's* suggestion with those officers who had elected to take their midday meal there. Few had any appetite and all were moody and depressed. Only Melville Clark snatched at the straw which the possibility of a petition offered, but the others shook their heads regretfully.

"They'll never be granted a retrial," the commander of A Troop asserted. He was a slow-voiced, pleasant captain named Henry Craigie, whose sympathies were clearly with the condemned sowars. "You know, I suppose, Sheridan, that two members of the court martial recommended the death penalty for all 85? By that criterion, they've been dealt with leniently . . . though I honestly believe that most of them would have preferred death to what was handed out to them this morning. The older men, certainly. They know they'll be left to rot in the Andaman Islands for what time is left to them. But"—he shrugged—"I'm going to the jail this evening, with Hugh Gough and Alfred Mackenzie. Come with us, by all means. You've been given B Troop, have you not?"

"Temporarily," Alex answered. "Until Major Harlow returns from leave."

"Then you come in your own right. We'll ride over about five, if that suits you?"

The discussion was continued as the four officers headed for the jail in the gathering dusk but so uncertain were they of the wisdom of raising false hopes that it was agreed between them that no mention of a possible petition should be made.

"We can sound the men as to their willingness to appeal for mercy," Henry Craigie said. "And provided a majority are willing, then we can bring the matter to the colonel's attention." He forestalled a question from young Lieutenant Gough with a wry, "I know, Hugh, I know. But *nothing* can be done without his knowledge and consent. He'd scotch it, if we tried. Don't you agree, Sheridan?"

Alex inclined his head. He was worried, not only about the condemned men but also about General Hewitt's reaction to the letters, which—if Archdale Wilson had kept his word—must surely have been shown to him by this time. Unless, of course, he reflected cynically, the station commander was so reluctant to disturb his superior's afternoon siesta that he had, on this account, delayed going to him. But the fact that he himself had been told nothing did not necessarily mean that the letters had not been delivered.

"Here we are," Captain Craigie announced, interrupting a somewhat heated exchange between Gough and Mackenzie on the subject of the missiles which had been hurled at their colonel during the punishment parade and the effect the mutineers' demonstration of hostility had had on him. "That is the City Jail." He pointed to a large, rambling building directly ahead of them, with heavily barred windows and a flat roof, standing behind an eight or nine foot high mud wall. There were red-coated sentries at the main gate—sepoys, Alex recognized, with some astonishment, of the 20th Native Infantry, in the charge of a *havildar*. They presented arms smartly when the small cavalcade halted at the gate and the *havildar* ordered it opened, took charge of the horses and summoned the European jailer from his house in the prison compound.

The 85 convicted sowars were confined apart from the other inmates, crowded into two dark, foul-smelling enclosures at the front of the jail, which clearly had been intended to accommodate half their number. The *charpoys* normally provided had been removed in order to make more room, the jailer explained apologetically, as he unlocked an iron-bound door between the two enclosures and stood aside to permit the visitors to enter. Craigie, looking about him distastefully, sent him for straw with which to

cover the damp, uneven mud floor and at the sound of his familiar voice, the fettered prisoners roused themselves from their
apathy and came swarming round him, begging eagerly for news.

"Captain Sahib—Allah be praised, I had not thought to see
the Sahib's face again! Is there word for us?"

"Are we to be shown mercy? Have our pleas been heard?"

"Captain Sahib, will the General Sahib release us? Will he
grant us forgiveness?"

The questions came thick and fast, but when the troop commander was compelled to shake his head, there was a stunned
silence. Some of the men turned away, weeping; others sank to
their knees, manacled hands grasping at Henry Craigie's boots,
beseeching him to help them and a few turned their backs, mut-
tering angrily. Gough and Mackenzie were also surrounded by
men of their troops and Alex, taking advantage of the fact that
he was a stranger to them, went in search of the old *daffadar,*
whom he found in the further room, his face buried in his hands,
weeping silently and alone.

"Ghulam Rasul!" he called softly and when the old man
looked up, startled, he took the medals from his pocket and held
them out to him. "These are yours, are they not?"

"Once I wore them, Sahib," the *daffadar* admitted. "But no
longer. Did you not see the white soldiers tear them from my
breast?"

"I saw, *daffadar-ji.* But they are yours, the reward of valor and
loyal service. I thought to restore them to you." Alex thrust the
medals towards him.

"The thought was generous, *huzoor.* But . . ." the bloodshot
eyes searched his face, went to his empty sleeve and then their
gaze rested once more on the two silver medals on his palm. "I
will take them, to keep hidden during my exile . . . for it will be

thus, Sahib, will it not? There is to be no pardon for us. We are to be sent into servitude?"

"I fear so," Alex said. "But we shall try to help you, if we can. Captain Craigie, Lieutenant Gough and the Adjutant Sahib, we shall all do what we can, Ghulam Rasul."

The old *daffadar* bowed his white head. He hesitated for a long moment, deep in thought and then, as if suddenly reaching a decision, leaned closer and said in a whisper, his lips to Alex's ear, "Bad things will happen, Sahib, if our pleas for mercy are ignored. Take warning, I beg you."

"Bad things, *daffadar-ji?* What manner of bad things?"

Ghulam Rasul turned away. "I cannot tell you, Sahib, for I do not know. I know only that our comrades will not desert us— the sepoys, as well as those of our own Faith and *paltan*—they will not see us suffer this injustice. There are those in the bazaars, holy men, *moulvis* and priests, who whisper that the John Company *Raj* will be ended very soon. We are the Company's men, Sahib, we have taken the Company's salt and its pay but they tell us that this is over—that we must end it, for our Faith. If we do not, then we shall see our Faith destroyed. These men speak of killing the *sahib-log*." The *daffadar's* gnarled brown hand, already sore and chafed by the raw iron of the fetters, came out to touch Alex's empty sleeve. "You, too, have fought the Company's battles, Sahib," he added softly. "And I would not see them kill you. Take heed."

Alex was thoughtful when he left the old man, every instinct crying out to him that what he had said was the truth. He went through the motions of paying off the men of his troop, obtaining their marks on the discharge papers and arranging that pitifully few coins to which each man was entitled should be paid to his dependents. When it was over and he and the other officers were on their way back to the lines, he repeated the *daffadar's* warning and Hugh Gough put in anxiously, "I was told much the same by my *rissaldar-major,* sir. Only he put it even more plainly. He came to my quarters, just before we set out for the jail, with some excuse about the troop accounts. The troop accounts, on a Saturday evening!"

"What did he say, Hugh?" Henry Craigie demanded.

"Well, he hinted that the troops would mutiny tomorrow—all of them, the Native Infantry regiments as well as ours. 'They will rise as one man,' he said, 'and free their comrades from the jail or die in the attempt.'"

"Why keep it to yourself?" Craigie reproached him. "You never mentioned anything to us and it could be damned serious, you know, if it's only half true."

"I went to the C.O., sir," Gough defended. "But he told me it was all nonsense and that I should be ashamed of myself for listening to such idle threats. He told me not to repeat it to anyone, but in view of what Captain Sheridan's just heard from the *daffadar,* I thought I'd better speak up. For one thing, there's a native guard on the jail and—"

"Quite so," Craigie agreed grimly. He heaved a sigh. "We'll go along to the Club, both of us, Hugh. And you too, Sheridan, if you're in agreement with the idea. General Wilson's usually there for a drink before dinner. We'll tell him. As station commander, he ought to know and at least, if he does nothing else, he might replace the jail guard with a detachment from the Rifles as a precaution. My wife is going to be annoyed—we have a dinner party this evening—but it can't be helped, this is too urgent to leave till after dinner. Alfred," he turned to the youthful Mackenzie, "be a good chap and ride over to my bungalow now, would you please? Say I've been unavoidably detained and hold the fort for me."

The boy obediently trotted off and Craigie glanced enquiringly at Alex. "Are you coming with us?"

"Certainly, if you think it will help. That guard *must* be changed."

"Don't be too optimistic," Craigie warned dryly. "Wilson probably ordered a sepoy guard, to show how implicitly he trusts them! Or possibly it was the G.O.C.'s idea, to demonstrate how effectively they've absorbed this morning's lesson that mutiny does not pay." He turned to head across the canal into Hill Street when someone called out to him and a horseman, a dim outline in the gathering darkness, came cantering to meet them. "It's Clark," he said. "What the devil! He seems in a hurry."

The adjutant drew rein beside them. "I'm glad I caught you," he exclaimed breathlessly. "I was just going to the jail, thinking you'd still be there. Captain Sheridan, the colonel wishes to see you," he told Alex.

"Trouble?" Craigie asked, frowning. "Oh, well, you'd better leave General Wilson to us, Sheridan. Don't worry. We'll make certain he hears the whole story. And perhaps *you* may succeed in convincing the colonel, where Hugh failed. Because *I* don't believe that these are all idle threats. I wish to heaven I did!" He and Gough rode on and Melville Clark glanced at Alex uncertainly.

"More of these rumors of mutiny, sir?" he suggested.

"I fear that they are more than rumors," Alex said, his tone bleak. He repeated what the old *daffadar* had told him and then Gough's account of the warning his *rissaldar-major* had brought, an hour or so earlier. "The colonel ridiculed Gough's warning," he added. "And told him to say nothing about it to anyone else. But he and Craigie have gone to the Club, hoping to speak to General Wilson, and I'd intended to go with them. *Someone* in authority must be persuaded to take action before it's too late, for God's sake!"

"The colonel won't," Clark asserted with unhappy conviction. "He insists that it's all talk. He's in a towering rage, I'm afraid— partly on your account, sir, but—"

"On *my* account? Why on my account, by all that's wonderful?"

"I believe he's had a message concerning you, by the electric telegraph from Lucknow," the adjutant explained. "I have not seen it, of course, but I gather it displeased him. I was ordered to find you at once and not to show my face in the Orderly Room again until I had!"

Sir Henry Lawrence's promised summons, Alex thought, and bit back a sigh. Last night he would have welcomed his recall but now, with this appalling crisis looming in Meerut, he wished that it could have been postponed for a few more days, until the threat of a mutiny of the native regiments had been averted. Until it was, General Hewitt could not be expected to send any of his British troops to Delhi. In fact, even if General Graves asked for them, he would have every justification in refusing the request.

His sigh must have been audible, he realized, when Melville Clark, evidently misunderstanding the reason for it, offered sympathetically, "I'm very sorry, sir. I'd have made a point of *not* finding you if I had dared to but when the C.O.'s in a mood like this . . . well, I've learned from painful experience that it's a mistake to try and cross him. It simply makes him worse and he doesn't forget, either." He hesitated, reining his horse to a trot as they crossed the cavalry parade ground. "Forgive my asking but . . . he doesn't like you, does he, sir? Didn't you serve with him before, in the Punjab?"

"Yes," Alex confirmed, "I did . . . and we got on quite well, I assure you. But . . ." he shrugged, remembering the cool reception accorded to him the previous evening. "He probably doesn't welcome ex-political officers back into the regimental fold. Few regimental commanders do, you know." They halted in front of the Orderly Room. "He's in here, not in the mess?"

Clark nodded, taking the rein as Alex dismounted from his horse. "He said he wanted to speak to you in private. I'll wait in the clerk's office, in case I'm wanted."

Colonel Carmichael Smyth was seated behind his desk when Alex tapped on the door of the inner office and, receiving permission, went in.

"You sent for me, sir?" he asked formally. "I'm sorry if I've kept you waiting. I went to the jail to—"

"To commiserate with the mutineers, who have been justly condemned and punished?" the colonel accused. He spoke without heat but a small pulse at the angle of his lean jaw was beating furiously.

"No, sir," Alex answered, taken by surprise. "To pay off those who were in my troop, as—"

"Not to organize a petition to the commander-in-chief, appealing for a new trial? I was told that this was your intention. My God, Sheridan, if it was—if you went behind my back to those men, I'll have you up before the general if it's the last thing I do!" All pretense of calm vanished; he was beside himself with rage, Alex realized. Of course, the *rissaldar* must have told him about the proposed petition; goaded or frightened by the threat of mutiny, probably, the native officer had claimed that an appeal for clemency was being organized, on the mutineers' behalf, by his new troop commander and the colonel had believed him, without attempting to verify his claim. He could hardly blame the unfortunate man, in the circumstances; it was a tense and difficult situation, following on the heartbreaking scene on the parade ground that morning.

"Permit me to explain, sir," he began. "I assure you, I—" but he was cut short.

"Explain?" Colonel Smyth flung at him. "What explanation is there for such conduct? Damn you, Sheridan, you've only been here for 24 hours and already you've started taking the law into your own hands, trying to teach me my business! Last night it was those infernal letters for which, perhaps, there was *some* excuse, since you brought the blasted things here. But today it's over a matter that is no concern of yours. This is *my* regiment and the miserable scum in the jail are—or were, until they proved themselves unworthy to be called soldiers—my men, and I shall deal with them as they deserve. Over my dead body will any sniveling petition be sent to the commander-in-chief, by you or anyone else, is that clear?"

"No petition has been organized to the best of my belief, sir," Alex told him, when the tirade came at last to an end. "Unless by the men themselves or by their comrades in the regiment. They—"

"Do you deny that it was for the purpose of organizing a petition that you went to the jail? Devil take you, Sheridan, I want the truth!"

Alex faced him, tight-lipped. "I was requested by my *rissaldar* to go there for that purpose, sir, but I made it very clear to him that there was little reason to hope that a petition would be permitted to leave here or that it would be heeded, if it were. Those, as I recollect, were my exact words to him. I did, however, offer to intercede with you, on behalf of the condemned men, if they asked me to and—"

"The devil you did! Intercede with *me,* for God's sake!" The colonel's voice shook. "The matter's out of my hands. I did not sentence them. They were tried and condemned by a properly constituted court martial, composed of their own countrymen. There's nothing I can do now." He rose and started to pace the room. "*Did* they ask you to intercede with me?"

Alex remained facing the desk. "Yes, sir, they did. On their knees, weeping. They begged for mercy, sir." He hesitated and, when the colonel said nothing, he repeated *Daffadar* Ghulam Rasul's warning. "I believe that Lieutenant Gough was given a similar warning, sir, which he reported to you?"

Carmichael Smyth drew in his breath sharply. "He did and I told him he was a damned young fool. These are just threats, calculated to force my hand. I'm not yielding to threats from my own sowars."

"Ghulam Rasul wasn't making any threats, Colonel. He was a good soldier and he's afraid. He doesn't want the regiment to mutiny but he believes that they will raid the jail in an attempt to free those who are imprisoned with him. If they do, it *will* be mutiny. If the infantry rise with them, there will be hell to pay."

"The infantry regiments won't rise with them. They're Hindus, why should they? In any case, if they should, we have enough British troops here to teach them a lesson." The colonel moved to the window, to stand looking out, jingling the coins in his pocket. He sounded less angry now and almost aggressively confident. "General Wilson isn't worried and he has his finger on the pulse of things. He's convinced that the worst is over. Look out there"—his gesture took in the rows of white painted mud huts, now visible in the light of the rising moon—"it's peaceful enough.

No fires, no excited voices. If they really meant business, they'd be milling about out there, yelling and shouting."

"Gough's *rissaldar* told him that it would be tomorrow," Alex pointed out. He tried a final appeal. "Isn't it possible to show those prisoners a small measure of clemency, sir? I truly believe that if they were allowed to appeal to General Hewitt, all danger of mutiny would be averted."

"The general wouldn't listen to an appeal, any more than I would, in these circumstances. It's too late, in any case. He can't overrule the verdict of a court martial."

"Then may I suggest, sir, that a British guard is placed on the jail?" Alex said wearily. "At present the 20th are on guard there."

"Oh, for God's sake, Sheridan!" The colonel turned irritably from the window. "It's up to the station commander whether the jail guard is British or native. I have no damned say in it. And whether we have a mutiny here or not is no concern of yours. I was forgetting I'd received a telegraphic message for you, from Lucknow. It's here somewhere." He made a pretense of searching among the papers on his desk and, watching him, Alex sensed that he had neither forgotten the telegram nor mislaid it. For reasons of his own, he had chosen to question him on the subject of the petition before making any mention of Sir Henry Lawrence's message. "Yes, here it is. You are recalled to Lucknow, by authority of the commander-in-chief to whom, it would appear, your friend and patron, Sir Henry Lawrence, has made an urgent request for your services. To command his cavalry, no less and," Smyth's tone was derisive, "with the brevet rank of lieutenant-colonel. Damn, I wish I had your influence!"

The reason for the delay in acquainting him with the news contained in the telegram now became clear but, for the second time during their brief interview, Alex was taken by surprise.

Sir Henry had promised him a step in rank, it was true, but he had expected it to be a local and acting rank, not a brevet authorized by the commander-in-chief, and his conscience pricked him. The promotion had been made now and in this manner to enable him to approach General Hewitt, of course.

"Since there is no room for two lieutenant-colonels in the Third Light Cavalry," Carmichael Smyth went on, "I take it you'll be leaving for Lucknow pretty well at once, Colonel Sheridan?"

Alex recovered himself. "I have to see General Hewitt before I can leave. Was he shown the Delhi letters, do you know?"

"Yes, he was shown them. Archdale Wilson went round with them before *tiffin*. The general did what we both knew he would. He sent them to Graves in Delhi, where they should have gone in the first place." There was a certain malicious satisfaction in the announcement and Smyth added, smiling, "If you must see him, then you must. But take my advice and request permission to call on him tomorrow; about midday is his best time. No, wait— tomorrow's Sunday, is it not? Make your request on Monday. The general likes to preserve the sanctity of the Sabbath Day, with Church Parade for the British regiments and all that, and tomorrow will be no different. Unless, of course, your gloomy forecasts come true and we have a mutiny on our hands. If you're wrong, at least you'll have a better chance of persuading the general to send a British detachment to Delhi, I imagine. I'll send a *chitti* to his house, if you wish, asking for an appointment for you on Monday."

Alex bowed, careful not to show his feelings. "Thank you, Colonel, I'd be obliged if you would."

His late commanding officer rose to his feet, still smiling. "Your promotion calls for a drink, but that will have to be postponed too, I'm afraid, because I'm dining out. Still, there'll be time enough for it tomorrow and naturally the hospitality of my mess is yours, for as long as you remain here. You'll be relieved of your duties with my regiment, of course. Gough can take over command of B Troop." He shouted for his horse and led the way out of the office, cramming on his shako, and Alex went after him, joined by Melville Clark a moment or so later. The adjutant glanced from one to the other of them nervously and, as they stood together on the steps of the Orderly Room waiting for their horses, Colonel Smyth said crisply, "Oh, Clark—post Lieutenant Gough to command of B Troop on Monday, will you? He'll have to act until Major Harlow returns from Simla."

"Very good, sir," Clark acknowledged. "Er . . . excuse me, sir, but is Captain Sheridan—"

"*Colonel* Sheridan has been posted to Lucknow on promotion. He'll be leaving us on Monday or Tuesday and—" He was interrupted by the sudden, sharp crack of a rifle and he swore angrily, ducking his head as the bullet passed between Alex and himself to bury itself harmlessly in the wall behind them. "What the devil! *Who* the devil fired that shot?"

"It came from over there, sir," Clark told him pointing. "I just glimpsed the flash—from behind B Troop office, I think."

"Then after him, you young idiot! And turn out the guard. I want him caught, whoever he is! If he's one of my men, I'll hang him! The devil take it! Orderly, where's my horse?"

Clark started to run, tugging at the pistol in his belt but Alex was before him. He too, had seen the flash of the rifle shot and he had seen something else as well: the dark silhouette of a big horse standing, with ears pricked and head lifted in alarm, beside a clump of mango trees on the road side of the parade ground.

There was no mistaking that noble head, even in the moonlight, and Alex's heart leaped. "Turn out the guard. Don't go after him yourself!" he shouted over his shoulder to the running Clark. "He'll make for the race-course if he can. He's left his horse there."

He himself ran towards the tethered horse, calling softly and, to his joy, he heard the animal whinny in response, saw him tug at the head-rope that held him. He was still thirty yards from his objective when the rifle spoke again and he felt the smack of the bullet as it struck his boot heel, the impact bringing him to his knees. The thud of hooves and a yell from Colonel Smyth brought his head round and he saw, as he dragged himself up again, that the colonel, mounted now, was thundering towards him, Clark and five or six of the quarter-guard at his heels.

"There he is!" the colonel bawled. He emptied his pistol, aiming at some target beyond Alex's line of vision and two of the guard knelt, carbines to their shoulders, ready to fire as soon as anything came into their sights. But nothing moved and Alex called back a warning of his own presence and ran on, relieved to find that he felt no pain in either foot.

He reached Sultan and bent to untie the head-rope when a dark body leaped on him without warning from the shadows and the moonlight glinted on naked steel. Ismail Khan, he realized, had not come alone. Unable to get to his pistol, he warded off the first blow with his upflung left arm and then attempted to grapple with his attacker, only to realize, to his dismay, that the man was naked, body and limbs smeared with oil, so that his groping fingers could not retain their grasp of his wrist. The menacing blade came nearer, aimed at his throat and he was compelled to give ground, thrusting out a foot over which, fortunately, his opponent tripped.

The man was up in an instant but now Sultan reared in alarm and Alex was able to put the plunging horse between himself and the would-be assassin for long enough to take his pistol from its holster. It was a six-shot Adams, which he had purchased recently in order to offset his difficulty in loading any weapon with one hand, and he brought it up with a brusque warning. His attacker let the knife fall and dived for the cover of the mango clump, the roar of the discharging pistol echoed by a volley from the guards' carbines. Alex was still endeavouring to calm the excited Sultan when two of the sowars dragged a limp black body from beneath the trees and laid it, grinning triumphantly, at his feet.

"What of the other *budmash?*" he asked breathlessly. "Did you get him?"

The grins widened. "The Colonel Sahib has him. See, Sahib, behind you!"

Alex turned. Ismail Khan, also naked, was being driven across the dusty parade ground, hands held above his head in token of surrender, the colonel trotting after him, grim-faced and uncompromising. His temper was swiftly restored, however, when Alex identified the prisoner. "A horse thief, is he? Well, he can be sent to the civil jail, to rot until he's brought to trial. Thank God it wasn't one of my men. For a moment or two I was afraid it might be. You'll forgive me, I trust, if I admit that I'm glad it was *you* he was after, Sheridan, and not myself. Whatever you may think, I don't *want* my regiment to mutiny." He smiled, the smile quite devoid of malice, as he looked at Sultan. "A fine piece of horse-flesh. I don't wonder the fellow was tempted. You'll be delighted to get him back."

"I am, sir," Alex confessed. "More than delighted . . . and grateful to you for laying the thief by the heels. He has a couple of charges of murder to answer for, as well as the theft."

"Don't thank me; I rather enjoyed the hunt, once I realized

he wasn't one of ours. Well, I'll have to get off to my dinner party. Pity you're not coming too, when you've so much to celebrate. But the adjutant will look after you in my absence—eh, Clark? You'll see that Colonel Sheridan is suitably entertained. Order champagne, my boy, and put it down to me."

"Certainly, sir," Melville Clark promised readily. "Only too happy, sir."

Hugh Gough was in the anteroom when Alex entered the 3rd Light Cavalry mess, half an hour later, after seeing Sultan bedded down for the night, with both Partap Singh and the *chokra,* Sukh Lal, in beaming attendance. He felt tired but in better spirits than he had felt all day and even Gough's apologetic announcement that he had "got no change out of General Wilson" failed to depress him as much as it might have done earlier.

"Well, it can't be helped, I suppose," he offered consolingly. "You did what you could. What reason did he give for not relieving the sepoy guard?"

Gough shrugged. "Oh, he said that the general was fully satisfied that they were carrying out their duties in exemplary fashion and that to relieve them now would make matters worse, because they'd think they weren't trusted. Then he gave us both, Henry Craigie and me, a lecture on not believing everything we heard! I tell you, I felt about two inches high." He stared moodily into his tankard of ale. "'When you've served for as long as I have, gentlemen,' he said. 'You'll learn to distinguish between the threat of revolt and the real thing. This is all talk. It will all blow over. The Meerut garrison won't mutiny and certainly your regiment will be the last to do so, in my considered opinion. They were taught a sharp lesson today and I'll take my oath it's one they won't forget when the chips are down.' That was what he told us, sir, more or less word for word, and I suppose I must believe him. He's got a lot more service than I have. Damn it, he *must* know what he's talking about!"

It was to be hoped that he did, Alex thought. He was spared the necessity of a reply by the arrival of Melville Clark and half a dozen of the other officers, attended by two immaculately uniformed mess orderlies, bearing trays of brimming champagne glasses.

"Bubbly, gentlemen!" Clark announced. "By courtesy of the commanding officer, who regrets his inability to join us owing to a prior engagement. Help yourselves!"

Young Gough swore softly. "What are we celebrating?" he asked. "The fact that the regiment was taught a sharp lesson today? Or are we simply fiddling while Rome burns?"

"Don't be an ass, Hugh," Clark bade him. "Here"—he thrust a glass into his friend's hand—"cheer up, for God's sake! We're celebrating a well-deserved promotion." He met Alex's eye and, ignoring his embarrassed headshake, raised his glass. "Your good health, Colonel Sheridan, sir! Speaking personally, I'm sorry that your association with this regiment is so soon to be terminated."

They drank the toast and crowded around, offering congratulations, wringing his hand, asking eager questions and Alex thanked them, very red of face, wishing that he could tell them the real reason for his sudden elevation in rank. But they seemed pleased by it and the champagne helped to dispel the gloom that had haunted them since early morning. He ordered more and the tense, unhappy young faces relaxed, as the memory of the pain and humiliation they had endured on the Rifles' parade ground was cast—temporarily, at least—into oblivion, and they laughed again, as few of them had hoped to laugh when they had marched back with their regiment that morning.

"Come on, my bonnie boys!" Gough invited, when the mess bugle sounded and they prepared to troop into dinner. "Eat, drink and be merry, for tomorrow . . ." he broke off, grinning. "Oh, hell, no, that's not right, is it? We aren't going to die tomorrow, on the word of Brigadier-General Archdale Wilson, who knows the John Company sepoy so much better than we do! *He* says there'll be no mutiny. D'you hear that, gentlemen?" He resisted Melville Clark's attempt to restrain him. "*You* told me to cheer up, Nobby old son."

"I didn't tell you to get drunk, you idiot," Clark reproached him. "And in the colonel's presence, too!"

"I am *not* drunk," Gough insisted. He bowed to Alex, the grin fading and a look of very adult disillusionment in his blue eyes. "No offense, Colonel Sheridan, sir, believe me. I'll alter the end of that quotation, shall I? Eat, drink and be merry, for tomorrow we *live*. Not that it matters either way, for what have the Third Cavalry got to live for now? Eighty-five poor devils of sowars chained up in the jail and the rest of us going round with hang-dog expressions, apologizing for them and expecting to be insulted! That's not life, is it? Well *is* it, gentlemen?" No one answered him and he added, with a flash of anger, "Whatever Wilson thinks, I'd stake my oath on our sowars having the guts to try and free those poor sods in the jail. Dammit, for two pins I'd help 'em!"

There was a shocked silence and Gough, realizing that he had gone too far, rose from his seat at the long table, apologized to the mess president and excused himself.

Alex also took his leave soon after the meal was over, aware that in his new rank his presence was bound to inhibit them from indulging in the schoolboy horseplay that would act as a safety valve, and they insisted on chairing him to the door of the mess.

Not entirely to his surprise, a sober Gough joined him and

together, on borrowed troop horses, they made a tour of the lines. All was quiet; they could detect no sign of tension or excitement and Alex returned to his quarters in an optimistic mood, which owed only a little to the champagne he had consumed. He wrote a report to Sir Henry Lawrence, sent Partap Singh to the *dak* with it and retired, his conscience a trifle eased by its confession of failure.

CHAPTER FIVE

SUNDAY, MAY 10th, dawned hot and overcast and all day the heat increased, with scarcely the hint of breeze to bring relief from it.

Alex attended early morning service in the garrison church, paid another visit to the lines with Gough, who was orderly officer and then, in common with most of the other Europeans and their families, he lay down on his bed and attempted to sleep through the long, sweltering afternoon. But sleep eluded him; despite the appearance of calm and the sight of the off-duty sowars, in their white, undress uniforms, squatting under the trees in the lines and passing the stems of their hubble-bubble pipes from hand to hand, he was uneasy. He felt instinctively that it was too quiet. The men talked in whispers, falling silent when anyone, even a servant, came within earshot, and the sullenness of yesterday had gone from their faces, replaced by a bright-eyed watchfulness which, of itself, was alarming.

Partap Singh, returning from the Sudder Bazaar just before five, reported that all the shops were open and plying their trade as usual.

"The white soldier-sahibs were there," he said, in answer to Alex's enquiry. "But they left before I did, Sahib. It seems they have a church parade, put back until the hour of six on account of the heat." The Rifles, Alex thought, frowning. They would parade for church, according to hot weather custom, in white drill with sidearms only. Their Lee-Pritchetts would be left in the barrack-rooms, chained in their racks, and the ammunition for them locked up in the armory. Why, he wondered helplessly, hadn't the darned church parade been cancelled and the regiment kept standing by, if only as a precaution? He sat up, with a smothered exclamation and Partap Singh, misunderstanding the reason for his sudden movement, pushed the tea tray closer to his hand.

"I noticed some *budmashes,* Sahib," he volunteered. "Men from outside the city, a *Bunnia* told me, although he could not say what had brought them to the bazaar. And I heard a rumor that there had been some trouble in the Street of the Harlots."

"Trouble?" Alex echoed. "What kind of trouble?"

The orderly shrugged. "The Sahib's tea is getting cold," he pointed out. "As to the nature of the trouble, I do not know exactly. It was said that the women offered taunts to some of the Light Cavalry sowars, accusing them of cowardice because they had come seeking pleasure while their comrades lie in chains, in the prison."

Alex waited to hear no more. "Saddle my horse, Partap Singh," he ordered urgently. "*Jeldi* . . . all right," he said, as the man hesitated, "I can dress without your help. Get Sultan!"

He was buckling on his sabre when Partap Singh came rushing back to the shuttered room, his return heralded by a burst of musketry from somewhere alarmingly near at hand.

"Sahib, Sahib—the sowars have set fire to the lines and they are riding for the jail!"

So it had come, Alex told himself, feeling his stomach turn to water. What he had feared and dreaded was about to happen although, perhaps, it was not too late to ride after the sowars to the jail. If only the cavalry had broken they might, even now, listen to reason. He ran out on to the veranda, the acrid smell of smoke in his nostrils, to encounter Gough, with a *rissaldar* and two men, already mounted.

"My *rissaldar* says that the Native Infantry have risen too," the orderly officer shouted breathlessly, as Alex grabbed Sultan's rein from his waiting *syce* and flung himself into the saddle.

"Has Colonel Smyth been informed?" he asked.

Gough nodded. "I've just told him, sir. He's Field Officer of the Week. He's gone to General Wilson, to have the Rifles' church parade cancelled. He told me to collect as many of our officers as I could and try to hold the men in the lines. I've sent for the others."

"Then they can follow us," Alex decided. "Come on!" He set spurs to Sultan, hearing, as Gough and his escort thundered after him, the faint, incongruous sound of the band in the Public Gardens, on the far side of The Mall, as it brought a brassy rendering of *The Last Rose of Summer* to a spirited crescendo. Praise be to heaven, he thought, most of the British wives and families would be there, in their carriages, listening to the evening concert, if they weren't on their way to church. Both church and gardens were close to the European barracks; they could seek safety there, if they were attacked. Although surely there was no reason why the sepoys should attack them, when all they wanted was the release of the 85 mutineers from the jail?

"My God, sir," Gough gasped, as they rounded the quarter-guard building. "Look at them! Have they gone mad?"

His horror was understandable, Alex saw. The normally neat, well-ordered rows of barrack huts had become a shambles, with men running this way and that, hurling lighted brands on to the thatched roofs which—tinder dry—instantly burst into flames. The sowars had broken open the bells-of-arms, in which their carbines were stored and, leaping and whirling in a frenzied dance, were firing into the air, screaming at each other in blood-curdling abandon.

In the swiftly gathering darkness, blinded by the glare of the blazing huts, they did not, for a few minutes, notice the arrival of the two officers but when they did, a concerted howl went up and a score of men leapt for their horses, which were tethered but not yet saddled.

"*Maro! Maro!* Kill! kill the *feringhi!* For the Faith, brothers. Strike a blow for the Faith!"

Carbines were raised and a ragged but ill-aimed volley passed over their heads as Gough's *rissaldar,* in a shaken voice, pleaded with them to flee. "Sahib, we must leave or we shall all be killed! I beg you, Sahib."

Gough looked round uncertainly. The mounted men had halted, apparently lacking a leader and Alex said, "B Troop—come on, they haven't set fire to their block yet. Let's see if we can rally them." They swung their horses right and, pursued by a few random shots, made for the row of huts on the far side of the lines.

But even here, although there were no fires, there was ample evidence of mutiny. The magazine had been broken into and the men of B Troop were engaged in dragging out crates of ammunition, breaking them open and distributing cartridges to their comrades. Gough yelled at them to stop but the sowars ignored him, although they offered no violence and made no attempt to fire on any of the new arrivals. Alex, spotting a young trumpeter on the edge of the crowd, trotted forward and rode him off, driving him back to where Gough and his escort were waiting, a spurred boot pressed to the small of his back.

"Sound Assembly," he ordered sternly and the youth, cringing from him in terror, put his instrument to his trembling lips and sounded the call. Half a dozen men, all N.C.O.s responded, amongst them the *rissaldar* who had sought his aid to present a petition to the commander-in-chief. He held a carbine in his left hand and there was a bulging cartridge pouch suspended from his sword belt; but he came to attention and saluted smartly.

"This is not the way, *Rissaldar* Sahib," Alex told him, more shocked by the sight of his hitherto trustworthy native officer in such compromising circumstances than by anything that had gone before. "You, surely, are not a mutineer?"

"It is the only way left to us, Sheridan Sahib," the man answered, a catch in his voice. "We cannot leave our comrades to rot in their chains. They are our brothers, they are of our Faith. We cannot desert them in their hour of need. I went yesterday to the Colonel Sahib, to plead for them, but he would not listen."

"But soon the Rifles will be here and the Dragoons," Alex said. "And these men will have to suffer the penalty for what they have done . . . only it will not be ten years' transportation for this night's work, it will be death. Can you not help us to restore order?" He was conscious of genuine grief when the *rissaldar* shook his head.

"*Nahin,* Sahib, I cannot. We shall release our brothers from the jail and then we shall go. But we intend you no harm, Sahib. I will select some reliable men to escort you back to your quarters. You must go at once, it is dangerous for you here. There are wild ones, who think only to kill. If you and Gough Sahib will wait until I can get the men mounted, I will myself ensure that you are unmolested."

"What do you think, sir?" Gough asked, when the *rissaldar* had gone. "Can we do any good here if we stay?"

"I doubt it," Alex confessed regretfully. "But when we've collected our escort, I think we should try our luck at the jail. They can't all have gone mad and it's possible that we might be able to reason with them when they've done what they set out to do."

"Released the prisoners, you mean?"

"Yes. But—" hearing the thud of galloping hooves, and a fresh outbreak of firing coming from the road that ran past the west side of the Sudder Bazaar, he stiffened. From behind the blazing huts two horsemen appeared, bent low in their saddles, both with sabres drawn, followed by a third, who was evidently wounded, and then a fourth horse, to which two riders clung, came pounding bareback after them. The first two drew rein and turned to face the mob of white-clad mutineers who were pursuing them, with the obvious intention of giving the other three time to escape, and a concerted howl went up from the mob.

"My God, that looks like Henry Craigie!" Gough exclaimed, drawing his own sabre. He and Alex galloped to join the two who had halted, Alex letting his knotted reins lie loose on Sultan's neck to enable him to draw his pistol, urging the horse on with knees and heels. The escort with which they had started did not follow them but when, after a brief exchange of sabre thrusts and pistol shots, they ranged themselves beside the other two, the mob surprisingly drew off, still screaming for their blood but, for some reason, reluctant to take it. They retreated slowly to the shelter of the darkened magazine, where they found the other fugitives being guarded by the Indian noncommissioned officers who had responded to the bugle call.

"Wait here, Sahib," a *daffadar* of B Troop advised Alex, in an urgent whisper. "We go to get our horses and then we will take the wounded sahibs to the hospital."

They vanished and Henry Craigie wiped the sweat from his brow with a shaking hand. "That was a close call," he said wryly. "Thanks for your timely assistance." He gestured in the direction in which the *daffadar* had gone. "Are those all the men who are with us?"

"Not quite all. My *rissaldar* has promised to provide a reliable escort for us," Alex told him. "When—if—he keeps his word, we intend going after the rest to the jail, to see if we can reason with them."

"I see. Well, I'll try to rally some of my troop to join you. But," he lowered his voice, "it's a damned ugly situation, Sheridan. And it's a hell of a lot worse in the Infantry lines. The two who were with us just managed to escape with their lives. They're both officers of the 11th and they've both been hit. They'd have been killed if they hadn't found a riderless horse. The third fellow we picked up on our way here; I don't know who he is, but he's badly hurt and . . ." he sighed despondently as Gough and young Alfred Mackenzie, who had gone to the aid of the wounded officer, lowered him to the ground and, meeting his mutely questioning gaze, shook their heads. "Poor devil! Well, that's another they'll have to answer for, damn them."

"What happened, do you know?" Alex asked. He was attempting to reload his Adams and Craigie took it from him. "Here, let me do that for you," he offered. "As to what happened, one of them told me that they went with their C.O., Colonel Finnis, to try and steady their men. The colonel's a popular officer and, backed up by his Indian N.C.O.s, he'd apparently succeeded in holding them when some madman started yelling that the 20th were coming to attack them."

"The *Twentieth?*" Alex echoed. "But for God's sake—"

"Yes, I know, the whole blasted thing's crazy," Craigie admitted. "But poor Finnis went to the 20th's lines and they shot him down and then turned on the rest of their officers. The 11th promptly did the same and now they're running amok, breaking out their arms and burning their huts as our men appear to have done. So far, though, they haven't left their own lines and if we can keep them there until . . . where the devil *are* the Rifles and the Dragoons? Have they been told what's going on, for heaven's sake?"

It was Gough who answered him. "I went to the C.O. as soon as I heard that our men had broken out, sir. He said he would inform General Wilson at once and told me to do what I could here. Colonel Sheridan and I have been here ever since."

"*Colonel* Sheridan?" Craigie returned the loaded pistol, a brief smile twisting his smoke-blackened lips. "Then you're in command, sir. What orders do you have?"

"It looks as if that's been decided for me," Alex answered. He pointed to where, under one of their own *rissaldars,* the men of the 3rd Light Cavalry were forming up in orderly ranks, mounted and properly accoutered. There were about two hundred of them and they might have been mustering for duty, so perfect was their turnout, so disciplined their response to the shouted commands. But when the *rissaldar* stood up in his stirrups, with sabre raised, and ordered them to the jail, the cheers that went up from the packed ranks were chilling in their savagery.

"*Din! Din!*" came the roar, from two hundred throats. "For

the Faith! The Company's *Raj* is ended. . . . Death to the *feringhi!*"

"We shall have to go after them, Captain Craigie," Alex warned. "With or without an escort. They've *got* to be stopped, but we'll have to summon help. Lieutenant Gough!" Gough was at his side, blue eyes blazing. "Ride for the Artillery barracks, as fast as you can make it. Tell whoever's in command that the jail is about to be attacked and we require Horse Artillery support, and then inform the C.O. of the Rifles. Captain Craigie and I are going after them and we'll take Mackenzie with us. The two wounded officers had better go with you but don't delay on their account, they'll have to fend for themselves. It's to be hoped that the Dragoons are already on their way here but if they're not, then get a message sent to them." He hesitated, assailed by a sudden, nagging fear. The destination of the 3rd Light Cavalry was in no doubt. But what of the two mutinous infantry regiments?

Gough saw his hesitation and asked quietly, "Anything else, sir?"

"Yes," Alex told him, tight-lipped. "I'm taking it for granted that steps will have been taken to send British troops to protect the cantonment bungalows but if they have not, then for God's sweet sake impress on any senior officer you can find that it is imperative they should be. I'll give you the best escort I can but don't stop for anything or anyone, d'you understand? It's vital that you get through."

"I understand, sir." Gough's face was white. "But with two Queen's regiments available *and* the artillery, surely—" he did not complete his sentence and Craigie said, shaken, "My wife and Alfred Mackenzie's sister were on their way to church. I waited to see them off. But they must have got there by now, they *must* have! Pray heaven they've stayed there."

"Ride past Captain Craigie's bungalow, Gough," Alex ordered. "To make sure it's empty. If you should find the ladies there, take them with you to the Dragoons' guardroom and go by Circular Road. Don't attempt to go through the bazaar in any case."

"Thanks," Henry Craigie acknowledged briefly. "I . . ." his voice lost some of its anxiety. "Look, sir, our escort. Ten, no, by God, twelve of them have kept their word! That has restored my faith in miracles. Give me five minutes, will you please, to see if I can induce a few more to follow their example? There are still some of my troop saddling up over there and they're good men. I might be able to talk them around."

Alex agreed without hesitation. He sent Gough's original escort and half the newly arrived men to accompany him on his errand and when they had gone, with the two wounded officers of the 11th Infantry in their midst, he occupied the time of waiting by looping the ends of his reins round his stirrups, so as to leave his single arm free. The old *rissaldar* watched him for a moment and then, dismounting, came to his aid.

"The Sahib is wise," he approved, with unconscious irony. "For he may well need to draw his *tulwar* before this night is over. Mackenzie Sahib"—his gaze went to where young Alfred Mackenzie was draping a horse blanket over the body of the unknown officer who had died of his wounds—"Mackenzie Sahib is saying that you would go to the jail. That, Sahib, is not wise."

"It is my duty," Alex told him. "I ask that you will come also, *Rissaldar* Sahib, but I shall not order you to do so. We would speak to the men, that is all. I shall not draw my *tulwar* save in my own defense. I have sent for guns but I shall bid them hold their fire if the men will hear me."

"They will not hear you, Sahib. They have gone too far. They are deaf to all but the call of their Faith. It would be better not to go."

"I have to go. Do you come or stay?"

The old native officer was silent but finally he bowed his head. "I will come," he agreed reluctantly. "I gave my word and I will keep it if I can. But if the white soldiers attack, I must fight with my brothers." He smiled, with unexpected warmth. "And that may not be wise but I have my duty also. Does the Sahib understand?"

"I understand, *Rissaldar-ji,* although with sadness." Alex offered his hand and the *rissaldar* took it, his smile fading. "This is a sad day, Sheridan Sahib. I would it were over."

"Captain Craigie's coming, sir," Mackenzie warned, swinging himself into his saddle. Alex glanced round and felt his heart lift as he saw that some thirty sowars were cantering at their troop commander's back, with Melville Clark riding beside him, bareheaded and on a foam-flecked horse. They set off at once after the main body and Clark said breathlessly, as they circled the still smouldering huts, "I've just got here, sir. The colonel sent me to alert the Carabineers but I never expected this." He looked about him in stunned disbelief. "Oh, God, what an appalling sight!"

"*Did* you alert the Carabineers?" Alex demanded. "Are they on their way?"

The adjutant shook his head. "They were ordered to the Rifles' parade ground. They'd gone when I got there, two mounted squadrons and the rest on foot, the guard commander told me. The general's orders, he said, sir."

Alex stared at him. "How long ago was that?"

"About . . . oh, about an hour ago, I think. I ran into several parties of the N.I., making for the Sudder Bazaar and I got this," he indicated a sabre cut which had severed his left shoulder-chain and slashed through the cloth of his sleeve, "from a sepoy of the 11th, who must have stolen an officer's horse. He nearly did for me, because I didn't see him coming and I had to run him through, because it was either him or me." He talked on excitedly but Alex scarcely heard him.

If the general had ordered the Dragoons to the Rifles' parade ground, presumably this must be with the intention of mustering all his British troops, including the Artillery, preparatory to sending them to the native lines. No doubt patrols had already been despatched and some must, by this time, have returned with their reports. Hugh Gough might well have met and joined up with one of them but, even if he hadn't, he should soon be at the Rifles' barracks, so support would not be long delayed.

"I gave your Sikh orderly my twelve-bore," Melville Clark was saying. "And told him to stand guard in our quarters. I was afraid that . . ." his words died in his throat. "Oh, my God, sir, look at them! Every *budmash* from the bazaar is out!"

They emerged into Suddar Street and Alex saw that he was right. A vast crowd was milling about, screaming and shouting wildly as the sepoys had done for the blood of the *feringhi*. Most of them were armed with clubs and spears, a few with matchlocks and almost all carried flaming brands and torches with which they were setting fire to every building they passed. Over to his left, he saw with mounting dismay, the British cantonments were a sea of flames and men were running, uniformed infantry sepoys among them, laden with plunder of every description, from silverware to furniture and he did not need a second glance to tell him that it had come from looted British bungalows.

Alex's first instinct was to charge and disperse the howling predators and, glancing at Craigie, he saw his own thoughts mirrored in the troop commander's grimly set face.

"What do you think?" he asked and Craigie regretfully shook his head.

"We daren't trust them, sir. I'm sorry. I wish I could say we could. But they've only agreed to escort us to the jail. They . . ." He swore. "Sweet Mother in Heaven, look! It's a British woman!"

A palanquin-*gharry*—a boxed-in carriage, drawn by a single horse—came careering drunkenly towards them from a side street. There was no driver, the terrified horse was out of control and riding beside it, his sabre raised, was a sowar of the 3rd Light Cavalry. As they watched, the heavy blade descended on the hapless occupant of the *gharry* and was raised again, ominously stained. Without waiting for orders, Craigie and Mackenzie spurred forward to meet the *gharry* and Craigie's sabre took the sowar across the back of the neck. He fell with a shriek and behind them, Alex heard angry murmurs from their escort.

"You are soldiers!" he reminded them, in ringing tones. "Not murderers of defenseless women!" and the murmurs were stilled. The crowd, however, was not so easily appeased; they had recognized the four British officers riding at the head of what they had, at first, taken to be a body of mutineers on their way to free their comrades from the jail, and shouts went up, calling on their escort to turn on them.

"Death, death to the *sahib-log!*"

"Why do you ride at their heels, like cowed dogs?"

"Kill them! kill them! Would you betray us, who come to fight your battle with you?"

"Maro—sab lal hogea! Maro, maro!"

The cries came from all sides and one man, a butcher by the look of him, made a dash for Mackenzie, aiming a blow with a meat-axe at his horse. Alex felled him with a single shot from his pistol and the crowd retreated, suddenly silent. Their escort, in obedience to his shouted command, spread out, driving the mob before them, offering no violence but gaining their ascendancy by disciplined steadiness.

All might have been well had not Mackenzie's horse, shying away from the butcher's fallen body, carried him to the road verge, where a trailing wire—the severed telegraph cable, Alex afterwards realized—whipped around the upper part of his body and brought him thudding to the ground. With commendable presence of mind, the boy retained his grasp of the reins but several of the sowars rode over him before he was able to drag himself, shaken and covered with dust, back into the saddle, calling out breathlessly that he was all right.

They were nearing the junction of the canal and the Grand Trunk Road now, still without seeing any sign of British patrols or reinforcements and everywhere they looked, it seemed, looters and arsonists were running riot, and more and more buildings were being set alight. The smoke was suffocating, clouds of ash were blown into their faces and the glare from the flames revealed corpses, hideously mutilated, lying beside the road or in the trampled, smoke-shrouded gardens of blazing bungalows. These were the Civil Lines and many hapless Eurasian and Indian Christian families had evidently been the first victims of the crowd's bloodlust. Alex saw, with a sense of shocked revulsion, that the blue-uniformed civil police, armed with their steel-tipped *lathis,* were at the forefront of several of the rioting mobs.

He said, uneasily, to Craigie, "I'm worried about the cantonment bungalows and the British married families' quarters, not to mention our own." He jerked his head in the direction of The Mall. "It may be my imagination, but I believe I can see fires burning over there."

"It's not just your imagination," Craigie answered thickly.

"They are. In heaven's name, what are the Queen's regiments *doing?* They must have got patrols out by now. They've had over two thousand men, mustered and under arms, on the Rifles' parade ground for well over an hour."

"It's more like two," Clark put in glumly. "It took me an hour to get to our lines from the Dragoons' barracks, Henry, and it's taken us over half an hour to get this far. And I haven't seen a patrol or heard any firing, have you?"

They looked at each other, unwilling to believe that the British regiments could have remained inactive for so long.

"They may have gone to the jail," Clark said, without conviction. "Or be on their way there, with the gunners. The Dragoons had two troops mounted."

Henry Craigie groaned. "I hope to God you're right! Dammit, you must be. The Rifles are a first-rate regiment and their C.O., Colonel Jones, isn't the sort of fellow to sit back and do nothing when the whole place is going up in smoke. Probably they've brought all the women and children into barracks by this time— their own, at all events. I'm not so sure about ours. And of course, if the general . . ." He swallowed hard, reluctant, even now, to express his doubts concerning General Hewitt's competence.

Remembering the obese, tottering old man who had stood on the saluting base the previous day, looking about him with lackluster eyes, Alex felt fear clutch at his throat. If the senile old general were in command then the inactivity was understandable but there was Wilson who, for all his unwillingness to accept the possibility of a mutiny, was an efficient and experienced officer. "The general would surely listen to advice from his staff, Craigie," he suggested.

"Perhaps. Oh, God grant that my wife and Liz Mackenzie

didn't try to get back to the bungalow! Because if they did, if they went back after Hugh Gough called there, then they . . . oh, God have mercy on them!"

"Go back," Alex urged, feeling acutely sorry for him. "You and Mackenzie. Call for volunteers to accompany you and take as many men as you need."

"And who will go to the jail?" Craigie objected. "You and Clark can't go alone."

"We'll go with the *rissaldar* and half a dozen men. W are probably too late now to prevent them releasing the prisoners, unless Gough got through with my message and we find the Horse Artillery battery and a British patrol there. If we do, all may yet be well and we shan't need you in any case. But if we don't and I find we can't do anything useful there, then Clark can join you with the rest of our men and I'll go to the Rifles' barracks and," Alex's mouth hardened, "I'll demand action, if they break me for it!"

"Right, sir," Craigie agreed. "I'm grateful. It's not only my wife I'm anxious about. There are several others, who may have stayed at home. Charlotte Chambers, whose husband is adjutant of the 11th, for one. She's pregnant and very near her time." He laid a hand on Alex's knee, forcing a smile, "I'll do what I can, sir, and thank you again. Good luck and I hope you find the Gunners waiting for you!"

He had no difficulty in obtaining his volunteers and he and Mackenzie turned and were off at a gallop in the direction from which they had come, the sowars clattering obediently after them and the mob, which had been following at their heels, parting with shrill shrieks and curses to let them through.

There was another, much larger and more dangerous mob

gathered about the jail when Alex, with Melville Clark and their now diminished escort approached it at a cautious trot. By the gate, a number of blacksmiths had set up anvils and lighted fires, beside which they waited expectantly, swinging their hammers and jesting with the crowd—evidence, Alex's mind registered, that the release of the prisoners had been planned and was about to take place. A few red-coated sepoys stood with them but of the British troops he had hoped to find there he could see no sign and his heart sank.

"We shan't have a hope of stopping them now, sir," Melville Clark said bitterly, putting his thoughts into words as the *rissaldar* hissed at them to draw rein. "The devil take those Queen's regiments! With even half a troop of Dragoons we might have done it but as it is . . ." He passed a hand across his smoke-grimed face. "Look, here they come!"

As the first of the prisoners emerged through the smashed iron gratings, assisted by the guards and their fellow cavalrymen, a frenzied cheer sounded above the crash of tumbling masonry and the roar of flames from the blazing courthouse nearby. Borne on the shoulders of their comrades, the prisoners were taken to the waiting anvils and the bazaar smiths, wielding their hammers dexterously, made short work of their leg irons and manacles, to the accompaniment of triumphant shouts from the line of mounted sowars drawn up to receive them. As each man was freed, he was given a horse and his uniform—the white undress jacket and pantaloons, normally worn off duty—and mounting, he drew his sabre, to join in the excited cheering which greeted every new addition to the ranks.

It was, Alex thought, for all the babble of voices, a disciplined and well-ordered operation. The men kept their ranks and obeyed the orders of their N.C.O.s; the European jailer and his wife stood, under guard but unharmed, by the door of his house, which, unlike those in the immediate vicinity, had not been set on fire. When all the 85 condemned men had been restored to the status they had lost, an Indian officer called them to attention and, ignoring the frantic appeals from other inmates of the jail who were watching from behind its barred windows, prepared to move them off. In threes, in perfect alignment, the regiment wheeled and Alex spurred to meet them. It was now or never, he knew. If any appeal to reason were to be made, he dared delay no longer.

But he had covered only a few yards when the old *rissaldar* and two of his escort closed around him, jerking Sultan back on his haunches with a brutal tug at his bridle.

"No, Sahib, no!" the *rissaldar* implored him.

"But I must speak to them. I must!"

"They would not listen. They would tear you limb from limb. You cannot stop them now." The man's fear was very real, Alex recognized; it was in his voice, in his dark, anxious eyes and in the trembling of his hand as it closed about Sultan's rein. "Come, Sahib, I beg you. We will take you and Clark Sahib to safety and then we will go."

"*You* will go, *Rissaldar* Sahib? But you have committed no crime, you have not joined the mutiny. Where will you go?"

"To join my regiment," the old man answered defiantly. "The 3rd Light Cavalry will march to Delhi, with the infantry *paltans,* at once. We shall pledge our lives and our *tulwars* to the service of Bahadur Shah, to whom we shall restore the throne of the great Mogul emperors, which is his by right. It is written, Sahib, that the Company's *Raj* will be ended throughout India. It is the will of Allah! And, as you have seen, we have struck the first blow and gained the first victory. The white soldiers have not opposed us. Allah is great!"

His words and the calm certainty with which they were uttered struck into Alex's heart. He did not argue, he could not, aware that any contradiction he might offer would evoke only scorn. In the absence of all opposition on the part of the British regiments to the orgy of arson and looting, as well as to the release of the prisoners, any mutineer might be justified if he claimed victory and attributed that victory to the will of his god, be it Allah or Ram.

He met Clark's shamed gaze, as their escort bustled them on through the ruined streets and the sacked houses, each with its quota of dead, and the younger man burst out wretchedly, "I never thought that I would live to see Meerut destroyed and no effort made to save it! I almost wish that I were lying there, with those poor murdered souls. It might be preferable to feeling ashamed of the uniform I wear and the race I represent!" He shuddered, as a group of native servants ran, screeching gleefully, from a nearby garden, the plunder they had amassed piled into a handcart. "Even the servants have turned on their masters and betrayed them and there's nothing we can do to stop them or avenge those they have slaughtered! We've saved our own skins, thanks to the loyalty of a few men like these and *they* intend to desert us as soon as they can, so that they can march on Delhi."

"They must not be allowed to reach Delhi," Alex told him uncompromisingly, thinking of Sir Henry Lawrence's grim prediction. "They will have to be stopped, no matter what the cost, and if we can help to stop them then at least it gives us a valid reason for saving our skins."

Clark said nothing. White and exhausted, he sat slumped in his saddle and only roused himself when, half a mile from the Rifles' barracks, their escort took leave of them, with a courteous

"Khuda hafiz" from the old *rissaldar* and a blow with the flat of his sabre across the sweat-soaked quarters of Clark's horse.

"The soldier-sahibs guard the *maidan* on which they drill," he called after them, with thinly veiled scorn. "Against an attack we have not made and do not intend to make."

"Is it possible that he's speaking the truth?" Clark asked incredulously.

"It would appear so," Alex was forced to concede. They turned into Boundary Road, now a wilderness of trampled gardens and burnt-out British bungalows and glimpsed the retreating backs of a score or so of 3rd Light Cavalry sepoys—the first they had seen engaged in undisciplined pillage. But there were others, Alex soon realized, as a fusillade of shots drew his attention to one of the houses standing back from the road and he saw a mob of scarlet-coated sepoys milling about outside. Encouraged by the savage screams of an audience of bazaar riff-raff, the sepoys were exchanging shots with the occupants of the house and hurling lighted torches into it, in an attempt to smoke out the defenders.

"Come on," Alex said, gritting his teeth. "There's someone alive in there. Let's try and get them out!"

Sabres drawn, they both put their horses at the mob, jumping over the low wall of the garden and taking the sepoys in the rear. The first blow Alex contrived to strike was at a dismounted sowar, with lance-*daffadar*'s stripes on his arm and, despite the difficulty of controlling Sultan with his legs, he knew a moment of almost savage satisfaction when the man went down before him, his head half-severed from his body. Clark was striking about him with equal fury and the mutineers, after resisting their assault for a few minutes, scattered and took flight, contenting themselves with firing a few spasmodic shots from a safe distance, jeered at by their erstwhile supporters from the bazaar.

CHAPTER SIX
➤➤➤ • ⋘

THE bungalow's defenders—three weary civilians, in bloodstained evening dress—came down from the roof, their smoking shot-guns still grasped in their hands and from somewhere in the rear of the house, where they had been crouched in terror, emerged the wife of one of them, with two white-faced little boys. As their rescuers stood guard, they made a dash for the stables, har-nessed two horses to a carriage and, profuse in their thanks, set off at a gallop for the Rifles' barracks. The bodies of the children's *ayah* and an old, white-bearded bearer, lying on the verandah, bore mute witness to the fact that some of the native servants had remained faithful and paid for their fidelity with their lives.

Alex and Melville Clark rode after the carriage through the rear gate of the compound, pausing there to make sure that it was unmolested and then, with common accord, riding into the next compound and the next. Their shouts were greeted by silence; in the fourth house they came to, they found the body of a woman, so mutilated as to be unrecognizable, and they turned their eyes away, sickened, from the two small, pathetic white bodies impaled on the wooden fence separating the rear veranda from the cook-house.

"It's no bloody use, sir," Clark said, a sob in his voice. "We shan't find anyone alive here now. We're too late. But in the name of God, what have those damned Queen's regiments been doing, while this was going on? They are barely half a mile away. Could they not hear the shooting, the infernal row that mob kicked up, the screams of that poor woman and her children?"

Craigie's wife, young Mackenzie's sister, and the pregnant Mrs Chambers—if they had stayed in or returned to their homes—were nearly two miles away, Alex thought, his throat suddenly tight. Some of the occupants of these bungalows might have escaped, might have found safety in the European barracks before the marauding sepoys struck. Pray God they had. But those living as far away as Mrs Craigie would have had no chance, unless Gough had got there in time.

"Heaven alone knows, Nobby," he answered bitterly. "But I think we'd better go and find out. If it costs me my commission, I'm going to see that they take action to stop our men and the sepoys from marching on Delhi!"

They spurred their flagging horses into a gallop and met the first skirmishers of the 60th Rifles advancing, with fixed sword-bayonets and their commanding officer at their head, down Chapel Street. From a furiously angry and despairingly outspoken Colonel Jones, who stopped them for information, they learned the reason for the delay.

"My regiment mustered for church parade at six o'clock," he said. "The alarm was sounded, the R.S.M. quite properly sent them to change into greens—you can't fight night actions in white. There was a slight hold-up because the magazine was locked and the men had only their emergency ten rounds. I had the infernal magazine broken into and issued a hundred rounds per man, which took about half an hour. We were ready by a quarter to seven. I'd given orders to march off, leaving one company to secure the European lines and intending to take a column of eight hundred men to the race-course, so as to confine the mutinous regiments to their own lines. I'd sent notice of my intentions to Colonel Custance of the Carabineers and to the Bengal

Artillery, requesting their immediate support and then . . ." He made an effort to control his indignation. "That damned fool Wilson arrived and ordered me to wait, if you please!"

"To wait, Colonel?" Alex echoed, in shocked bewilderment. "For what?"

Colonel Jones roared an order to his adjutant, who cantered off obediently, and then said, with a disgust he made no attempt to hide, "For General Hewitt, of course. As station commander, Wilson insisted that he could issue no orders when the divisional commander was present and the doddering old imbecile duly arrived in his blasted mobile bath-chair five minutes later! They then engaged in a lengthy conference, to which I was not admitted, sent for the Dragoons and the Artillery and formed us all up on our parade ground . . . to repel an attack, I was eventually told, which the mutinous regiments were supposed to be launching from the Sudder Bazaar! Needless to tell you, there was no blasted attack. Your miserable Pandies were too busy breaking into the jail and setting fire to the place to attack *us*. And they had more sense, damn them to hell!" He peered short-sightedly at the devastation about him, his eyes behind the thick lenses of his pince-nez holding a steely glint. "While they were shooting down their officers and slaughtering English women and children, *I* was permitted to send a single detachment of fifty men to secure the Treasury. It's beyond belief, isn't it? They should both be court-martialed for this, Hewitt *and* Wilson."

"I sent an officer, Lieutenant Gough, to ask for cavalry, and Horse Artillery support to prevent the attack on the jail, sir," Alex said grimly, keeping pace with him as he started to move on. "Didn't he get through?"

Colonel Jones snorted. "Oh, he got through all right and was sent packing with a flea in his ear! General Wilson told him that there were more important things to worry about than a raid on the jail." A flash of white in the darkened compound of one of the bungalows they were passing caught the alert eye of a corporal and the Rifles' commanding officer broke off as a band of belated looters let fall the proceeds of their raid and attempted to make their escape. A dozen Enfields spoke and the corporal's party made a swift end of the white-robed thieves with their sword-bayonets. "Good man!" Jones approved. "Are they sepoys?"

The corporal shook his head regretfully and, turning to Alex again, the colonel went on, his tone sarcastic, "Pity. They were only bazaar ruffians, *goojurs* by the look of them. But we are, at long last, on our way to avenge our dead by attacking the mutineers. Those are my orders . . . issued by General Wilson who, it appears, has now taken command of the brigade, notwithstanding the presence of the divisional commander, who is following behind the column in his bloody bath-chair. We're to deploy across the racecourse, supported by cavalry and artillery, and occupy the native lines."

"The *lines,* Colonel?" Alex was taken aback. He saw the advancing skirmishers turn right-handed into Circular Road, and reined in with a smothered exclamation. "I doubt whether you'll find more than a few stragglers in the lines now. There's nothing there, they've burnt everything in sight and, according to my information, all three native regiments intend to make for Delhi. That means they'll head for the Trunk Road. If you cut across to the Begum's Bridge now, you may be able to stop them."

"Contrary to my orders, Sheridan?" Colonel Jones swore. "Damn, they've got to be stopped, though, haven't they?" He frowned, shading his eyes from the glare of a burning *godown,* as he peered anxiously into the darkness beyond. "A battery of Horse Artillery and the two squadrons Custance has mounted ought to do it, if they can establish a blockade on that road now. We could back them up. How far d'you suppose your sowars could have got?"

"They can't have got far, sir—a mile or so, perhaps, if they set off at once, which I doubt. Some of them had only watering bridles and blankets on their horses. They'd have to saddle up and—"

"And the infantry will have to march, won't they? Right, I'll come back with you and we'll *both* talk to Wilson." The dapper little colonel, for all his unmilitary appearance and his myopia, was a man after his own heart, Alex decided, warming to him as he brought his skirmishers to a halt and issued a crisp order to his second-in-command.

Accompanied by Melville Clark, they rode back past the main body of the Rifles and Alex asked, as a sudden fear assailed him, "Colonel, do you know if any warning of this outbreak has been sent to Delhi?"

"Warning? The telegraph wire has been cut but I understand a message was sent about an hour ago. Hewitt dictated it." Colonel Jones added cynically, "He said 'I am holding my position.' If you can call *that* a warning, then yes, Delhi has been warned." He glanced around at Alex's shocked face. "Saving your presence, Sheridan, I say perdition take all Company's officers! India appears to soften their brains, if—as in the case of General Hewitt I take leave to doubt—they were born with any brains in the first place! Ah, there's Wilson, in conference with his superior, as usual. It might be better, for all concerned if *you* talked to him. I'm afraid I may lose my temper."

General Wilson received them without enthusiasm, sitting his horse in silence beside the divisional commander's buggy. Alex repeated what his *rissaldar* had told him but was cut short when he attempted to offer his own appraisal of the situation.

"You are asking me to believe the claim of a mutineer, who simply *told* you that his regiment was going to Delhi?"

"Not a mutineer, sir—a reliable native officer."

"Who, on your own admission, has now joined his regiment in mutiny? Did he, or any of the other sowars who escorted you to the jail, make any attempt to prevent the release of the prisoners?" Wilson's tone was cutting.

"No sir," Alex was forced to admit, feeling impotent anger catch at his throat. "There were barely a dozen of us and at least two hundred of them, in addition to a mob of several thousand. There was nothing we could do. I sent Lieutenant Gough to ask for support from your troops but—"

"I had no troops to spare," Wilson told him coldly. "We had to secure the European cantonment and barracks." He glanced at General Hewitt, who sat, his eyes closed, apparently taking no interest in the discussion, and added, with a warning cough, "A decision with which the general entirely agreed, did you not, sir?"

Thus appealed to, the old man opened his eyes, subjected Alex to a frowning scrutiny and grunted peevishly, "Damn, of course I did! We had to be ready for an attack." He looked about him, saw that the column had stopped and demanded the reason.

Wilson told him. "*Colonel* Sheridan," he finished, with heavy emphasis on the title, "wants us to accept the word of a mutinous native officer that the Light Cavalry, and presumably the other native regiments, are planning to take themselves off to Delhi. He's suggesting that, instead of attacking the native lines, we ought to establish a blockade of the Delhi Road."

"Sheridan?" the General interrupted sharply. "Isn't he the

damned feller who brought those letters, the ones the *Shahzada* are supposed to have written . . . Lawrence's man?"

"Yes, sir, he is."

"There's no blasted mutiny in Delhi, is there? Is there, Sheridan?" The bloodshot eyes bored into his and Alex shook his head. "No, not yet, sir. But if those regiments get there—"

"Who says they're going? A blasted Pandy? Damn, that could be a trap, a deliberate attempt to deceive you! No, we'll stick to our original decision. We'll secure the native lines and teach these insolent, murdering devils a lesson they won't forget in a hurry. Eh, General Wilson? I take it you concur, don't you?"

"I do, sir," Archdale Wilson answered promptly. "No sense in going on a wild goose chase, without reliable intelligence. Oblige me, Colonel Jones, by continuing your advance on the racecourse, if you please. I want to get this over. I'm not happy about leaving the European cantonment so lightly guarded, not happy at all."

Jones said nothing. He took off his pince-nez and started to polish them vigorously, opened his mouth to speak and then closed it again as a young captain in the uniform of the 6th Dragoon Guards, who was riding with the brigadier's staff, ventured diffidently, "Excuse me, sir?"

"What is it? Who are you, sir?"

"Rosser, sir—Carabineers. If you would permit me to take one mounted squadron of my regiment, and a half troop of the Horse Artillery, I could blockade the road, sir, and make sure the mutineers don't make for Delhi."

"A squadron?" Wilson exclaimed. "Good God, you've only got two mounted squadrons, haven't you? We need them—*and* the Horse Artillery—to cover our attack."

"Then let me take a patrol, sir," the captain pleaded. "I could confirm whether Colonel Sheridan's information is correct.

Indeed, he might care to come with me, and we could be back with a report by the time you—"

It was General Hewitt who silenced him. "Certainly not, Captain Rosser! We're facing over two thousand armed and mutinous sepoys. I will *not* have my force weakened. Dammit, we need every man we've got. Now, for God's sake, let us get this column moving or it'll be daylight before we even set foot on the race-course!"

Wilson turned again to Colonel Jones and snapped irritably, "Continue your advance, Colonel, if you please."

"Very well, sir," Jones acknowledged. "If you insist." He motioned Alex to follow him and, when he was once more at the head of the column, gave the order to advance in a controlled voice, which clearly cost him an effort. To one of his officers, who enquired whether they were to shoot to kill any uniformed sepoys remaining in the lines, he answered testily, "By all means, my dear Muter. If you can find anyone at all to shoot at, execute them."

Half an hour later, the Rifles deployed on the smooth turf of the race-course and, flanked by the two mounted Carabineer squadrons, advanced at the regulation one hundred and forty paces a minute on their objective. The Horse Artillery troop unlimbered, loaded their four nine-pounder guns with grape and waited for the order to open fire.

There were no sepoys in sight but, hearing a babel of voices coming from behind a clump of brushwood on the perimeter of the parade ground, General Wilson gave the expected order. The Rifles obediently fired two volleys; the nine-pounders discharged their hail of grape and then Colonel Jones despatched a company in extended order through the smoldering line of huts, with instructions to bring out any British bodies which might be lying there. They repeated the process in the infantry lines, led this time by the dismounted Carabineers but, apart from the bodies of Colonel Finnis and some of the other murdered officers, they found only devastation, a rifled magazine and a few loose and injured horses.

At Alex's urgent request, the Rifles' commander was about to send search parties into some of the burnt-out bungalows which had housed the married Company officers' families, when an A.D.C. galloped up with orders for the column to retire immediately to The Mall and their own barracks. As this order was being reluctantly obeyed, Alex and Clark, joined by two surviving officers of the 11th Native Infantry, contrived to make their own brief search. With the single exception of Henry Craigie's— which was untouched but deserted—every house had been looted and set on fire, furniture that was too heavy to carry away smashed and littering the once neatly tended gardens. In the garden next to Craigie's they found the body of the unhappy Charlotte Chambers and they all four turned away, sick with horror at the realization of the ghastly torture she must have endured, before death put an end to her sufferings. Alex, thinking of Emmy, found himself retching uncontrollably as his gaze fell on the trampled remains of a child, prematurely delivered by those who had butchered its poor young mother.

"I'll find whoever did this to her if it's the last thing I ever do," Lieutenant Möller of the 11th vowed thickly, as he knelt to cover the two pathetic bodies with a charred curtain, tears streaming down his grimly set face. "And by God I'll kill him, with my bare hands if I have to!"

Anxious to find Henry Craigie, Alex and Melville Clark left him to his grief and extended their search over as wide an area as they could but without success.

"They must have made their escape, sir," Clark said, when they were recalled to the column by Colonel Jones. "Odd that Henry's bungalow wasn't touched, though, wasn't it? I wonder if his sowars mounted guard over it until the bazaar mobs made off?"

It was a possibility, Alex thought, and infinitely to Craigie's credit if the men of his troop had stayed with him to ensure his safety, as well as that of his house, before riding off to join the rest of their regiment.

"Where's Hugh Gough?" he asked wearily. "I haven't seen him, have you?"

Clark shook his head. "No, I haven't, sir. But knowing Hugh, I should think he came back here to help the Craigies, after General Wilson sent him packing. Which leads me to hope that they're all safe. We may even find them when we get back to the European lines. Shall I have a look for them?"

"Yes, do that," Alex agreed. "I'm going to find Rosser of the Carabineers. Perhaps, once he's satisfied that the European lines are secured and in no serious danger of attack, Wilson will give us permission to set up a blockade on the Delhi road, or at least let us take out a mounted patrol to ascertain what *is* happening and how far the mutineers have got. We can't just sit here all night, damn it, it's only 38 miles to Delhi! They could be there by tomorrow morning, if something isn't done to stop them."

Captain Rosser, when he found him preparing to obey the order to bivouac in The Mall for what remained of the night, was in a state of angry exasperation.

"It's confirmed, you know. And, of course, you were right, Colonel. All three blasted regiments are making for Delhi! A police officer came in from Hapur with the news. He ran slap into a bunch of them and was lucky to escape with his life."

Alex expelled his breath in an anxious sigh. "Does the general know?" he asked flatly.

Rosser nodded. "General Wilson does. Shall we endeavour to approach him again?"

"That was what I came to suggest. There may still be time to intercept them if we act now."

Rosser called for his horse. "Get those remounts over here," he bade to the sergeant who answered his shout, and turning to Alex, said eagerly, "After the appalling fiasco he's just led us into, Wilson surely cannot refuse to let me have my squadron, on fresh horses, and a couple of guns. We must have guns, obviously, if we're to have a hope of stopping them but we could call for volunteers, could we not, if he's unwilling to spare any of his gunners? A party of officers, perhaps. I feel sure that some of the Company's officers would be willing to volunteer and—"

"They will volunteer to a man, sir!" Alex recognized young Möller's voice, coming from behind him, and reined in, to enable him to catch up.

"And you're the first of them?" he suggested.

"Indeed I am, sir. After what I have seen tonight, I'd give my immortal soul for the chance to make my sepoys answer for the innocent blood they have shed." Möller broke off and added, with restraint, "More to the point, sir, I served for a year with the Bengal Artillery, so permit me to come with you to General Wilson and add my voice to yours. He's on the Rifles' parade ground; I've just seen him there."

"And General Hewitt?" Rosser enquired, his voice carefully expressionless.

"He's gone to his own house, I understand, sir, to write a report for the commander-in-chief."

"Then I fear he will have to perjure himself," the Dragoon officer observed under his breath. Meeting Alex's gaze, he smiled. "But let us thank heaven for small mercies, Colonel Sheridan. We may be able to persuade the brigadier to listen to us this time. You know, I suppose, that following your subaltern's appeal, General Wilson had second thoughts and ordered me to your support at the jail earlier this evening?"

"No, I didn't know," Alex confessed. "Should I ask what prevented you from obeying that order?"

"Do you need to, sir? General Hewitt countermanded the order, of course. He insisted he could see your Light Cavalry preparing to attack us." Rosser laughed shortly. "As it happened about a dozen of them did come to ascertain what we were doing but, needless to tell you, they made off at speed without firing a shot when they saw that we were more than ready to receive them! Probably considered themselves fortunate that they were able to do so, in the circumstances. Since then, I believe, the entire jail has been emptied of its inmates. Ah, there's Wilson! Will you make the initial approach or shall I?"

"It might be better received, if it comes from you, Captain Rosser."

"Then here's hoping," Rosser said dryly. He rode forward, with Alex and Möller at his heels, and saluted. "If you please, sir . . ."

Archdale Wilson had Colonel Smyth with him, Alex saw. Both looked tired and harassed, their faces and uniforms caked with ash and it was clear that neither welcomed the interruption.

"Well, what is it?" the brigade commander demanded. He listened with weary resignation to Rosser's request and his refusal was emphatic. "Nothing more can be done until daylight, gentlemen. Those are General Hewitt's orders and I can't disregard them. Besides, the report I have just received is that the mutineers are in force all along the road and are guarding the first river bridge. You'd be wiped out if you tried to intercept them. I can't afford to lose a squadron of cavalry, even if you are prepared to throw your own lives away."

"With guns, sir," Alex began, "I feel confident that we—"

"Guns, Sheridan? For God's sake, we have only one troop of Horse Artillery and a single field battery, from which every lascar has fled! I can't let you have any guns. If you lost them to the sepoys, there really would be hell to pay. Don't you agree, George?"

Carmichael Smyth mopped at his brow with a torn and blood-stained handkerchief. There was a livid weal across one cheek, as if a bullet had creased it. "Most certainly, General. In my view it would be madness. You'd risk running into an ambush, Sheridan, if you went after them in darkness. As I've just told the general, I believe the mutineers had no definite plan to go to Delhi. It will have been a last-minute decision, based on the fear of retribution because they know damned well that we shall be after them, as soon as we've dealt with the escaped convicts and *budmashes* here."

"But, Colonel," Alex said, trying vainly to bide his impatience, "Delhi is only 38 miles away and—"

"Exactly!" Colonel Smyth exclaimed. "It's the nearest place where they can hope to find sanctuary. They're hoping to throw themselves on the old king's mercy. They probably imagine that he'll hide them in the Red Fort. Well, they're in for a disappointment. . . . They'll come up against an ordered brigade in Delhi, which will swiftly put an end to any ideas of that kind."

"But only if the Delhi Brigade receives adequate warning, sir. General Graves—"

"Sir," Möller put in, unable to contain himself, "General Wilson, may I be permitted to try to get through to Delhi with a warning? I could ride across country, sir, and if I left now I—"

"You'd never get there,"Wilson told him irritably. "In any case a warning has been sent by native courier. A native might contrive to get through but any British officer would be seen and recognized before he'd gone half a mile. Enough of these heroics, gentlemen. I appreciate your zeal, but I've told you General Hewitt's orders. Nothing more can be done until daylight. This brigade will bivouac in a full state of readiness and, at first light, we shall commence mopping up operations in cantonments and in the Sudder Bazaar and the native city, from whence most of this trouble has sprung. The sepoys weren't responsible for half the arson and looting that has taken place . . . or the murders. We can thank the escaped convicts and the blasted *goojurs* for that! When order has been restored here, we can think about Delhi, although we probably won't have to, since I am confident that General Graves has sufficient disciplined native troops under his command to arrest and disarm any disorganized mob of mutineers which may reach Delhi."

Rosser and Alex looked at one another in dismay.

"For God's sake!" the Dragoon officer whispered, as Wilson started to turn away. "Isn't there anything we can do?"

Alex reached a swift decision. "Forgive me, sir," he said quietly. "But as Colonel Smyth will confirm, I have been appointed to the Lucknow command, for service in Oudh under the chief commissioner. May I have your permission to leave this brigade and return to Lucknow?"

"What the devil . . ." Archdale Wilson swore loudly and venomously. He glanced at Smyth, who nodded, his mouth tight with disapproval.

"That is quite correct, sir," he admitted reluctantly. "Sheridan has been appointed to the Lucknow Brigade, with brevet promotion, on the authority of the commander-in-chief. I was notified of the appointment by the electric telegraph two days ago and I removed his name from the active roll of my regiment. He is no longer under my command, sir."

"Nor is he under mine, it would appear." Wilson shrugged, looking more relieved than annoyed, Alex observed wryly. "Very well, Colonel Sheridan, by all means carry out your orders. I would advise you, however, to delay your departure until day-light. You understand, of course, that I cannot be expected to take the responsibility for your safety by whatever route you may elect to travel? And I can't provide you with an escort, either, I regret to say, although you're at liberty to recruit one. There are pensioners and unemployed officers who may be at your disposal."

"Thank you, sir," Alex acknowledged. "I understand the position." He nudged Rosser's knee with his own, bowed and swung his horse around; the other two saluted and trotted after him.

"Well?" Rosser said, when they were out of earshot of the brigade commander and his staff. "I take it you'll try to get to Delhi?"

"Yes. Obviously someone has to. But I shall need a fresh horse." Alex spoke regretfully. But it would, he knew, be asking too much even of Sultan's gallant heart to attempt to ride him over a grueling, forty-mile cross-country route, much of which would, of necessity, have to be covered at speed, under the blistering heat of the sun, for he could not hope to reach Delhi much before noon. And there would be two rivers to cross.

"I'll give you the pick of my remounts," Rosser promised. "And look after that fine creature of yours until you're able to reclaim him."

"I have an orderly here—a Sikh, Partap Singh—and a couple of *syces*. Perhaps you'd be so good as to hand the horse over to them . . . or to one of my brother officers, the adjutant or Hugh Gough."

"Yes, of course, most gladly," the carabineer assented. "But aren't you taking your orderly with you? Are you going without any escort at all?"

Alex nodded and meeting Möller's reproachful gaze, said crisply, "My best chance is alone. A small escort would attract attention, besides being of little use if it were attacked. I'm sorry, Möller, but we'd be going deliberately against General Wilson's orders if I let you come with me. I tell you what though. While I'm changing horses, see if you can rake up a native *chuddar* for me, would you? I think it might be advisable to conceal my uniform."

"Yes, of course, sir." The boy reined in. "I'll see what I can find. My bearer will probably have one."

Alex's preparations, such as they were, were soon completed. Mounted on a lively chestnut waler, with a dragoon's saddle stripped of its accouterments, an ancient and somewhat strong-smelling white *chuddar* girt about him and a turban, also the property of Möller's bearer, wound about his head in place of his shako, he was ready to set off on his long ride. Rosser escorted him past the now silent Sudder Bazaar, a dozen tall dragoons hiding him from any curious eyes that might be watching and, not entirely to his surprise, an A.D.C. caught up with him just before he parted from his escort, to thrust a sealed letter into his hand.

"From General Wilson, sir," the young officer told him. "He said you'd know for whom it's intended."

Rosser laughed aloud, as the A.D.C. cantered off.

"By heaven, he's an opportunist, is he not? If you get through, he'll take the credit for having sent you and if you don't, then he can't be blamed. There's no address on it, is there, sir?"

Alex grinned. "None. However," he tucked the despatch into his breast pocket, "I'll do my best to deliver it. *Au revoir,* Rosser . . . and my thanks for your assistance."

"I wish I were coming with you, Colonel Sheridan. Godspeed and a safe journey!" The Dragoon Guards officer saluted smartly and was gone, his troopers clattering after him, as Alex set his face in the opposite direction and spurred his own horse into a canter.

For the first hour and a half, he made good progress, keeping to the shadows at the road verge and heading steadily south-westward. He encountered few other travelers and those he did meet were on foot—country people for the most part, returning to their villages laden with the spoils of a night of looting—as anxious, on this account, to avoid him as he was to pass them by. He saw no sepoys, although some of the white-robed looters he passed might well have been mutineers, who had discarded their uniforms in order to seek a safe anonymity with those who had aided them in the sack of the Meerut cantonment. All were armed, one or two with firearms, the rest with clubs and spears, but none attempted to molest him and, satisfied that, at all events by moonlight, his disguise was effective, Alex rode on with increasing confidence, intent on putting as many miles as possible behind him before dawn.

After a while, however, he heard the rhythmic tramp of marching feet ahead of him and was compelled to leave the road and make a detour across cultivated fields. It was heavy going through shoulder-high sugar cane but he continued, pausing now and then to listen, only returning to the road when he had assured himself that he had out-distanced the marchers. They appeared, from the occasional glimpses he caught of them, to be a band of stragglers, in Native Infantry uniform, belatedly endeavouring to

overtake their comrades. They were marching in a disciplined for-
mation, with shouldered arms, to the beat of drums and fifes
which, incongruously, were playing a British marching tune.

Once past them, the road was again virtually deserted for a
further ten or twelve miles and he was able to increase his speed,
halting at regular intervals to dismount, loosen his girths and give
his horse a breather. The borrowed charger was fit and willing
enough but with an iron-hard mouth and no manners, like the
country-bred he had ridden for so many weary miles on his outward journey from Lucknow. The dragoon's saddle, too, was less
supple than his own and Alex himself was beginning to tire when,
dismounting in order to stretch his legs and fight off an overwhelming desire for sleep, a sound was borne to him which swiftly
banished all thought of sleep from his mind.

Faintly at first but quite unmistakable as it came nearer, he
heard the thud of hooves and, judging this to herald the approach
of a party of at least a dozen mounted men, he dragged his sweat-
ing chestnut back into the thin cover of the sugar canes and
waited tensely for the horsemen to make their appearance. They
did so, a few minutes later, and he counted fifteen of them, darkly
silhouetted against the still reddish glow of the sky above Meerut.
They were making a good deal of noise, shouting and laughing
and seemingly in the best of spirits as, to Alex's dismay, they jerked
their lathered horses to a standstill only a few yards from him and,
as he had done earlier, dismounted to loosen girths and permit
their animals to drink from a small stream which flowed sluggishly near the road from an irrigation ditch among the canes.

He recognized them, without difficulty, as sowars of the 3rd
Light Cavalry in white undress uniforms, armed with lances and
sabres, and with carbines slung from their saddles. It was evident
from their carefree attitude that they expected no pursuit and, in

the absence of their officers, that all of them were reveling in their unaccustomed freedom from discipline, like children playing truant from school. But these were not children. Their uniforms were stained with blood and smoke, their saddles bore proof that they, like the *goojur* villagers, had been engaged in looting and worse. Alex, making strenuous efforts to calm his restive horse, knew that he could expect no mercy at their hands, if they discovered him here.

With infinite caution, he started to move away but their shouts and the milling horses had excited his borrowed mount, and when it reared and cannoned into him, he was knocked off balance, losing his hold on its rein. Compelled to let it go, he flung himself flat in the hope that the horse might distract their attention for long enough to enable him to find more adequate concealment in the ditch or further into the field, but this hope was short-lived. The dragoon horse, neighing shrilly, plunged into the road and then, eluding the hands stretched out to capture it, to Alex's intense chagrin, it returned to him. He managed to scramble back into the saddle but the next moment the sowars were clustering round him and one of them grabbed his bridle, effectively preventing his escape. In the shadows, unable to make out the colour of his skin and seeing the *chuddar* and the turban wound, Moslem fashion, about his head, they took him at first for one of their own faith and jested with him good-humoredly.

"So thou hast stolen a *lal-kote* soldier's horse? And killed its owner, doubtless?"

"Do not fear us, brother. We, too, have *feringhi* blood on our hands!"

"Art thou perchance a fugitive from the jail? Is that why thou seekest to hide from us? Shame on thee. It was we who brought about thy liberation! See . . ." A hand was thrust forward, so that he might observe the still raw galling of the fetters. "I still bear the mark on my arm. But we have thrown off our chains. The Company's *Raj* is ended. Allah is good. We go to Delhi to fight for our Faith and the Shah Bahadur!"

Aware that his voice would betray him if he attempted to answer them, Alex muttered something and slumped in his saddle, keeping his head averted and praying that they would take him for a dim-witted peasant and let him go. They seemed on the point of doing so when one of them, his suspicions suddenly aroused, leaned forward and wrenched the *chuddar* roughly from his shoulders.

"This is no dumb *ryot*. He is a *feringhi*, my brothers! A sahib, see, wearing the uniform of our *paltan!*" the man exclaimed, jumping back as if he had inadvertently uncovered a venomous snake, and a chorus of shocked and angry shouts went up from the rest of the sowars. They had all dismounted and, in the brief panic which followed their discovery of his identity, Alex made a bid for escape. He spurred for the sugar canes, careless of which direction he took and seeking only to put as great a distance between himself and them as he could before they could remount their horses and come in pursuit of him.

He heard a spasmodic volley of musketry and several shots spattered the cane foliage ahead and on either side of him and then they were pounding after him, baying like a pack of hounds for his blood. If his horse had been fresh—or, he thought despairingly, if he had been on Sultan—he might have eluded them, but the animal he rode was tired and blown. It stumbled and almost precipitated him over its head, picked itself up and then, to his horror, he found himself clear of the canes and in an open field, crisscrossed by a maze of irrigation ditches and devoid of cover.

He jerked his horse's head round and had come within ten

yards of the cane field he had left when a single shot rang out and he felt his horse stagger, slither a few yards and then come crashing to the ground. He was leaning low over its neck and was flung clear but, having only one arm with which to try to break his fall, he landed heavily and rolled over, the breath temporarily driven from his lungs. As he lay helpless, struggling for breath, he saw his unfortunate horse drag itself up and, with a courage he had not expected of it, continue its flight across the open ground.

Seven or eight of the sowars broke cover and went after the wounded horse and he contrived to claw his way back into the canes before, realizing that their quarry was riderless, the men abandoned their chase and came back to look for him. Alex, drawing air into his tortured lungs at last, took his pistol from his belt and, glimpsing a ditch to his right, lowered himself into it, resolved to sell his life dearly if they found him.

They were yelling advice and instructions to each other and threshing about in the canes, some with sabres drawn and others probing the undergrowth with their lances. He kept well down and three of them rode right over him, leaping their horses across the ditch and, by some miracle, failing to see him as he crouched in the damp mud beneath them. The pursuit did not slacken but it was moving farther afield and he was beginning to hope that he had managed to make good his escape when the sound of voices, coming from the direction of the road, effectively dashed his hopes.

Cursing under his breath, Alex raised himself cautiously, parted the leafy screen in front of him with the muzzle of his pistol and was just able to make out the dark figures of two sowars coming towards him across a patch of open ground to his right. They were evidently the men who had been firing at him, for they were on foot, he saw, their horses' reins looped over their arms and their carbines at the ready. He aimed his pistol at the nearer of the two and waited for the range to shorten, uneasily conscious that once he opened fire on them, he could not afford to miss, since the sound of firing must inevitably bring the others back. But at least with only two of them, the odds were more even than they had been before.

"His horse fell here. He cannot have gone far," he heard one of them say. "See, here are the tracks. Thy aim was true, *daffadar-ji!* Let us search the ditch; the accursed sahib may be hiding there."

"Didst thou see who he was?" the second man asked.

"*Nahin.* I saw only that he was a *feringhi.*" The first speaker laughed derisively. "What matters it who he was?"

"He had one arm. The sahib who restored my medals to me had lost his sword arm—in the Crimea, they say, when the Queen's Light Cavalry charged the Russian guns, in just such a charge as we made against the Sikh guns at Chillianwala." Alex tensed, remembering the old *daffadar* whose plight had moved him to pity during the punishment parade, as the man added, a note of regret in his voice, "It was a kindly and noble thought that prompted him to bring me my medals, a soldier's thought, Ramzan. I would not see that sahib dead."

"All the *sahib-log* must die, Ghulam Rasul. Thou knowest in thy heart that it is so," his companion reproached him. "He would not spare thy life, were thou to meet him now. And why does he ride to Delhi, if not to give warning of our approach, so that the sahibs there may meet us with cannon?" He kicked with a booted foot at the canes and spat his contempt of such manifest weakness. "If mine eyes have the good fortune to light on him, nothing shall stay my hand on the trigger!" His second kick came nearer and Alex, accepting his logic, depressed the trigger of the Adams.

The explosion sounded unnaturally loud and, for a moment, he feared that he had missed, for the sowar remained standing, a look of ludicrous surprise on his face. Then he fell forward without a sound and Alex, the smoking pistol still in his hand, found himself looking into the muzzle of the *daffadar's* carbine, which pointed steadily at his heart. They faced each other for a long moment in silence; then the old *daffadar* said, almost apologetically, "The Sahib has not reloaded his pistol."

"It has six bullets in it," Alex told him. "Five are left, Ghulam Rasul."

"And you would kill me, Sahib?"

"No, *daffadar-ji*. Not unless you prevent me from doing what is my duty. I need a horse—I must ride to Delhi." Excited shouts were coming now from amongst the canes; in a matter of minutes, Alex knew, the rest of the men would return. They had heard the shot and would come to investigate and he had somehow to appeal to this old man's dormant loyalty before his comrades could remind him of the new cause for which he must fight. *"Daffadar-ji,"* he began, "you—" The old man cut him short.

"Do you ride to Delhi in order to prepare cannon to receive us, Sahib?" he asked.

"I ride to warn my people, in order to avoid the shedding of innocent blood," Alex answered and added, with bleak honesty, "If cannon are necessary to preserve the peace, then I will ask for them to be turned against you."

"Take the horse, Sahib." Ghulam Rasul offered him his rein. "But first put a pistol ball into me, for I break faith with my brothers."

Alex shook his head. He thrust the pistol into his belt and vaulted into the saddle. He had covered a scant half of the distance separating him from the road when he heard the crack of a carbine and the horse he was riding emitted a high-pitched squeal and pitched forward on to its knees. This time he fell awkwardly sideways and the animal rolled on top of him, the whole weight of its now inert body on his legs, pinning him down. As he lay there, unable to free himself, he heard running footsteps and looked up to see a white-robed figure standing over him, the carbine gripped in both hands like a club.

Its butt descended and, in the instant before it smashed into his skull, he caught sight of two small circles of silver pinned to the chest of his assailant.

"You should have killed me, Sheridan Sahib," *daffadar* Ghulam Rasul reproved him sadly, but Alex, sinking into a dark and bottomless pit, did not hear him and gave him no answer. The old cavalryman bent and dragged his victim from beneath the dead horse and, when the others galloped up, he called on them to aid him in concealing the sahib's body. Two of them dismounted and did as he had asked and, when the dusty sugar canes had once again served as a hiding place, he urged them to delay no longer.

"We must go on to Delhi, brothers, and not draw rein until we see the face of Shah Bahadur, for who knows? We have stopped one messenger but there may be others. And with daylight the *lal-kote paltans* will be after us. On, on to Delhi!"

The sowars raised a cheer and spurred after him.

CHAPTER SEVEN

⇛ • ⇚

THE NATIVE courier sent by Meerut's civil authorities had left ahead of the mutineers and, by dint of hard riding and two fresh horses, he reached Delhi late on Sunday evening. Presenting himself at the residence of the commissioner, which was situated some distance outside the Kashmir Gate of the city, he handed his despatch to a servant with the statement that it was of extreme importance.

The commissioner, Simon Fraser, had fallen asleep in his chair and although his bearer, impressed by the messenger's urgency, made strenuous efforts to waken him, when he finally did so, Fraser blinked at him uncomprehendingly and thrust the letter, unopened, into his pocket and resumed his interrupted slumbers. It was not until the following day that he remembered having received it and, when he had absorbed its contents, he at once ordered his carriage and drove the two miles to Brigadier-General Graves' house, in the military cantonment, to pass on the warning. By the time he drew up outside, he found that other messengers had reported seeing the approach of a strong body of cavalry, already crossing by the Bridge of Boats over the Jumna from the Meerut road.

After requesting the general to send troops into the city in case of trouble, the commissioner despatched one of his staff to warn Lieutenant Willoughby, the officer in command of the Delhi magazine and, joined by the Collector Ross Harrison and Captain Douglas, the commandant of the king's bodyguard, he hurried to the Calcutta Gate, which he ordered to be closed against the newly arrived cavalry sowars. An attempt to send a telegraphic enquiry to Meerut was met with the information that the line had been cut and, realizing from this that the situation was serious, the civil police were called out and Brigadier Graves sent for Colonel Ripley, of the 54th Native Infantry, and ordered him to take his regiment, with two guns, into the city at once.

Of the three regiments in the Delhi brigade, the least reliable and the one which had recently exhibited signs of disaffection was the 38th and, by ill-chance, all the guards—including that on the city magazine—had been supplied, according to the weekly roster, by the 38th. The Calcutta Gate guard obeyed the order to bar entry to the Meerut cavalry sullenly but there was another way into the Royal Palace at the Selimgarh, to which access could be obtained by the simple expedient of riding along the dry river bed, and the sowars took it gleefully. All the one hundred and fifty men who formed the advance party of mutineers had changed into their French grey and silver uniforms and, with sabres drawn and in perfect order, they lined up outside the windows of the palace, the traditional place from which petitions were delivered, and called on the king for succor and protection.

The eighty-year-old Shah Bahadur, accompanied by the commander of his bodyguard, looked down on them apprehensively from a tower, the Musammun Burj, which jutted out over the river.

"We come to fight for thee, O King!" the sowars shouted. "Open the gates and let us in. We will restore thee to thy throne! For the Faith, we come to fight for the Faith!"

The old man, roused from his opium-inspired dreams and leaning heavily on the arm of his physician, flinched from these warlike cries and, turning to Captain Douglas, besought him to send them away. Hands cupped about his mouth, Douglas sternly bade them be gone, adding that they should present their petition to the king in the usual orderly manner, not with weapons in their hands.

For answer, one of the sowars unslung his carbine and fired a shot at him and instantly pandemonium broke out. A number of them forced their way in by a small, unguarded gateway in the palace wall and, augmented by another fifty or sixty men who had just crossed by the Bridge of Boats, they opened the Calcutta Gate without opposition from the sepoy guard. As more mutineers galloped across to the gate, they split up. One party made for the jail, where the guard and the convicts they released joined their ranks; another smaller party of native officers entered the palace and demanded immediate audience of the king. The main body, gathering support as they went, charged through the great bazaar in the center of the city, known as the Chandni Chouk, some screaming their bloodcurdling warcry "*Deen! Deen!* For the Faith!" and others claiming, at the pitch of their lungs, that the Company's *Raj* was ended.

Moslem butchers, Afghan merchants and the scum of the bazaar flocked to them and when the crowds became too dense they again divided, one mob making for the Bank and Civil Lines between the magazine and the Kashmir Gate, where most of the public buildings were situated, the other for the Darya Ganj, a European suburb beyond the palace, occupied by government clerks and pensioners and their families.

Both mobs were bent on slaughter, but neither had reached its destination when Captain Douglas dashed breathlessly down to the Calcutta Gate, where he was joined by the commissioner and several of his civil officials, including the chief magistrate, Sir Theo Metcalfe. They endeavoured bravely but unavailingly to restore order but were shouted down; the guard and Douglas's own command now, it seemed, affected by the madness. When a sowar fired at him, Fraser called on the sepoys of the guard to do their duty and was met by sullen silence; grabbing a musket from one of the policemen standing impotently by, the commissioner shot down the man who had fired at him and instantly found himself under attack.

With one of his party dead and one wounded, he was forced to make his escape. Driving at full speed in his carriage, with the wounded Hutchinson beside him, he gained the comparative safety of the Lahore Gate, where he pulled up and waited for the others.

Metcalfe went to try to rally the police in the Chandni Chouk but Douglas, compelled to jump into the fort ditch to avoid being torn to pieces by the sepoys of his own bodyguard, was injured and had to be carried to his quarters above the gate. Here he was tended by the chaplain of Delhi, the Reverend Midgley Jennings who, with his daughter Annie and her friend, Mary Clifford, occupied adjoining rooms, but the mob had been close on his heels and their respite was short-lived.

Joined by a yelling crowd of palace menials, a band of sepoys and Light Cavalry sowars surged about the steps of the gatehouse, in a frenzied demonstration of hatred, and the commissioner was cut down as he made a last appeal for reason. The old king's retainers slashed his body to a bloody pulp and then, waving their dripping *tulwars,* they rushed up the steps to the apartment where Douglas lay helpless, seeking fresh victims, and finding them in the persons of the chaplain and the two women. Jennings defended himself and them most valiantly, laying about him with a sword but the odds against him were too heavy and he went down beneath a shrieking wave of brown bodies, and the two terrified girls were dragged from the cupboard in which they had taken refuge.

When they, Douglas and Hutchinson were dead, one of the sowars picked up the bodyguard commander's severed head, impaled it on his lance-tip and, leaping on to his horse, led his motley band of murderers on to the Government College where, he promised them, they would find more Christians to be killed for the Faith.

Other, similar bands were now on the rampage in the Delhi and London Bank, in the offices of the *Delhi Gazette* and in St John's Church, killing, looting, burning, while in the Darya Ganj a terrible, cold-blooded massacre had just begun, from which only a handful were to escape.

In the great audience chamber of the palace, the old king had, at last and with reluctance, consented to receive a deputation of the mutineers. Informed of the death of the commissioner, he watched with trepidation as the Light Cavalry rode their horses across the carefully tended flower-beds and, joined by two hundred sepoys of the 11th and 20th Native Infantry who had lately arrived from Meerut, came thronging into his palace.

Faced by so many armed and threatening men, the king could do little save accept the allegiance they offered him. With what dignity he could muster, he seated himself on the throne of his ancestors and, as they knelt before him, in the name of Ghazi-ud-Din Mohammed Bahadur Shah, he gave them his blessing in a thin, quavering voice and then, bidding them disturb him no more, he retired unhappily to his own quarters.

Colonel John Ripley, at the head of his regiment—the hitherto loyal and well-disciplined 54th Native Infantry—approached the Main Guard at the Kashmir Gate with confidence. His two guns were following behind, under the command of an artillery subaltern, Lieutenant Wilson, and escorted by two companies of the 54th. It had taken a little while to muster them but, as General Graves had reminded him, there were two thousand British troops in Meerut and these must surely be on their way by now and could be counted on to quell the disturbance, if the 54th were unable to do so. The colonel anticipated no serious trouble, once he had gained entrance to the city and, even when a message reached him from Lieutenant Willoughby, with news that a mob was threatening the magazine, he was not unduly worried. He sent the messenger back to inform his commander that relief was at hand and rode through the inner wooden gate of the Main Guard without haste.

The guard of the 38th presented arms and watched him uncertainly as, flanked by six of his officers and his European sergeant-major, he emerged into the open square beyond the gates, to be met by a large party of mounted Light Cavalry sowars. Backed by an armed and noisy crowd, they barred his way; the colonel ordered his own men to load and continue their advance, with bayonets fixed but, to his shocked surprise, the order was ignored. Instead, his men broke ranks and started to fraternize with the mutineers, who opened fire on the advancing group of officers. Six were killed and the colonel was ruthlessly cut down and, while lying on the ground, bayoneted by his own men and left for dead.

The 54th, now in open mutiny, dispersed to join their comrades from Meerut in carnage and looting and the mortally wounded colonel managed, somehow, to drag himself to the inner gate. From there, at his own request, he was taken back in a borrowed carriage to cantonments by the regimental surgeon, to make his horrifying report to General Graves.

The remaining two companies of the regiment, arriving with

the guns, refused for a time to join the mutiny and both they and the guard of the 38th stayed at their posts. None attempted to molest the flood of frightened fugitives, mainly women and children from the Civil Lines, who came to seek refuge in the guardhouse. Those with conveyances were permitted to go on to the Flagstaff Tower on the Ridge, where General Graves had now directed all families to assemble. The rest stayed, with the surviving officers of the 54th, concealing themselves as best they could in the quarters of the guard commander—two small rooms at the summit of the gate.

In the magazine, which was situated between the Kashmir and Calcutta Gates, Lieutenant George Willoughby listened to the howling of the mob outside the walls and waited in vain for the succor he had been assured was soon to reach him. With his small staff of Europeans—Lieutenant George Forrest, his second-in-command, Lieutenant William Raynor, Conductors Buckley, Shaw and Scully, Sub-Conductor Crow and Sergeants Edwards and Stewart—he had made what preparations he could to ward off the expected attack. Inside the gate leading to the park, he had placed two 6-pounder guns, double-charged with grape; two more stood at the principal gate of the magazine, covered by another pair mounted in a bastion in its vicinity and, in front of the office, were ranged three more 6-pounders and a 24-pounder howitzer. As a precaution, the young ordnance commissary had caused a powder-train to be laid from the main powder store to the foot of a lime tree in the yard, where he stationed Conductor Scully, with orders to fire the train on receipt of a signal from his fellow Conductor Buckley, who would wave his hat if it was decided that the magazine could not be held.

The sun rose higher and the heat grew almost unbearable as the nine soldiers and a civilian clerk called Rayley, who had joined them from the judge's office, stood grimly to their guns. A demand from the king, brought by his son and grandson, with a force of mutineers, called on them to yield the magazine, was refused and soon they heard the scrape of scaling ladders being placed against the walls as, from the tops of tombs in an old Christian cemetery which towered above them, the king's bodyguard started to fire down on them.

On the Ridge, two miles outside the city, General Henry Graves waited in growing despair for the arrival of the expected relief column of British troops from Meerut. Two messengers who had volunteered to carry a request for aid to General Hewitt had failed to get through. The first, a young civilian named Marshall, had been shot down by a sentry of the 38th as he was fording the river. The second, the 74th's surgeon, Dr Batson, had attempted to disguise himself as a native but he, too, had been seen and recognized and was now believed to be in the hands of the mutineers.

Graves had taken what steps were in his power to protect his position on the Ridge, with pickets drawn from the best and steadiest of his three regiments, the 74th; and these were still carrying out their duties with heartening loyalty, but the brigadier had received the report from Colonel Ripley with both incredulity and dismay. His dismay increased when intelligence of the Darya Ganj massacre was brought to him, but when this was followed by an appeal for reinforcements from the Kashmir Gate, he decided that he had no alternative save to answer it.

His call for volunteers was insolently rejected by the 38th, but answered en masse by the 74th, and he sent them, under their commanding officer, Major Abbott, with two more guns, to the city at midday, keeping back only a detachment to guard the Ridge against a surprise attack. Of necessity, he also kept those of the 38th, who were not on guard duty—about two hundred men—aware that, if he allowed them to go to the city, they would immediately make common cause with the mutineers. His attempt to replace their guard at the main magazine on the Ridge met with ignominious failure, the sentries firing on the officer who brought the order for their withdrawal.

As news from the city became more alarming, the brigade commander ordered all women and children to leave cantonments and make their way up to the Ridge. The Flagstaff Tower, a round, 150-foot-high stone edifice, standing on the rocky spine of the Ridge itself, was the logical choice as a refuge for noncombatants and he set about making it secure. De Teissier's last two guns were mounted at its foot and a detachment of native Christian bandboys placed behind them to supply ammunition to the gunners, but as the day wore on and more and more terrified fugitives crowded into the small, hot, airless building, it rapidly became untenable. There was no water supply; few, if any, of the women had been able to bring food with them, they were anxious for the safety of their menfolk, exhausted and afraid, the children fractious. Many of those who had escaped from the Civil Lines were panic-stricken; some had seen their husbands butchered in front of them and each new arrival added to the general despondency with a fresh tale of horror.

General Graves, still hoping for the appearance of the British troops he was convinced that his superior must have sent from Meerut, was reluctant to abandon his position, but by 3:30 P.M. he had received no word of their coming and nothing stirred on the Meerut road.

Watching that road with equal despair, from a bastion overlooking the Bridge of Boats, Lieutenant Willoughby shook his head and returned to his gun. For five hours he and his small party had defended the magazine, but now the walls were swarming with yelling rebels who leapt down from their scaling ladders to pour a withering fire on them, before making a concerted rush to force open the barricaded doors.

There were hundreds of them inside the walls and the six-pounders did terrible execution, but the defenders had no time to reload. Crow and Edwards, running back to the howitzer, were dead before they could reach it; Forrest and Buckley were both wounded. George Willoughby shouted to Buckley, who seized his hat with his uninjured hand and waved it high above his head. Conductor John Scully touched his lighted portfire to the powder-train and, with earth-shaking force, the whole building exploded, hurtling skywards in a red-tinged mushroom of smoke and taking over four hundred of the besiegers with it. Incredibly, six of the defenders made their escape, blackened and bleeding. Raynor and Buckley scrambled over the crumbling ruin of the wall and eventually reached Meerut; Willoughby, Forrest, Shaw and Stewart staggered to the Main Guard at the Kashmir Gate, Willoughby to meet his death in a village a few miles from Meerut.

With the roar of the explosion still ringing in his ears, General Graves decided that nothing more could be done to save Delhi, in view of the limited means now at his disposal and in the absence of the hoped-for aid from Meerut. Anxious to protect the evacuation of the fugitives from the Flagstaff Tower, he ordered the recall of the 74th and the two guns from the Kashmir Gate. This order was obeyed reluctantly by Major Abbott, and no sooner had he withdrawn his small and still loyal force than the guard of the 38th closed the gate and opened fire on those officers who had remained, killing three of them. The survivors, including the badly wounded Lieutenant Forrest, made a lifeline with their sword-slings and lowered the women 25 feet into the ditch below, then jumped down after them and, under heavy fire from the sepoys of the guard, scrambled up the almost perpendicular counterscarp, to find cover in the undergrowth on the far side. There they crouched until the fall of darkness enabled them to begin the long and perilous journey across country to Meerut.

With the return of the 74th, the exodus from the Flagstaff Tower was also beginning. Major Abbott had brought back just over half the men he had originally led to the stricken city; now, having seen their officers safely back to the Tower, even these men deserted, urging the major not to delay his own departure from the Ridge. Those on picket duty remained, however, among them some forty sepoys of the 38th, who assured their company commander, Captain Robert Tytler, that they would not harm him or oppose the retreat of any of the British officers and their families but, they insisted, the retreat must begin at once. They even offered their escort, on condition that Tytler would himself command them and that they would not be called upon to fire on their comrades but this was refused by the brigadier, and their impatience increased.

"Go, Sahib," they bade Tytler. "This is no longer a place for you."

In buggies, in carriages carrying three times their normal load, in carts and artillery tumbrils, on horseback and even on foot, the refugees left the Ridge, some hoping to reach Kurnal, nearly eighty miles to the north, others going towards Meerut in the conviction that they would meet the British relief column, on its belated way to their rescue.

Finally only General Graves, his brigade major, Captain Nicolls and a surgeon named Stewart remained. Graves, unable to contact Meerut because the telegraph line had not been repaired, had managed to send a report of his plight to Ambala, 160 miles to the north, with the request that it should be forwarded to the commander-in-chief in Simla. An eighteen-year-old telegraph operator, William Brendish, had also sent his own version of the tragic happenings in Delhi to his fellow operator in Ambala, and Graves could only pray that both messages had got through. His own message, sent in the early afternoon, when he had ordered the telegraph office reopened, had been dictated before the full extent of the mutiny was known, and had read: *"Cantonments in a state of siege. Mutineers from Meerut 3rd Light Cavalry. Numbers not known, said to be 150 men. Cut off communication with Meerut. Taken possession of Bridge of Boats. 54th N.I. sent against them but would not act. Several officers killed and wounded. City in a state of considerable excitement. Troops sent down but nothing known yet. Further information will be forwarded."*

He had been able to forward no further information, because the office had been burnt down and the line cut; Todd, the telegraph master, had been killed when searching for the break in the line to Meerut and his possession of the Bridge of Boats had lasted only until the second party of mutineers had crossed it from the Meerut road, but the brigadier at Ambala would surely read between the lines. Even so, the nearest help he could expect would have to come from Kurnal, since General Hewitt at Meerut had inexplicably failed to pursue the mutineers. Had they all been killed in Meerut, he wondered, and then dismissed the thought. It was impossible; Hewitt had two thousand British troops under his command and the despatch Commissioner Fraser had received from Meerut had not suggested anything of the kind. A few officers shot down by their own men, the native lines set on fire, some families murdered. . . . The sowars of the 3rd Light Cavalry had, it seemed, reserved the full force of their treacherous fury for the unhappy Christian inhabitants of Delhi, and Hewitt, damn his soul, had not even seen fit to send his British cavalry after them! What, in God's name, *was* he doing with his Carabineers, his Rifles and his Horse Artillery . . . still defending his position from a few bazaar *budmashes* and escaped convicts, when in Delhi the streets were running in blood?

"Huzoor," a *subadar* of the 74th said urgently, "the men grow impatient to join their comrades in the city. General Sahib," there were tears in his eyes, Henry Graves saw, "we have served together for many years, you have commanded my regiment and I love you as my father. Go from here, I beg you, lest those Moslem devils of sowars come in search of you, with murder in their hearts. My men will not fire on them, even to save your life, *huzoor.* Will you not go, while there is yet time?"

The general turned to him sadly. "I have one last duty to perform, *Subadar* Sahib. Bid my bugler sound Assembly."

The native officer hesitated, then motioned to the bugler to obey the order. The man raised his instrument to his lips and, as darkness fell over the Ridge, the shrill, clear notes of the call to the Colours sounded eerily. Always in the past, the sepoys of John Company had obeyed it; now only the *subadar* heard and answered the summons. He stood rigidly to attention, a lone, dark figure against the red glow now rising skywards from the deserted cantonment bungalows, as the looters and arsonists commenced their work of destruction; but the others remained where they were.

The commander of the Delhi Brigade turned away. Mounting his horse, he saluted the *subadar* and dismissed him. To the rest he said, "We shall come back and exact retribution for what has been done here this day. I thank you for the loyalty you have shown . . . but remember my words. If you betray your salt, the punishment is death!"

"The Company's *Raj* is ended!" one of the sepoys called after him and added tauntingly, "No white soldiers have come from Meerut. All are dead! *We* shall not die!"

Graves gave him no answer; there was, he thought bitterly, no answer to give. They were hauling down the Union Jack from the Flagstaff Tower; even de Teissier's last two guns were coming back to the city, in the hands of their native drivers and, further along the Ridge, he did not doubt, the guard of the 38th would be breaking open the magazine. He set his face to the north and rode on, shoulders bunched and head bowed, praying that he would be able to make good his promise to return.

In the Kishnagurh Rajah's house, forty men, women and children who had fled there from the carnage of the Darya Ganj, still held out bravely, without water or food, defending themselves with sporting guns and hog spears—and even stones and kitchen knives—against several thousand frenzied besiegers. They were not all British, many were Eurasian clerks, with skins as dark as those of the mob outside but theirs, although they did not know it, was the last pocket of British resistance left in Delhi. It was to last for two hot, endless days and, a week after their honorable surrender, they were all to be dragged out and publicly butchered by the king's sons to celebrate a Mogul victory.

"Sahib . . . Sahib! Waken, I beg you, Sheridan Sahib!"

Alex heard the voice but did not recognize it. He opened his eyes dazedly, conscious of pain. Shafts of sunlight slanting through the foliage above him set his head throbbing; the light hurt his eyes and he closed them again but a hand shook his shoulder, gently at first and then with rough urgency, and the voice continued to call to him by name.

"Sheridan Sahib, it is not safe for you here. I must take you to a safer place. Waken, Sahib. Hear me, I beseech you. There are wicked men roaming the road, *budmashes* who would rob you and slit your throat. Terrible things have happened in Delhi this day, things I would gladly forget if I could, for I have had a small part in them. Waken, Sahib. If you would live, you must waken!"

Alex made an effort to answer, his own voice sounding like that of a stranger—a stranger, as this man who knelt beside him appeared to be, this man who was nevertheless calling him by name. His vision cleared a little and he stared up into a dark, bearded face, the hair of the beard grey . . . an old man, then, dressed in the white *chuddar* of a civilian, yet the face was a soldier's face beneath the green turban. Stern, even cruel, with the hawk-nose and black, somber eyes. Damn it, who was he? Why had he come when . . . memory returned.

"*Daffadar—Daffadar* Ghulam Rasul!"

Relief lit the dark eyes. "*Ji-han,* Sheridan Sahib. If you would endeavour to sit up . . . we must go from here, you understand."

Assisted by the *daffadar,* Alex dragged himself into a sitting position, the sky whirling about him and nausea catching at his throat. The sun was setting, he noticed. Dear God, for how long had he lain here? He had been on his way to Delhi, in darkness, when the sowars had attacked him—on his way to Delhi, with the note General Wilson had scribbled, to warn the commander of the Delhi Brigade that the three regiments which had mutinied were also on their way. But that, heaven help them, had been the *previous* night. The mutineers must have reached Delhi by this time unless, of course, Hewitt and Wilson had sent the Carabineers and the Rifles to stop them. Wilson had said that nothing more could be done until daylight but they had had twelve hours of daylight—time enough for the cavalry and Horse Artillery, at any rate, to have got there. Rosser's two squadrons had fresh horses. He felt in his waistband. Archdale Wilson's note was still there.

"Delhi," he managed hoarsely. "Ghulam Rasul, what has happened in Delhi?"

"Terrible things," the old *daffadar* answered. "Of which I fear to speak, Sahib. The sowars of my *paltan* were seized by a madness, the like of which I have never before seen." He shivered and again urged Alex to try to get up. "I have a horse, tethered by the roadside. If you can get to your feet, Sahib, I will fetch it and—"

"Wait," Alex bade him sternly. "Have the *lal-kote* cavalry and the *Riffel-ka-paltan* reached Delhi?"

The old man rose. He shook his head almost angrily to the question. "No, Sahib, none have left Meerut that I am aware of . . . perhaps they come now but I have seen no sign of them on the road." He helped Alex to his feet, holding him in strong arms as he swayed dizzily.

"Why did you come back to me, *daffadar-ji?* You could have stayed in Delhi."

Ghulam Rasul eyed him in silence for a moment. Then he sighed. "I have served the Company for twenty years, Sahib, and I have taken pride in my service. An old dog cannot learn new tricks and I . . . I am too old to learn what I should have to learn, were I to stay in Delhi. The men I commanded have become arrogant madmen, seeking only to kill, like butchers, not as soldiers. They rode through the Darya Ganj sabreing every white passer-by they could see, women, children, even babes in their mothers' arms. I have no stomach for such slaughter and I . . ." he smiled briefly. "I had the Sahib on my conscience. Last night you could have taken my life but you did not, Sheridan Sahib, even though I gave it to you."

"You hit me an almighty blow with your carbine," Alex reminded him. He put up a cautious hand and felt the swelling at the back of his head ruefully.

"I had no choice," Ghulam Rasul answered. "If I had not done so, the others would have cut you to pieces. I told them that you were dead and carried your body to conceal it among the sugar canes. But I did not think I had struck you too hard. I came back to make sure that you were *not* dead, Sahib." His smile faded and he frowned up at the darkening sky. "I will get the horse. There is no time to be lost. The Sahib is fortunate that he was not seen by those of the infantry *paltans* who passed by in the night . . . and still more fortunate that no villagers found him before I did."

He vanished and Alex moved a few uncertain paces after him, still dazed and finding difficulty in holding himself upright. Just beyond the edge of the canes, he saw the carcass of a horse, already almost picked clean by a flock of scavenging vultures and, a few yards further on, the remains of what had once been a man. That body might well have been his, he thought, sickened, as three or four of the noisome birds, clumsy in their satiation, took wing reluctantly at his approach. But Ghulam Rasul had struck him with calculated force and, before leaving him, had fashioned a protective screen of cane stalks to hide him from both human and animal scavengers. He sighed, feeling the lump at the back of his head again, as the *daffadar* came towards him with a lathered and weary horse.

"The Sahib's pistol," the old cavalryman said, holding out the Adams. "I took it last night." He bent, offering his hand. "If the Sahib will mount, we can be on our way. My horse is tired but he will carry us both a few miles from the road."

As they set off across country at a shambling walk, Alex again questioned his rescuer about the happenings in Delhi and, in a low, shamed voice, Ghulam Rasul gave him an account first of what he had seen and then of what he had learned from others. It was a terrible story; worse, infinitely worse than he had expected and, as he listened, Alex found himself wondering whether this was a nightmare, imagined rather than real, an ugly dream from which he would wake, looking up into the dusty tops of the sugar cane, still with the night before him in which to carry his warning to Delhi. He dismissed the hope; Ghulam Rasul's account was too detailed, too factual to be a figment of his imagination.

He told of the audience with old Shah Bahadur and of how, once they had gained his promise to embrace their cause, the mutineers had taken possession of the palace, ousting the body-guard which, after admitting them, had gone with a mob of the king's rapacious retainers to join the scum of the bazaar in an orgy of killing and looting.

"They tethered their horses in the courtyard, watered them at the royal fountains, Sahib," the *daffadar* said. "Showing little respect, even to the emperor himself. Some of them spread their bedding rolls on the marble floors of the inner chamber and lay down to rest. Others attempted to raid the harem, firing their carbines into the air if any said them nay. The Begum and her son, Janna Bakht and the other princes, offered them encouragement but I—I could not stomach such conduct, so I returned to the city. I saw the sepoys of the 54th shoot down their officers at the Kashmir Gate, aided by our men, and later I saw them destroy the Christian church of the *sahib-log* and set it on fire."

"Did all the sepoys of the Delhi regiments join in the mutiny?" Alex asked.

"Not quite all, Sahib. Many of the 74th remained true to their salt and two companies of the 54th also . . . until they saw that it was hopeless. All the *sahib-log* are gone from cantonments and from the Ridge. The sepoys who were with them saw them go on their way unharmed before they, too, went to join their comrades in the city. . . ." The old *daffadar's* voice droned on, telling of fresh horrors, fresh humiliations but Alex scarcely heard him, his numbed brain unable to take in any more.

If General Hewitt had acted as any general worthy of the name would have acted, he thought bitterly, this might not have happened. If he had sent even half the British troops under his command in pursuit of the mutineers at once, when Charles Rosser had offered to lead them, how many lives might have been saved, how much tragedy averted!

"Let a mutiny succeed in Delhi," Sir Henry Lawrence had said. *"And it will be the signal for an uprising all over the country, from the Afghan border to Calcutta. . . ."* Well, the mutiny had succeeded in Delhi, due largely to Hewitt's incompetence. Dear heaven, why hadn't Archdale Wilson taken those letters seriously, why hadn't he *listened* to Lawrence's sage advice? Rosser's two squadrons of dragoons, a Horse Artillery troop and even two companies of the Rifles, under the command of Colonel Jones might have been sent 24 hours ago and, with British troops behind them at the Kashmir gate, the 54th would not have cut down their officers! Even if they had reached Delhi after the mutineers, the small force he and Rosser had visualized might have deterred many of them from entering Delhi and could have held the Ridge and the magazine, until the Rifles arrived to support them.

But now, if Lawrence was right, every ploughshare in Delhi would be turned into a sword and all India would rise against the British *Raj*. Delhi was the key and it was in the hands of the plotters; in hundreds of stations where there were only native troops, the pattern would be repeated in all its tragic horror. The very ease with which the ancient capital of the Moguls had been taken would inspire contempt for British authority and British military prestige, and the sepoys would rise in Adjodhabad, in Cawnpore, in Allahabad and throughout Oudh—perhaps even in Lucknow, where Lawrence had only one British regiment, heavily outnumbered. He must return to Lucknow, Alex told himself, but first he would go back to Meerut and add his voice to those who, he was certain, would now be demanding that General Hewitt should take action, however futile and belated it might be. If every man in the Meerut garrison died in the attempt, it would be a small price to pay for the recapture of Delhi and the attempt had to be made, if all India were not to be lost. He felt the sweat break out on his brow, as he heard Ghulam Rusal voice his own bitter conclusion.

"Sahib, we expected that the *lal-kote* soldiers would pursue us. Throughout the night, we listened in fear for their coming. We posted men on the road and on the Bridge of Boats to give warning of their approach, so that we might take flight before they attacked us. Why did they not come, Sheridan Sahib?"

"I do not know, Ghulam Rasul," Alex answered. "Before God, I do not know. But they *will* come, of that I am sure."

"They will be too late," the old *daffadar* said, with conviction. "My comrades and the people of Delhi will not yield to them now. And other *paltans* will rise and march to their aid. The day for the uprising is not yet, it was planned for the end of this month but when the news is spread that Delhi has fallen, I tell you, Sahib, they will all rise."

Lawrence's prophecy, Alex thought, a bitter taste in his mouth. The weary horse stumbled and he asked, with genuine concern, "*Daffadar-ji,* why do you stay with me? You have saved my life, you have done all and more than I have the right to ask of you. Why do you not return now to your comrades?"

"I told you, Sahib. I am too old a dog to learn new tricks. I will stay with you, if you will permit this, and serve you. If need be, I will die with you. I ask only that when we reach Meerut, you will not send me back to the prison from which I made my escape."

"You have my word on that, Ghulam Rasul," Alex promised. The old man slid from the saddle. In the darkness, he held up his hand and Alex took it, sealing the bond.

"The horse tires, Sahib," the *daffadar* said quietly. "I will walk for a while, to ease him of his double burden."

They halted when the animal could go no further. Ghulam Rasul removed the saddle and, like the good cavalryman he was, rubbed the poor creature down with wisps of grass, tethered it to a tree and went in search of water.

"There is a village not far from here. No doubt there will be a well. Rest, Sahib, for you, I think, are also very tired. I will be as quick as I can."

Alex did as he had suggested. He was still feeling the effects of the blow from the carbine and his head was throbbing unmercifully, so that he was grateful for the respite and lay down beside the tethered horse. Often in the past, he had lain down to sleep on the open ground or made camp at the roadside, anticipating no danger from villagers living nearby and he anticipated none now—the villagers were simple *ryots,* peaceful cultivators of the soil who, even if tempted by avarice, were usually afraid to rob a British officer. He lay between sleeping and waking, glad just to close his eyes and let his aching muscles relax and he did not move when he heard voices coming towards him, supposing that

Ghulam Rasul had returned from the village with some of its inhabitants, perhaps bringing food with them.

Then, as the voices came within earshot and he was able to make out what they said, he felt a sudden chill about his heart. A woman's voice, an English voice speaking halting Hindustani, was pleading for mercy. "We are wounded . . . weary from walking. You have our carriage and the horse, our money . . . even our clothes. Please let us go. We are from Delhi, we have suffered enough. We seek only to reach Meerut. Help us and you will be rewarded. You . . ."

She was brutally silenced and Alex sat up, feeling for his pistol, every sense alert now, yet—in that moment—more stunned than shocked by the realization that an Indian peasant had dared to strike a British memsahib.

"All the *sahib-log* in Meerut are dead, how will they reward us?" The question was insolently phrased. "Likewise in Delhi, it is said, the streets run with their blood, and the Company's *Raj* is over. All will die, *sab lal hogea!* Why should we spare you?"

On his feet, crouching low, Alex moved swiftly. He could see them now in the light of the torches some of them carried. There were about eight or ten villagers, two of whom were leading a battered carriage, drawn by a single horse. The woman whose voice he had heard was grey-haired, clad only in a torn shift, hatless and barefooted and behind her, evidently badly wounded, staggered a man, stripped naked save for a blood-soaked bandage wound about his chest, leaning heavily for support on the arm of a girl with long, flowing fair hair.

She replied to the *ryot's* taunting question with a quiet, dignified courage which impressed Alex deeply as he heard it.

"If it is your intention to take our lives, then kill us here," she bade the man, her Hindustani fluent and accentless. "We can offer no resistance. But do not humiliate us by taking us as we are to your village, for your women to mock our nakedness. We have not deserved that of you and you would shame yourselves if you do it."

One of the villagers raised his hand as if to silence her in the same ruthless manner as her grey-haired companion had been silenced but Alex took aim at him and the crack of the pistol was followed by a shrill scream of pain as the man rolled over, clutching his shattered arm. The two who were leading the horse relinquished its reins and ran for cover, too frightened to look back; one, the only one who was armed with a flintlock, brought his weapon to his shoulder and as quickly lowered it, when he saw that the pistol was leveled at his head.

"We meant no harm, Sahib," he whimpered. "We did but jest. Truly, we could not have hurt the *sahib-log,* we—"

"Cowardly dogs! Misbegotten curs, back to your kennels!" Alex roared at them, beside himself with rage. "Defilers of women, why should I spare *you?* Give the memsahibs their garments and then go from my sight before my pistol speaks again!"

They quailed before the fury in his voice and, when Ghulam Rasul ran from the darkness to stand by his side, the *chuddar* opened to reveal his uniform, even the owner of the flintlock took to his heels, crying out a terrified warning that the soldiers had come to seek vengeance on them for what they had done.

"Our clothes are in the carriage," the girl said. "I will get them." Gently she lowered the wounded man to the ground, whispered a word of reassurance to him and crossed to the carriage, walking like a queen in the mudspattered petticoat that was her only covering. The older woman dropped to her knees beside the prostrate form on the ground, shaken by sobs, and when Alex picked up one of the discarded torches and carried it over to her, she thanked him brokenly.

"My husband has been very badly wounded—a musket-ball in the chest. I . . . I fear that there is little I can do for him. He . . . we were taking him in the carriage, you see, but they made him leave it and walk. If the bleeding has started again . . . poor soul, he has endured so much pain, I—"

"Permit me to look at the wound, ma'am," Alex requested. She yielded her place to him, bravely biting back the tears as Ghulam Rasul, carbine in hand, crossed the intervening space to offer him one of the water-bottles he had filled.

"It will not be wise to linger here, Sheridan Sahib," he said, lowering his voice. "It is a big village. They will come back when they find out how few we are. I will keep watch and call to you if they come."

Alex nodded his understanding and bent over the wounded man, holding the water-bottle to his lips and noticed, as he did so, that the bandage wound about his chest was unusually bulky and that a braided scarlet cord held it in place.

"My regimental . . . Colour," the wounded man whispered faintly. "The sepoys of my company . . . gave it to me before they deserted. I had it . . . wrapped round me when . . . one of the 38th . . . fired at me from the . . . Main Guard. My men . . . two companies of them . . . did not offer me violence. They waited . . . all day for . . . the British troops from . . . Meerut but they did not come. I—" He attempted to raise himself but Alex gently restrained him.

"Don't try to talk, sir," he advised.

"It can do me . . . no harm, sir. I'm . . . done for, I'm afraid.

But you . . . my wife and daughter—if you could save them, I . . . would be more grateful than I . . . and the Colour. You . . . you'll take the Colour, won't you, when I—"

"Of course, sir," Alex assured him. The wound had, he saw, opened again, as his wife had feared it would and a glance told him that it was mortal. He was endeavouring to tighten the bandage when the girl, dressed now in a muslin gown that had once been white, came to relieve him of the task. She was very young, seventeen or eighteen, at the most, and he marvelled at her calm competence as she deftly secured the bulky dressing, smiling down at her father as if she had not a care in the world.

"There, dearest Papa, that's better. I'm going to tie my sash round you, to make sure this doesn't slip again. And then . . ." the sash in place, she kissed his pale cheek and rose. "We will get you into the carriage and drive on to Meerut. It can't be very far now and when we get there the surgeons will make up for my clumsiness and have you well again in no time. You—" her eyes met Alex's and he was shocked by the pain they held, although she went on smiling and her voice was steady and controlled. She continued to smile and to talk encouragingly as, between them, they helped her father into the carriage. "You ride with him, Mamma," she suggested. "He should not be alone."

Her mother, drying her tears, got in beside the wounded man, pillowing his head on her lap. The girl squeezed her hand, then reached for a pistol which had been hidden somewhere in the interior of the carriage and offered it to Alex.

"It will save you reloading yours," she said practically. "I could not find it, when those men from the village surrounded us. But if I had, I . . ." she stifled a sigh. "Shall I drive and you sit on the box beside me? Then you'll have your hand free if they . . . if they come after us."

Alex nodded, not trusting himself to speak. She reminded him of Emmy, as she had been when he had taken leave of her in Windsor, on the eve of his departure for India, never expecting that he would see either her or her elder sister, Charlotte, again. This girl, whose name he did not know, had something of Emmy's childlike candor, her earnestness and certainly her courage, he thought, conscious of a pang as he watched her take up the reins. She had probably never driven a horse and carriage before but no one would have guessed it as she whipped up the horse and the clumsy vehicle started to move forward at a snail's pace along the uneven, rutted track, its sorely tried springs creaking in protest. Thank God that Emmy had been spared the ordeal that this poor child had endured. For all her protests, he was thankful that he had persuaded her to go to Calcutta.

"Better head across country," he told the girl, as Ghulam Rasul mounted his own horse and trotted after them, shaking his head to Alex's mute enquiry. "This track leads to the village and I think we had better give it a wide berth. As soon as we can, though, we'll return to the road, so as to save your poor father too much jolting. Bear left towards those trees."

She followed his directions without demur. "How far is it to Meerut?"

"About twenty miles. Perhaps a little more. But don't worry, we'll see you get there."

"If those men don't come after us. Do you—do you think they will?" He shook his head and saw her smile. "Well, at least we'll give a better account of ourselves, with *your* help, than Mother and I were able to . . . and once it's light, they won't dare to attack us, will they?"

Daylight might bring worse perils, Alex reflected grimly. The news of Delhi's fall must have spread like wildfire and now, unless

General Hewitt sent out patrols to search for and aid the fugitives, those who were unprotected and unarmed might find every man's hand against them. But surely even Hewitt could not have failed to send out patrols?

"Our name is Patterson," the girl volunteered. "My father is Major Patterson of the 54th and I'm Lavinia." Alex introduced himself and she bowed solemnly in acknowledgement. "Your *daffadar*—I noticed his uniform—isn't he of the Light Cavalry, the —the ones who caused all this trouble?"

"Yes, Miss Patterson, he is . . . but he has remained loyal and, indeed, he saved my life, not once but twice. You may trust him completely."

"I'm glad that one of them stayed true to his salt, Colonel Sheridan. My father's sepoys stayed with him all day at the Kashmir Gate, you know. If the British troops from Meerut had come, he says that they would not have mutinied." There was a catch in her voice. "*Why* didn't Meerut send us help? Didn't they know what was likely to happen? Didn't they even try to stop the mutineers from reaching us?"

"I cannot tell you, Miss Patterson," Alex evaded, his tone carefully expressionless. "I don't know the reason for the general's decision or what steps were taken after I left."

"But you were there, were you not?" Lavinia Patterson persisted. "There was a rumor that all the British troops in Meerut had been wiped out. I heard it, when Mother and I were in the Flagstaff Tower but none of us could believe it. Two thousand British troops—the *Rifles,* one of the best regiments in the British army . . . we all agreed that it was impossible. It *was,* wasn't it? I mean, they weren't all killed. The mutineers didn't defeat them, surely?"

"No," Alex confessed reluctantly. "They were not defeated and they suffered no casualties that I am aware of. Some of the Company's officers were killed but . . ." He gave her a brief account of what had happened in Meerut and saw her small, grave face pucker in bewilderment.

"Then *why,* Colonel Sheridan? It's only 38 miles and—"

"I honestly do not know, Miss Patterson. But no doubt we shall learn the reason when we reach Meerut." Alex called to Ghulam Rasul, anxious to change the subject, and when the *daffadar* trotted up, they agreed, after a whispered consultation, to return to the road, now plainly visible in the moonlight and not more than half a mile distant. Mrs Patterson replied reassuringly to his enquiry as to her husband's condition and he said, more in an attempt to keep the girl's spirits up than because he really believed it, "We'll probably meet a cavalry patrol soon."

"Do you really think we will?" She spoke bitterly.

"I'm sure there's a good chance of it. In any case, the road is the most likely place to find one and, for your father's sake, the sooner we get on to a smoother surface, the better."

"Yes, of course." She applied her whip across the tired horse's quarters in a gentle flick, clicking her tongue to it encouragingly. "Poor old Rastus! We usually have two horses to draw this carriage—a matched pair that Papa was so proud of—but the coachman stole them and Rastus was the only one left. He's my hack, not a carriage horse at all, really, but he's done very well, hasn't he?"

"He has indeed," Alex agreed warmly. He laid his hand on her arm. "And so have you, my dear child."

She flushed and was silent until Ghulam Rasul signed to her to pull up under cover of a clump of trees, while he trotted ahead to reconnoitre the road. Then she asked, in a whisper, so that her mother should not hear, "Colonel Sheridan, do you think there's any chance that my father will live? If we get him to Meerut, I mean?"

The question caught Alex off guard. She was looking at him, he realized, her blue eyes very direct and searching as they met his and he knew that he could not fob her off with a half-truth. "It's a nasty wound," he said. "And he's lost a good deal of blood. I'm no surgeon, of course, but I would not rate his chances very highly, I'm afraid. Where there's life there's hope, though."

"Thank you," Lavinia answered, as if he had conferred a favour on her. "That was what I . . . what I thought." Her lower lip trembled but she controlled it and went on, her voice flat and devoid of emotion, "The road *is* more dangerous than the way we've been going, isn't it—unless we meet a cavalry patrol?"

There were *goojur* villages close to the road from which, in the present state of affairs, danger might be expected. Alex shrugged. "We're more easily seen, that's all, but there's not much in it. On the credit side, your father will not be so badly jarred and we should be able to travel a little faster on the road."

"He would not want you to risk your life, Colonel Sheridan, just for the sake of his comfort. I know he wouldn't. So if you—" Alex cut her short.

"My *daffadar*'s giving us the all clear, Miss Patterson," he pointed out. "So I think we'll try the road for a bit. But thank you for your suggestion." Again he found himself admiring her courage. "Perhaps," he added, smiling, "if you asked it of him, your old Rastus might be able to raise his pace a little. How about it, eh?"

Her smile echoed his, although her eyes were brimming. "I'll ask him," she promised. "But I'm afraid he hasn't a trot left in him, poor old fellow." She leaned forward and, in response to her coaxing, the weary horse managed a few yards at a shambling trot and then lapsed back into its former labored gait, head down and breathing hard.

"I think I'd better lead him," Alex said. "We'll have to find some water for him, if we can." He had given the water-bottle to Mrs Patterson and he saw, glancing into the rear of the carriage, that she had used its contents to moisten a cloth for her husband's brow. He walked to the horse's head and started to lead it when Ghulam Rasul, observing their plight, turned back to join them. Slipping from his saddle, he poured the little that remained in his own water-bottle into his shako and held it out, and the old horse drank greedily.

"This horse cannot go much further, Sahib," he warned, lowering his voice.

"I don't think it can," Alex agreed. He did not want to call a halt but knew that he would have to, before long. If the carriage horse collapsed, they would have only Ghulam Rasul's charger, which was not harness-trained. "Look for somewhere where we can rest, *daffadar-ji,*" he ordered, shaking his head to the man's offer to take his place. "No, I'll lead the horse—you'll be more useful as you are, you've got two hands. Keep your carbine handy and go ahead of us. We'll need somewhere with enough cover to hide the carriage."

The *daffadar* replaced his shako and climbed stiffly back into the saddle. "Take care, Sahib," he cautioned anxiously. "There are some bad villages about here and I fear that not all the *goojurs* will be sleeping."

The darkness swallowed him up and the sound of his hoof-beats had scarcely receded when there was the flash of a musket from the road verge. Whoever had fired had taken careful aim and Alex was conscious of a sharp, stinging pain in his right shoulder.

But it was slight and he did not register the fact that he had been hit because the next moment the carriage was surrounded by a score of leaping, shouting figures, armed with clubs and knives, and he had just time to pull the girl down from the box before they were upon him and he was fighting for his life.

"Run!" he bade her urgently and, when she still lingered, he thrust the pistol she had given him into her hand. "In God's name, Lavinia, get under cover and use this if you have to! The *daffadar* will come back. Wait for him."

One of the attackers dived beneath the horse, his long dagger raised to hamstring the animal and Alex fired the Adams at point-blank range and saw him fall back, the dagger clattering to the ground. He brought down two more, who were attempting to climb into the carriage and Mrs Patterson, with a smothered cry, struck out at a third with the carriage whip, before the mob wrested it from her and she went down under a hail of blows.

The Adams had only one shot left in it but Alex used this to good effect on the man with the flintlock, recognizing the evil, pock-marked face as he fired. Those swine from the village they had left must have followed them, he thought savagely, bringing the butt of the pistol down on to the fellow's head, as he slithered, wounded but still dangerous, to the ground at his feet.

With the loss of their leader, the attackers seemed momentarily to lose heart and he managed to get the horse moving again while they hesitated, engaged in a shrill-voiced argument at the edge of the road. He drew his sabre, brought the flat of it down, none too gently, across the horse's quarters and released its head, praying that, of its own accord, it would continue along the road. He was turning, the sabre raised awkwardly in his left hand, when he glimpsed a flash of white a few yards from him and realized, to his dismay, that the girl was coming back in defiance of his injunction to hide herself.

"No!" he yelled at her. "Get away from here, Lavinia! There's nothing you can do. You—"

She ignored his frantic plea. Running to the horse's head, she seized the rein and brought the carriage to a standstill, calling out breathlessly over her shoulder, "There's a British cavalry patrol coming! Your *daffadar's* bringing them to . . . help us!"

Alex heard the drumming of hoof beats, coming rapidly nearer and then an English voice shouted an order. He lowered his sabre and breathed a prayer of thankfulness, feeling some of the tension drain out of him. The *goojurs* heard and recognized these sounds, too, and vanished, slinking into the shadows like jackals hearing the roar of a tiger. Only their dead remained when the patrol clattered up. Their dead and . . . Lavinia Patterson went to the rear of the carriage, mounted the step and turned away with a little broken cry, to bury her face in her hands, even her courage not proof against what she had seen there.

Alex took a pace towards her, sick with pity but one of the newly arrived officers was before him, slipping from his horse to enfold her in comforting arms and he halted, as two of the others rode up to him, calling his name in mingled astonishment and relief.

"My God, sir, I'm glad to see you!" Henry Craigie dismounted to wring his hand and he recognized Hugh Gough behind him, grinning broadly, with Ghulam Rasul at his side.

"Not nearly as glad," Alex told them, his voice not steady, "not nearly as glad as I am to see *you,* my friends, believe me!"

"It was by the grace of God that we came," Gough said, his

smile fading abruptly. "We're a volunteer patrol, sir, composed mainly of Company's officers, who now lack regimental employment. But you, I see, have brought one of our regiment back?" He gestured to the *daffadar.*

"The only one, I fear," Alex said. "And I owe my life to him twice over."

Craigie unstrapped a flask from his saddle and offered it. "The most appalling rumors concerning the situation in Delhi have been filtering through to us all day and we set out—with the general's grudging consent—in the hope of *disproving* them." He broke off, to stare into Alex's white, exhausted face, the light of horrified understanding slowly dawning in his eyes. "*Are* the rumors true, sir? Is Delhi now in the hands of the mutineers?"

"Without a single British regiment to stand in their way, they had only to walk in," Alex answered bitterly. "To be received by the king with open arms and joined by the native population and most of the Delhi Brigade. Oh, yes, Delhi is now in the mutineers' hands all right!" He controlled himself and went on, his voice expressionless, "I failed to get there but the two people in that carriage were among the fugitives and the poor child who is weeping for them is their daughter. You'll find the 54th's Colour wrapped about Major Patterson's body." He gave brief details and heard Gough swearing impotently beneath his breath. "They waited all day for the troops from Meerut, while the mobs indulged in an orgy of slaughter and then, when the regiments that might, with British backing, have stood firm, finally deserted them, they had no choice but to flee. *I* could not answer the question they asked me but perhaps you can. Why, in the name of all humanity, gentlemen, were no British regiments sent from Meerut?"

The little group of officers looked at one another in unhappy silence and then Henry Craigie said, an edge to his voice, "I am afraid that only General Hewitt can tell you that, sir."

Cold fury caught at Alex's throat. "You mean that General Hewitt deliberately refused to . . . ?" He could not go on.

"Colonel Custance and Colonel Jones, together with Major Tombs, of the Bengal Artillery, pleaded with him for over an hour, sir, and at least a score of junior officers volunteered to go to Delhi in any capacity," Gough said. "But he simply would not listen. I believe he told Colonel Custance that he considered it his first duty to provide for the protection of his own station. After that, he refused to see any of them!"

The others confirmed this incredible statement and Craigie added, his mouth tight, "As to protecting Meerut, Colonel Sheridan, he didn't do that very effectively either. While his entire force was ordered to bivouac in The Mall, my wife and I, with Alfred Mackenzie and his sister, were hiding in a Hindu temple less than a mile away, with a mob from the bazaar hunting high and low for us. We only escaped from them at dawn, when Hugh Gough and a few volunteers came to our rescue. We owe our lives to the sowars who hid us in the temple before they left for Delhi, and to my old bearer, who brought us a couple of sporting guns from the bungalow with which to defend ourselves! But to General Hewitt—" He sighed, in remembered frustration, and went on cynically, "There are, I understand, a number of mutinous officers in Meerut at this moment, who would consider the loss of their commissions a small price to pay for the satisfaction of telling the divisional commander, to his face, what they think of him. But he's barricaded himself in his house, with sentries posted on the door, and left General Wilson to cope with complaints. And Wilson won't issue any orders without his authority!"

"The only order be *did* give, sir," another officer put in, "was for the arrest of Lieutenant Möller, of the 11th, because he went into the Sudder Bazaar without permission to bring out the butcher who murdered poor Mrs Chambers. The fellow was boasting about what he'd done, quite openly, sir. However, General Wilson gave permission for a drumhead court martial and the butcher's been tried and condemned to death. So far, though, he's the only one who has."

Alex listened, unable to believe the evidence of his own ears. This was worse, infinitely worse than he had expected, even of the obese and senile Hewitt. He glanced anxiously to where Lavinia Patterson had been standing and saw that she was being lifted onto his saddle-bow by the young officer who had tried to comfort her. The carriage, with its tragic burden, had been moved from her immediate vicinity, he was relieved to notice, and Gough said, reading his thoughts, "She's with her brother, sir—young Luke Patterson of the 11th. He told us his parents and sister were in Delhi. Er—I'll see about a horse for you, shall I?"

Alex nodded his thanks. The brandy in Craigie's flask was going to his head a little but he was grateful for it, nonetheless. "You'll continue the patrol, will you not?" he asked Craigie, returning the flask. "There will be other fugitives, quite a number of them, probably, and they'll need help as much as we did."

"Our orders," the younger man said, avoiding his gaze, "were to return to Meerut before daylight. But," he shrugged, "I'm in no mood to adhere strictly to General Hewitt's orders, I must confess. We'll send you back, sir, with Miss Patterson, and I'll take a few of our fellows and see if we can find anyone else. I can depend on you to make our excuses to General Wilson, can I not, sir?"

"You can," Alex assured him grimly. "Yes, by heaven, you can!"

Gough was coming with a spare horse, he saw, and he turned, preparing to mount it when suddenly, without warning, his vision blurred. He put his foot into the stirrup, feeling for it blindly, the night sky revolving in crazy circles above his head. The brandy, he thought, fool that he was to have taken it on an empty stomach; he hadn't eaten for 24 hours, of course it had gone to his head. Bracing himself, he made another attempt to mount.

"Are you all right, sir?" Gough asked, concerned.

He swayed and would have fallen had not Craigie moved swiftly to break his fall.

"The colonel's wounded!" he heard someone exclaim, the voice seeming to come from a long way away. "Good God, he's been hit—taken a musket ball in the shoulder, I think. Yes, look, the back of his jacket is covered with blood. The poor fellow only has one arm . . . we'd better get him to a surgeon as fast as we can, I think. He . . ."

The voices faded into silence as once again the dark and bottomless pit opened to receive him.

A long time later, he wakened in a lamp-lit room, to find a stranger bending over him.

"All right, sir," the stranger told him cheerfully. "You're in hospital in Meerut and I've taken a musket ball out of the top of your scapula. No serious damage, the bone's nicked, that's all, and I've had to put a few stitches in the back of your head. But you'll live to fight another day, so don't worry. Try to sleep now, if you can."

Alex accepted his advice gratefully and let his heavy lids fall.

CHAPTER EIGHT

⋙ • ⋘

NEWS of the outbreak of mutiny in Meerut and the subsequent fall of Delhi was brought by an officer on horseback from Ambala, where the telegraph line terminated, to the commander-in-chief in Simla on May 12th. General Anson was at dinner when the message was handed to him. Because there were ladies present, Anson slipped the note under his plate and courteously waited until the port was being circulated before reading it . . . but having done so, he took action at once. His aides were sent posthaste to order all British troops on furlough in the hills to march to Ambala and he reached there himself, 36 hours later, to establish telegraphic communication with the governor-general in Calcutta and with Sir John Lawrence in the Punjab.

Thereafter, preceded by rumor and speculation, the news spread throughout the length and breadth of India; to be received with jubilation by the plotters and with stunned incredulity by the Company's British officials.

Emmy Sheridan heard it in Cawnpore on the 15th, from the midwife who had assisted at the premature birth of her son, ten days previously and at first she, too, had difficulty in believing it. Then, when realization of what the disaster meant slowly sank into her numbed mind, she wept, feeling as if her heart would break and the midwife, a rough but kindly woman, offered what comfort she could.

"There, ma'am, there," she soothed, seating herself on the bed and enfolding the sobbing girl in her plump, motherly arms. "It's not the end of the world, is it? And it may not happen here. They say that General Wheeler has sent for reinforcements from Calcutta and, even if they don't get here in time, the Nana Sahib has promised us his protection . . . and besides, there are the entrenchments. My husband says we'll be safe enough inside the entrenchments, until a relief force arrives."

"I'm not worrying about *our* safety, Mrs Miller," Emmy whispered fiercely.

"No, of course not, ma'am. You're upset and it's only natural that you should be with the captain in Meerut But there weren't many of them killed in Meerut. There couldn't have been, with all those queen's regiments there; it stands to sense there couldn't. Although *my* husband says . . ." She talked on volubly, giving the views of her husband, who was the quartermaster-sergeant of the 53rd Native Infantry, but Emmy shut her ears to the sound.

She had received no letters from Alex, apart from the hurried note he had sent her from Lucknow to say that he was leaving for Meerut next day. She did not even know whether he had reached his destination, she thought wretchedly. She had written him an equally hurried note, after the baby's birth, in which she had endeavoured to explain to him how that unexpected event had rendered it impossible for her to keep the promise she had made him to accompany her sister and brother-in-law to Calcutta. Harry's orders had brooked no delay; she had been compelled to let the two of them go without her and it had been on the advice of the garrison doctor that she had done so . . . wise advice, as it had proved, for her labor had started within hours of their departure. But Alex, naturally—if he were able to write at all—would address his letters to her in Calcutta and it might be weeks, even months, before she heard from him. The mail would inevitably be delayed if there was trouble and some letters might not be delivered at all, her own included, so that Alex would have no more idea of her whereabouts than she had of his. According to the reports, it had been his regiment—the 3rd Light Cavalry— which had started the mutiny.

"A sepoy in my husband's regiment," Mrs Miller was saying indignantly. "He had the cheek to accost me in the bazaar this morning and tell me that none of us would be doing our shopping there much longer. And when I asked him what he meant, he spat, ma'am, spat at my feet, if you please, and said we'd none of us be alive two weeks from now! I gave him the sharp edge of my tongue, you may be sure."

"How horrible," Emmy exclaimed. She lay back on her pillows, evading Mrs Miller's embrace and the woman, realizing that she had allowed her indignation to carry her away, stood up, smoothing her apron and looking down at her anxiously.

"I'll order tea for you, ma'am," she promised. "And you can be drinking it while I see to the poor wee soul's needs, before I bring him to you."

She always referred thus to the baby, Emmy thought, having to make an effort to hide her resentment. He was pathetically small, it was true; a tiny, red-faced creature, with scarcely any flesh on his bones and a tendency to resume the curled-up position he had occupied before his premature arrival, but he was not a poor wee soul. And he was not, please God, destined to leave the world as precipitately as he had entered it, whatever might be Mrs Miller's opinion. Furthermore, he had a name; the chaplain had christened him, in a brief ceremony performed soon after his birth. At her request, the name William had been bestowed on him, after Alex's oldest and most valued friend, Colonel William Beatson, with whom they had both shared so many joys and sorrows during the Crimean War. Alex, she knew, had intended to invite him to act as godfather if the baby was a son but . . .

"I'll just plump up these pillows for you, Mrs Sheridan," the midwife said. A strong, work-roughened hand behind Emmy's head, she subjected the pillows to a vigorous pummelling, tucked in the sheet and finally bustled out, calling loudly for the bearer in a mixture of English and Hindustani. "*Koi hai—koi hai!* Oh, there you are, Bearer. Take tea to the memsahib, *chae lao, jeldi.* And you can bring me a pot too, while you're about it. I'll be attending to the baba-sahib." The voice receded at last and Emmy wearily closed her eyes.

It was hot in the bedroom, hot and airless; despite the *punkah* creaking above her head, she felt stifled, hardly able to breathe. Mrs Miller had drawn the sheet constrictingly tight. She sighed, lacking the energy to tug it loose. If only she knew where Alex was, she thought, if only there were some way of finding out what he was doing, what he intended to do. She could not, would not believe that he was dead; that was unthinkable. To believe anything of the kind would be to lose her own desire to live and, for the sake of the poor wee—for little William's sake, she must not give up hope. He would need all her care, all her love and pity if his frail hold on life were not to be broken and, if Mrs Miller was right, and they were all soon to be herded into General Wheeler's hastily constructed entrenchment, she would have to make an effort to regain her lost strength and courage, so that she might give her son the care he needed.

She thought of the entrenchment and bit back another sigh. Many members of the garrison considered that the general's choice of a site left much to be desired and Alex, she remembered, had shared this opinion but Sir Hugh Wheeler, having once made up his mind, was not to be turned from his purpose. The site he was now busy preparing for the reception of both civil and military inhabitants of the station was in the open, on the south side of the city and close to the Allahabad road. It contained two newly constructed European barracks, one of which was intended for use as a hospital and had additional sanitary outhouses and verandas built on to it—a fact by which the general set great store, according to his wife, Emmy remembered.

"With so many women and children to be accommodated, as well as civilians," Lady Wheeler had said, in her musical, persuasive Indian voice, "one *must* think of these things. And it is within sight of the road by which our reinforcements will come, in easy reach of the cantonment bungalows and close to our own residence. My dear husband is not a young man—he celebrated his 75th birthday quite recently—and I'm thankful that he has decided on the barracks site. At least it will mean that he does not have to ride six miles in the hot sun to supervise the preparations, as he would have had to, if the Magazine had been chosen."

Had this, Emmy wondered, been one of the general's reasons for rejecting the alternative possibility of the well-fortified, stone-built Magazine? She swiftly banished the thought, as unworthy and disloyal. Sir Hugh Wheeler was a good and upright man, an experienced commander, who had fought with great distinction in the Sikh wars. . . . He would never have put his own convenience before the safety of those for whose lives he was responsible. There were a great many, she knew. Cawnpore contained a large civil and business community and numerous Eurasian Christians; in addition there were the railway engineers, who had been preparing an embankment in readiness for the approaching line from Calcutta, as well as the wives and families of the 32nd Queen's, left behind when the regiment was posted to Lucknow. Lady Wheeler had estimated that there were at least three hundred women and children, for whose defense, she had added gravely, the general could muster fewer than two hundred trained British soldiers—some of them invalids—and perhaps two hundred able-bodied but untrained male civilians.

"My husband is doing his best with the means at his disposal, Mrs Sheridan," she had insisted. "A place of refuge and shelter for the European noncombatants is the first essential, if there should be an outbreak of mutiny here. And this he is providing, with a parapet to surround it and guns for its defense."

Emmy pressed a hand to her burning eyes. Before the birth of little William, she had gone with Harry and her sister to see the preparations being made. They had watched gangs of coolies toiling in the hot sun to construct an earthwork parapet on the rock-hard ground—a parapet little more than four feet high its mud walls two to three feet thick. Anne had looked at the single-storied hospital building, with its thatched roof, and shuddered.

"Thank God," she had whispered, a catch in her voice, "that we shall not have to stay here, depending on *this* place as a refuge!"

The Nana Sahib's hateful young advisor, Azimullah, had called the entrenchment "The Fort of Despair" someone had reported wryly, and even Harry Stirling, who liked and admired General Wheeler, had admitted that it was aptly named.

"Memsahib . . ." The door curtains parted, to reveal the bearded face of the old bearer. "I bring you tea, as the nurse-sahiba is asking. Also," he was beaming, Emmy saw, as he set down the tray on the table at her bedside, "a letter, Memsahib, which has come by the *dak* from Lucknow."

He placed it in her hand and Emmy's heart missed a beat, only to sink, when she looked at the envelope and saw that the writing on it was unfamiliar.

"From the Captain Sahib?" the bearer asked eagerly. "Is the Captain Sahib back in Lucknow?"

She shook her head regretfully. "No, it isn't from the Captain Sahib, Mohammed Bux, it *is* from Lucknow, so perhaps there may be news of him. Wait, I will read it."

She unfolded the flimsy sheet of paper, her fingers trembling in their haste, looking first at the signature. It was from Sir Henry Lawrence's secretary and it ran: *"Sir Henry has asked me to tell you that your husband has been summoned to Lucknow by telegraph, in order to assume command of a volunteer cavalry force, now being raised for our defense. With this appointment goes the brevet rank of lieutenant-colonel . . ."* Emmy stifled a little cry, the words blurring before her eyes. Then she read the message aloud to Mohammed Bux, and turning the page, saw that Sir Henry himself had added a paragraph, *"In view of the alarming news from Meerut, my dear Mrs Sheridan, I thought you would like to know that my telegraph was despatched before the mutiny of the native regiments and that your husband is, in all probability, on his way back to us now. I learned of your continued presence in Cawnpore, quite by chance from Sir Hugh Wheeler, the reason for which is, I understand, cause for congratulation, and I offer you mine most warmly."*

The kind old man, Emmy thought, her throat stiff, the dear, kind old man! With all the anxieties he was facing in Lucknow, he had still found time to endeavour to set her fears at rest . . . she must write at once, to thank him and she must write also to Alex, so that he would find the letter waiting for him when he returned.

"Bring me pen and paper, Mohammed Bux," she requested eagerly. "I have letters to write."

"To the Cap—to the *Colonel* Sahib?" the bearer suggested and she saw her pleasure and relief reflected in his lined brown face.

"Yes, of course to the Colonel Sahib," Emmy assured him. "Oh, I'm so thankful to receive this news! I was so afraid, I . . ." Mohammed Bux brought her the writing materials she had asked for and she thanked him, smiling through her tears, as he laid a book on the bed, on which to rest the paper, and opened the lid of the inkwell for her. "I must tell him about his son. He will come here, won't he, to see his son? Even if . . ." fear returned, full force, to torment her. The country would be unsettled, she told herself uneasily. When the fact that Delhi was in the hands of the mutineers became generally known, the roads—even the Grand Trunk Road—would be dangerous and Alex might have to brave those dangers with only Partap Singh and his two *syces*. Oh, but surely they would have given him an escort, if he had left Meerut before the native regiments rose? If he had left on the 10th—last Sunday—he would be well on his way by now and, once he reached Lucknow and received her letter, he would come to her, of that she was certain. He would come to take her and the baby to Lucknow and . . . she bit her lip. She would have to be ready to go with him. The doctor had told her that she was weak and run-down; he had left instructions with Mrs Miller to make sure that she did not overexert herself and had told her that she would need at least three weeks complete bed-rest before she put a foot to the ground, but all that was changed now. She *must* be ready when he came.

"Mohammed Bux," she said, with sudden resolution. "Send *ayah* to me with my clothes. I will sit up to write these letters."

"*Atcha,* Memsahib," the bearer acknowledged dutifully. "But nurse-sahiba is saying that you must rest. I do not think—"

"Send *ayah*," Emmy ordered. "Now, at once. And do not tell the nurse-sahiba. When the Colonel Sahib comes, I must be ready to go with him."

She was dressed and seated at the table, busy with her letters, when Mrs Miller came in carrying the tiny, blanket-wrapped bundle that was her son. "Here he is, ma'am," the woman began. "Here's the poor wee soul to—" she broke off with an exclamation of dismay. "Mrs Sheridan, have you taken leave of your senses? Don't you remember what the doctor said? Back to bed with you at once, ma'am, if you please or I won't be held responsible for the consequences!"

Emmy rose, with dignity, to her feet. "I'm perfectly all right, Mrs Miller, I assure you. If you will give me William . . ." She held out her arms for the child and the midwife reluctantly acceded to her request.

"It's not right, ma'am," she objected. "Truly it's not, and the doctor will blame me for permitting it." She became conscious of the change in her patient's demeanor and her homely face relaxed its professional sternness. "You look as if you'd received good news, ma'am. Is it that you have heard from the captain? Is that why you've decided to defy the doctor and get up?"

Emmy cradled her little son in her arms. "I've heard *of* him, Mrs Martin, although not, alas, from him yet. But I've reason to hope that he's on his way to Lucknow and that he'll come here for me—for us—much, much sooner than I expected. So you see I had to defy the doctor, as you call it, because I must be fit and well and ready to go with him when he arrives, mustn't I?"

"Well, yes, ma'am, I suppose you must," Mrs Martin conceded. "And I'm glad, real glad that you've had good news. All the same, if you're really set on being fit and well by the time the captain gets here, I think you'd best let me tuck you up in bed again, just for another day or two. Give the—give Master William his feed and finish your letters and then back to bed . . . will you do that?

We can ask the doctor tomorrow, when he calls, if he'll let you sit up in a chair for a few hours."

Reluctantly, Emmy gave in. When William had been returned, protesting weakly, to his cot and the letters given to Mohammed Bux to take to the *dak* office, she allowed Mrs Miller to help her back into the hot confines of the big double bed once more and lay back wearily against the plumped-up pillows. She was neither fit nor well yet, she was forced to admit but, if she did a little more each day, no doubt her strength would return. Even if Alex reached Lucknow on Sunday, which was three days hence, he would have duties to perform and his new command to attend to, so that the earliest she could expect him would be Monday.

A week later, on May 21st, General Wheeler ordered all non-combatants in the city and garrison of Cawnpore to take refuge inside the entrenchment and to sleep there at night. There had been no news of Alex and Emmy obeyed the order unhappily, bringing the baby, her *ayah* and the bearer, Mohammed Bux, with her. Four guns—nine-pounders—had been mounted, manned by British gunners, and inside the entrenchment all was confusion as people of every colour, sect and profession came crowding in. Officers' ladies, noncommissioned officers' wives and their children found themselves sharing the cramped accommodation inside the hospital and barracks with civilians, Eurasians and Indian servants and, with each hour that passed, more arrived, some on foot, others in buggies, *palki-gharis* and carriages, to add to the confusion and the overcrowding. The heat was intense, the noise almost unbearable; children wailed and mothers complained and Emmy, appalled by the disorganization, was tempted to return to her own bungalow.

"If anything makes the sepoys rise," she said bitterly to the young wife of a Native Infantry officer, with whom she was sharing one of the rough wooden mess tables in the hospital building, "it will surely be this demonstration that we have been herded in here because we are afraid of them!"

The girl opposite agreed tearfully. "My husband," she confessed, "has been ordered to sleep in the lines with his men, as proof that we *do* trust them. And they say that General Wheeler and his wife are remaining in their house, with all the doors and windows open, as further proof . . . and the brigadier and Judge Wiggins are doing the same."

By evening, the confusion had sorted itself out a little and Emmy, having managed to get William off to sleep it last, left him in the *ayah*'s charge and went with some of the other officers' wives to listen to the band, which was playing in cantonments. Rumor was rife; tales of unrest amongst the sepoys and in the bazaar were bandied about, only to be contradicted or superceded by others still more alarming a few hours later.

The following day a detachment of about eighty men of the 32nd Queen's arrived from Lucknow, together with a squadron of irregular cavalry under Captain Fletcher Hayes; the former, Emmy learnt, sent by Sir Henry Lawrence to aid in their defense. Anxiously she questioned them, at the first opportunity and was distressed when Captain Hayes told her that, to the best of his knowledge, Alex had not yet arrived in Lucknow. The irregulars left next morning with orders to pacify a district said to be in a state of insurrection and not long afterwards came a report that the sowars had mutinied, killing their commander. The report added to the despair of those who must nightly leave their homes and endure the heat and discomfort of the entrenchment.

There were now eight 9-pounder guns mounted at various strategic points behind the mud parapet and it was known that, in response to General Wheeler's request for aid, the Nana Sahib had sent a force of his own troops, amounting to over four hundred men, both cavalry and infantry, with two guns, under the command of his personal bodyguard, Tantia Topi. To this force were entrusted the Magazine, with its store of light and heavy cannon, ammunition and small arms, and the Treasury, which contained £100,000 in coin and bullion.

General Wheeler appeared less harassed after their arrival; he went regularly among the sepoys, by whom he had always been held in high regard, visiting each post and picket and continuing to sleep in his undefended residence, determined to display no lack of trust for as long as this was humanly possible. To those who urged him to destroy at least the powder in the Magazine, he returned an adamant refusal—to do so would indicate a lack of the trust he was trying so desperately to maintain. The Nana, he insisted, had made himself personally responsible for both ordnance stores and treasure.

For Emmy, as for most of the other women, the days of waiting seemed endless and now, to add to her fears for her husband's safety, little William's condition had begun to give cause for anxiety. By day, when she was permitted to return to her own bungalow, she did what she could for the frail little boy, trusting no one but herself to care for him. Cool sponges, to reduce the temperature he seemed always to be running, had little effect; his tiny body was red and covered with the scarlet spots of prickly heat but neither the ointments the doctor prescribed nor gentle bathing with spirit wrought any improvement. He was able to take very little in the way of nourishment, lacking the strength to suckle and her attempts to feed him with a spoon ended in dismal failure, however patiently she tried. His fretful crying, which had worried her during the first two or three nights spent on the veranda of the hospital, had now ceased and he lay, in silent apathy, in his cot, emitting no sound, his breathing so light and shallow that at times she had to place her ear to his chest, to make sure that he was breathing at all.

Even Mrs Miller, who had returned to her own healthy and numerous brood, when consulted, could suggest no remedy for William's malaise.

"I'm afraid the poor wee soul is not long for this wicked world, ma'am," was her verdict, delivered sadly, and she added, in a wry attempt at consolation, "Although, for all we know, Mrs Sheridan, he may be better off than we are if the truth were told. If we're to be kept cooped up in that awful enclosure for very much longer it may be the death of us all . . . *and* without a shot being fired at us! My husband says that, if the sepoys had been going to rise against us, they'd have done so already and I believe him. *His* men have volunteered to go to Delhi to drive out the mutineers and they're to be publicly thanked by the general, I believe. Between ourselves, Mrs Sheridan, the ones *I* don't trust are those sly monkeys the Nana's sent to guard the Treasury. They're more likely to rob it than the sepoys are, I'm quite sure!"

There were others who shared this opinion, Emmy knew. Certainly the sepoys were showing no evidence of disaffection and the whole garrison had been heartened by the 53rd's offer to march on Delhi. She sighed, blinking back the tears, as she knelt beside William's cot. "Please God," she prayed silently, "oh, please God help us to get away from here before it's too late for this poor child. . . ." The baby, as if he had heard her, turned his big, lackluster eyes on her in mute and sightless appeal. She rose and went to the shuttered window, unable to bear the sight of his suffering.

But when the festival of Id, which marked the end of the Moslem period of fasting, had passed and there had still been no rising, the Cawnpore garrison began to cherish fresh hope. The first of the promised reinforcements from Calcutta arrived—a company of the 84th Queen's Regiment and a small advance party of the Madras European Fusiliers, a Company's regiment from Fort George. Sir Hugh Wheeler, assured that the main body of the Fusiliers was on its way to him, sent all the new arrivals and the eighty men of the 32nd Queen's on to Lucknow, and despatched bullock carts and elephants toward Allahabad to assist in establishing a convoy system which would hasten the arrival of the next batch of reinforcements.

Before leaving, the officer commanding the 84th passed on the welcome news that the governor-general, Lord Canning, was making strenuous efforts to obtain reserves of British troops. He had recalled regiments from Burma and Persia and sent fast ships to Singapore, with orders to intercept all troop convoys en route from the Cape to China and direct them, instead, to India, so that any sepoy rising might be dealt with swiftly and summarily.

Wheeler was jubilant when still more encouraging news came in, via the electric telegraph, from Lucknow. The commander-in-chief, General Anson, hampered by lack of transport, had nonetheless reached Kurnal, seventy miles from Delhi, with a force of six thousand. There, unhappily, he had been stricken with a fatal attack of cholera and General Barnard had been appointed commander-in-chief in his stead. Despite this unexpected change in command, the Kurnal Brigade, the general at their head, had already left for Delhi and, marching from Meerut to meet them, the 60th Rifles and two squadrons of the 6th Dragoons under Brigadier Archdale Wilson, were reported to have crossed the Hindan River, inflicting a heavy defeat on a force of mutineers which had come from Delhi to oppose their crossing.

That evening, as the news was circulated, the band in cantonments played to a relieved and greatly heartened audience. Emmy, valiantly throwing off her cares, joined in the joyful singing of patriotic songs and in the final, belated tribute to the queen, whose official birthday had not been celebrated in Cawnpore on May 24th. Alex, she told herself, had probably joined the Meerut force for its advance on the Hindan—the force which had struck the first blow against the Delhi mutineers. At least its victory was proof that the Meerut Brigade had not been annihilated, as those first terrible bazaar rumors had claimed. . . . She sang the last verse of the National Anthem with a fervent prayer of thankfulness in her heart and then turned, in surprise, when someone called her name from the darkness behind her.

"Yes," she began uncertainly, "Who . . . ? " The voice was familiar, a woman's voice that she knew well, and yet she could not place it until its owner stepped into the glow of the lamps ringing the bandstand.

"It is Mrs Sheridan, is it not?" The woman was tall and thin-featured, with greying hair and pale, almost lashless blue eyes, dressed in a crumpled, dust-covered gown. She looked tired and oddly defeated and Emmy, who had always gone in awe of her in the past, dreading her sharp tongue and arrogant manner, stared at her in puzzled recognition.

"Mrs Chalmers! But you . . . I thought you were in Adjodhabad, you and the colonel. And Lucy, too, of course. What are you doing here?"

"Lucy and I are fugitives," Mrs Chalmers answered tonelessly. "We had to make our escape from Adjodhabad during the night, with nothing but the clothes we stood up in, when my husband's sowars broke out in rebellion. They killed him, in front of my eyes, as he was coming to warn us . . . they shot him and when he fell from his horse they—they hacked him to pieces with their sabres. I saw them; there was nothing I could do." She shivered and Emmy, sick with pity, put an arm about her shoulders.

"Don't talk about it, Mrs Chalmers," she begged. "It will distress you. I'm so sorry, so terribly sorry. If there is anything I can do, I—"

But Mrs Chalmers seemed not to have heard her. She went on, in the same bleak, expressionless voice, "We hid in a cupboard in the bungalow, Lucy and I, and the sowars searched for us. But the servants—heaven praise their courage and loyalty—told them we weren't there and then they helped us to escape, when it was dark and the mutineers had gone. We were on foot and alone and then we—we met your husband, Mrs Sheridan, and he—"

"Alex . . . you met *Alex?* I don't understand—where, *how* did you meet him? He was in Meerut." Emmy's heart was thudding wildly, her throat so stiff she could scarcely get the words out.

"He came with a small party of horsemen—natives, some of them. Pensioners, I believe he said, and two young officers. They were on their way to Lucknow and they heard about the mutiny, so they came and rescued as many of us as they could." Mrs Chalmers mentioned several names, all of them familiar to Emmy. "The magistrate, Mr Lee, was in his courtroom. He had barricaded himself in, and the mutineers or the townspeople, I'm not sure who, set the courthouse on fire but they managed to get him out. And then they brought us here."

"Here! Oh, Mrs Chalmers, is he . . . is Alex here?" It was too much to hope for, Emmy told herself, but she clung to the hope until Mrs Chalmers shattered it with a headshake. "No, he went on to Lucknow. He said he was overdue there and left at once.

We were too exhausted to go on with him but the men went, four of my poor husband's officers and Mr Lee." She broke off, looking at Emmy in some dismay. "Does he not know that you are here? Oh, but of course," the tired eyes lit briefly, as memory returned, "he told me you had gone to Calcutta. With your sister and brother-in-law, I think he said, so that your baby could be born. But you, you're not—"

"My baby was born here," Emmy told her. "He was premature; that was why I could not go to Calcutta." The lamps round the bandstand were being extinguished and those who had been grouped about it during the concert started to move, slowly and with evident reluctance, towards the entrenchment. Recovering herself, Emmy took Mrs Chalmers' arm. "We sleep inside the entrenchment, Mrs Chalmers, in the hospital. If you come with me, I'll find you a place to sleep, you and Lucy, on the veranda where it's a little cooler than it is inside. I'm afraid it's very crowded but one gets used to that and we are permitted to go back to our own bungalows in the daytime. I'll be able to find clothes for you and give you meals tomorrow."

She looked about her, seeing only a pale, thin girl in a torn and bloodstained dress, who looked through her with the blank, unresponsive stare of a stranger. Lucy Chalmers was a girl of barely eighteen, she remembered, gay and lighthearted and an incorrigible flirt. Surely this could not be Lucy? She drew in her breath sharply. "Where *is* Lucy, Mrs Chalmers?"

"She is standing beside you," Mrs Chalmers said, without resentment. "You didn't recognize her but that's understandable. She's very shocked, you see, and it's made her ill. She was so fond of her dear father and seeing him meet his end as he did was too much for her. Come, Lucy, my dear child. Mrs Sheridan is going to show us where we can sleep."

The girl moved forward with listless obedience, but without a word and Emmy, hiding her feelings as well as she could, led them into the entrenchment, where she gave up her *charpoy* to them and herself lay down on the wooden floor at its foot.

That night the sowars of the 2nd Cavalry rose. Followed by the native artillery and by the 1st Native Infantry, they made for the Nawabganj, first moving their families from the lines into the city. The Nana's troops offered no opposition and the exultant sowars broke into the jail, set fire to the public buildings, rifled the Treasury and finally took possession of the Magazine.

The sound of musketry and the sight of smoke and flames rising from burning buildings warned those in the entrenchment what was afoot, long before the alarm gun was fired. Sleep was out of the question and the women waited, tense and apprehensive, but the two remaining sepoy regiments were reported to have paraded at 2 A.M., fully accoutered and obedient to the orders of their officers. Dismissed to cook breakfast, however, the 56th marched off to join the mutinous regiments in a frenzy of looting and incendiarism in the city, first escorting their officers to the entrenchment.

Only the 53rd stood firm, the men continuing to squat over their cooking pots in the lines. Their native officers were in the act of entering the entrenchment to protest their loyalty when, apparently fearing that they were about to attack, a gunner on the northeast side of the parapet opened fire, sending a hail of grape into their lines. The sepoys leapt to their feet in shocked surprise and all but eighty of them fled, in an angry, frightened mob to join their comrades in the city. The eighty who remained shouldered arms and, in an extraordinary display of loyalty, marched up to General Wheeler and pledged themselves to fight in his defense—a promise echoed by their officers, which all were heroically to keep. Deeply moved, the old general saluted them and directed them to take their places behind the parapet.

A day of terrible uncertainty followed, as officers from the mutinous regiments came hastening into the entrenchment, accompanied by a few civilians who had made perilous journeys from the city and the Nawabganj. Each brought his own alarming account of what was going on but no officer had, it seemed, suffered violence at the hands of his own men and several had been protected by their men from the mobs of released convicts and *budmashes* now roaming the streets. The sepoys were looting but they were not killing and the majority were engaged in removing guns and ammunition from the Magazine, as if in preparation for a march on Delhi.

The day wore on and no attack was launched against the British garrison; only the distant rumble of artillery and spasmodic volleys of musketry told them that the danger still existed and hopes rose when, by nightfall, the expected attack had still not taken place.

Next morning, to the heartfelt joy and relief of the defenders, came news that all three native regiments, with an artillery train, were six miles away, at Kalianpore, on the road to Delhi.

"That is what the Nana Sahib told me they would do," General Wheeler said, when making this announcement. "Now all we have to do is hold firm until reinforcements reach us from Calcutta . . . in a few days, perhaps, if all goes well."

Prayers of thanksgiving were offered by the chaplain, the Reverend Edward Moncrieff, and Emmy, kneeling in the crowded hospital with the rest, offered her own glad thanks for the knowledge, so providentially brought to her, that Alex was alive and well.

"I can bear anything," she confided to Mrs Chalmers when,

the short service over, she took William from his cot to change and feed him. "Anything, even another week in this place, so long as Alex is safe. Because I know that he will come to me, to us, whenever he can."

William emitted a plaintive little cry and she held him to her breast, rocking him gently to and fro until his cries were stilled.

Mrs Chalmers said nothing but there were tears in her eyes as she watched Emmy's patient attempts to suckle him which, as always, ended with the tiny mouth closing and the head, with its fringe of dark hair, falling back in futile exhaustion.

In the plundered Treasury building at the Nawabganj, the plump, sallow-faced Nana Sahib, Maharajah of Bithoor, received a deputation of native officers from the regiments which had mutinied. Flanked by his two brothers, Baba Rao and Bala Bhat, and with the handsome Azimullah Khan at his elbow, he listened, frowning, to the pleas of the officers.

"Lead us to Delhi, Maharajah," *Rissaldar-Major* Teeka Singh of the 2nd Cavalry entreated him. "My sowars are eager to go. They will obey you and fight for you. We have guns and tumbrils of ammunition, bullocks and elephants to pull them, and the infantry are with us. We await only a leader."

"It is a long way to Delhi," the Nana objected. "And," he glanced at Azimullah, "and I have work to do here."

"Protecting the British?" a *subadar* of the 1st Sepoys suggested insolently. "A kingdom awaits you if you join our cause, Maharajah . . . but death if you take the side of our enemies."

"What have I to do with the British?" the Rajah retorted angrily. "They have robbed me of my inheritance. I am altogether yours."

"Our hearts are set on going to Delhi, *huzoor,*" Teeka Singh put in swiftly, motioning the *subadar* to silence. "There our brothers have raised the banners of Islam. They have proclaimed Bahadur Shah emperor, they have restored him to the Peacock Throne of his Mogul ancestors. We would go to offer him our *tulwars,* to find glory in fighting for our Faith. If you will lead us, Highness, a share of the glory will be yours. Our Hindu comrades of the infantry fight with us in this war against the *feringhi.*"

"Highness," Azimullah whispered, bending close so that the officers could not overhear him. "What profit lies in the long march to Delhi to espouse the cause of the Mogul emperor? I speak contrary to the dictates of my Faith but I am thy loyal servant in all things, even in this. There is greater glory for thee here—a kingdom to be had for the taking! What can the British offer thee to equal that—a pension they have always refused to restore to thee in the past?"

"I have sworn to protect them," the Nana reminded him uneasily.

"Promises can be broken, Highness. And what can those poor fools in their Fort of Despair hope to do, if we advance against them with an army at our backs? And guns . . . we shall have heavy guns, they have only nine-pounders and a mud wall a child could leap over!"

Sweat broke out on the Nana's brow and he brushed it away with a long, bejewelled hand. "I made promises also to the sons of old Shah Bahadur. I told them that I would send soldiers to their aid."

"They will not want for soldiers," Azimullah assured him. "From all over Bengal, the sepoy regiments will rise and march to Delhi. Keep these men here, Highness, under thine own command. Let them fight to build a kingdom for thee here."

"How can I persuade them to remain?" the Nana asked, his

frown deepening. "If their hearts are set on marching to Delhi with the rest?"

"Offer them rewards, Highness," Azimullah retorted confidently. "Pay for their men, promotion for themselves. They will stay."

The native officers were growing impatient and the *subadar* who had spoken insolently a few minutes before was, the Nana saw, arguing with some of the others. He raised a hand for silence. "Do not go to Delhi," he urged them. "Rather stay here and your names will be greater. I will be your leader if you remain. Kill every Englishman in Cawnpore and I will give you each a gold medal and unlimited plunder and I will see to it that your men are paid as regularly as the Company paid them." He pointed to Teeka Singh. "You, I will make my general. And you," he waved the *subadar* of the 1st Infantry to approach him, "shall be colonel of your regiment. Well, how say you? Will you stay and fight here against the British?"

They hesitated, looking at each other, still undecided. Then Teeka Singh dropped on one knee and offered his hand.

"I will serve you, Maharajah. But come with us, I beg you, to Kalianpore to address our men."

The Nana Sahib rose. The die was cast, he told himself. "Fetch me my horse," he ordered. "We will ride to Kalianpore."

Alex was stiff and saddle-sore when he reached Lucknow just after daybreak on June 4th. He and his small party of volunteers had ridden hard since leaving Meerut eleven days before. The first part of their journey had been, perforce, slow and mainly across country, for the whole area between Delhi and Meerut was in a dangerously unsettled state and they had twice had brushes with parties of mutineers.

Once on the Grand Trunk Road, however, and heading south-east, they had encountered no hostility from the country people, although in the towns and out-stations, the atmosphere was full of brooding menace. The British officers, both military and civil, were remaining grimly at their posts, whilst admitting that they felt as if they were seated on a powder keg which might, at any moment, explode in their faces. Most had made arrangements for the protection of noncombatants, arming and provisioning such forts or other strongholds as were available; a few had sent their women and children to places of greater safety but in many cases, the women had refused to leave and Alex's offer of escort had also been rejected. In Fatehgarh, through which they had passed before making a detour to Adjodhabad, the garrison commander, Colonel Simpson, had stated quite frankly that he could not trust his native troops. He had made arrangements to transfer one hundred and seventy civil residents and their families to Cawnpore by boat, he said and, in view of the number involved, Alex had been relieved that his escort had not been required, for it had enabled him to answer the request for help which had come in from Adjodhabad while he was still talking to the colonel.

"Go if you can, Sheridan," Simpson had begged. "I've no troops I dare send—the Tenth are merely waiting for an excuse to rise. You've friends there, haven't you? Then off you go, my dear fellow, with my grateful blessing!"

They had gone, of course and, although they had been almost too late, they had at least arrived in time to bring out those who had survived the treacherous attack launched on them by Colonel Chalmers' Irregulars, including the colonel's widow and his shocked and pathetically altered daughter.

Making his report to Sir Henry Lawrence over breakfast in the fortified Residency, within an hour of his return, Alex did not

dwell on the mutiny at Adjodhabad. There were other, more pressing matters on which the Chief Commissioner of Oudh needed
up-to-date information, and it had taken him the best part of an
hour to give chapter and verse of the events which had led up
to the capture of Delhi by the Meerut mutineers.

Sir Henry, who looked more ill and exhausted than on the
last occasion that they had met, belied the frailty of his appearance by his energetic grasp of the situation and by the crisp,
incisive comments he made.

"If anyone but Hewitt had been in command at Meerut none
of this need have happened," he said finally, when Alex came to
the end of his recital. "Can you imagine Hearsey behaving as he
did, or Outram? Either of them would have sent a detachment
of British troops to Delhi on reading those letters you delivered
and without waiting for permission from a commander-in-chief
out of touch with the situation in the hills. No, no"—he brushed
aside Alex's apologies—"you did not fail, you did everything in
your power. I doubt whether I could have done more, if I'd had
those wings I wished for. With a man in Hewitt's state of senil-
ity, nothing could be done. And his brigadier, Wilson, doesn't
appear to have acted much better . . . although he's redeemed
himself a little, as the result of his successful action at the Hindan
crossing. You heard about that, I suppose?"

"No, sir." Alex shook his head. "I knew that General Wilson
was commanding a force from Meerut. Lieutenant Hodson rode
from Ambala with orders from the commander-in-chief the day I
left." His eyes gleamed, as Sir Henry told him of the repulse of the
mutineers at the bridge over the Hindan River. Colonel Jones and
Colonel Custance would, he thought, be able at last to hold their
heads high again, and so, too, would the gallant Rosser, whose two
squadrons of recruits had captured five of the mutineers' guns.

"We had a sharp little action of our own here, last Sunday evening," Sir Henry went on. "We had been warned that the 71st intended to rise then and I was at dinner in the Mariaon cantonment, with a wing of the 32nd Queen's standing by. I had just said to young Wilson, 'Your friends are late,' when we heard a great commotion and the sound of firing coming from the native lines. I ordered my horse to ride over to the gun battery and the *subadar* commanding my guard asked me if he should order his men to load. The guard was found by the Thirteenth and I wasn't quite sure of them but," he smiled, "I said, 'Yes, load and see that no harm is done here lest I come back and hang you all.' They all stood firm and three hundred men of the regiment ranged themselves alongside the Europeans, followed by small parties from both the 48th and the 71st. That's on the credit side. On the debit side, alas, we lost Brigadier Handscombe and the adjutant of the 71st, Lieutenant Grant, killed and several others wounded and, of course, there was the usual crop of burnt and pillaged buildings."

"But you repulsed the mutineers, sir?" Alex suggested. "Judging by the calm at present reigning."

"We drove them on to the race-course," Sir Henry confirmed grimly. "And at dawn on Monday morning we drove them off and pursued them for several miles, taking sixty prisoners, a number of whom we have hanged. I'd have preferred to disarm the whole regiment before they mutinied, of course, but," he gave vent to a weary sigh, "I was afraid, if I did so, that it would provoke other regiments to mutiny, particularly those in the out-stations. Now I have moved all the women and children into the Residency area and organized our defenses to the best of my ability. We're provisioned for a siege. If necessary for a lengthy one. We have guns and ammunition and some six hundred sepoys have remained loyal and, I believe, will continue to remain so. Although Martin Gubbins, as you might expect, wants me to disarm them, except for the Sikhs in the Machi Bhawan, whom he's prepared to trust." He gave details of the various defensive positions, to which Alex listened with interest and admiration. Sir Henry Lawrence might be a sick man but his farsighted planning would have done credit to any general. The Residency was not a fort but he had done his best, by means of a series of gun batteries and linked earthworks, to make it defensible and to provide adequate shelter for invalids and noncombatants, even converting a two-story banqueting hall into a hospital. Its weakness lay in the fact that, although he had demolished a number of surrounding houses, he had refused to destroy the mosques which also overlooked his position and, admitting wryly that his engineers had strongly advised him to do so, he said with a shrug, "I told them they must spare the holy places. Perhaps I was wrong."

Perhaps he was, Alex thought; only time would tell.

Sir Henry poured himself a second cup of coffee and took out his silver hunter. "I am required to attend a council of war in half an hour. We have to decide whether or not to abandon the Machi Bhawan and the Mariaon cantonment and concentrate solely on this area for our defense. I feel we should try to hold all three positions for as long as we can." He repeated his shrug, "But I must learn to listen to advice, I suppose. In the meantime I want to bring in as many women and children from the outstations as I can, and that requires cavalry. You have added a third to my total of volunteer cavalry, Alex, and I shall need you not only to command them but also to train civilian volunteers."

"I'm at your service, sir," Alex responded readily.

"Are your men fit to go out this evening, to bring in fugitives from Sitapur?"

"We need fresh horses, sir, but the men are fit."

"I can give you horses. The trained men are what I lack. But," Sir Henry smiled, setting down his cup, "you, I trust, will rectify that. Take some of the volunteers with you." He gave his instructions and, taking this as his dismissal, Alex rose. Sir Henry's smile widened.

"It is good to have you here, Alex. Tell me, did you bring your wife and son from Cawnpore with you, after you left the unfortunate Mrs Chalmers there?"

"My wife, sir?" Alex stared at him in shocked incredulity. "My wife and *son*? But Emmy was to go to Calcutta with her sister! I had no idea, I . . ." he choked. His son, Emmy's son and his! Oh, dear God! And Emmy still in Cawnpore—surely that wasn't possible? Surely . . .

"My poor boy, how appallingly remiss of me to make no mention of this before," Sir Henry apologized, in genuine distress. "I was so certain that you knew! You came here from Cawnpore, so I took it for granted that you had seen your wife and, indeed, that you had brought her and the child with you. That was why I asked, so that accommodation could be arranged and . . . your son was born prematurely, Alex. That was why your Emmy was unable to make the journey to Calcutta. I had a letter from her about ten days ago. I have it somewhere. There is also one for you, which George Cooper was keeping for you, I believe." He looked at Alex's stricken face and laid a hand pityingly on his shoulder.

"I see, sir. Thank you, I—"

"She will be safe enough in Cawnpore, you know," Sir Henry went on. "Sir Hugh Wheeler has all noncombatants within the shelter of his entrenchments and he wrote me, only yesterday, to say that he believed the worst to be over. He had feared that his native troops would mutiny during Id but they did not. Indeed, he received the first reinforcements from Calcutta—a hundred and twenty men of the 84th Queen's and the Madras Fusiliers— and he sent them on to me here, to assist my defense, having been assured that the remainder of the Fusiliers, under their colonel, were on their way to him."

Alex listened in dazed silence. Sir Henry talked on reassuringly and, sending a servant for George Cooper, was able to give him Emmy's letter, as well as the one she had sent, by the same mail, to himself.

"What of the Nana Sahib, sir?" Alex asked, recovering himself. "Does General Wheeler continue to repose complete trust in him?"

Sir Henry sighed. "Yes, I fear he does. But again, my dear boy, I seem to have been proved wrong. Sir Hugh informed me that the Nana had responded at once to his request for aid, ten or eleven days ago. He sent several hundred of his own troops and has given a promise that the lives of all British subjects will be protected, even if the Cawnpore regiments do rise. You need not be unduly anxious."

"No, sir, of course not." Alex made to take his leave, Emmy's unopened letter in his hand. Sir Henry looked white with strain, he realized with compunction; he had no right to add to the burden of responsibility resting on those thin, bowed shoulders. The fault was his own; he should have waited, made enquiries last night, he reproached himself, instead of dashing on so precipitately to Lucknow. Fool that he was, he had never doubted that Emmy was in Calcutta. . . . He came to attention. "Forgive me for having taken up your time with my personal concerns, sir. I'll carry out your instructions regarding the Sitapur people." He could feel his control slipping. "Will that be all, sir?"

"*Is* it all, Alex?" Sir Henry reproved him gently.

Alex reddened under his grave-eyed scrutiny. "I hold my command under your orders, sir, and I am not asking for favours but I . . . I'd be grateful, should an opportunity arise for me to bring my wife and son here from Cawnpore, if I might be permitted to take it."

"The first opportunity that arises shall be afforded to you," Lawrence assured him, smiling now. "You have my word on that."

The opportunity came with unexpected suddenness during the afternoon. Alex was dressing, after a snatched sleep, when George Cooper sought him out.

"Colonel Sheridan, a courier has just come in from Cawnpore," the secretary told him, his voice strained. "The whole brigade has mutinied, it seems—with the intention, according to General Wheeler's intelligence, of marching to Delhi . . . although there's no confirmation of this as yet. The courier reports that both the Magazine and the Treasury are in their hands but so far there has been no attack on the entrenchment and no officers of native regiments have been harmed by their men. They've indulged in the usual looting and incendiarism, and cut the telegraph wires, but that's all."

"And the Nana's troops?" Alex asked grimly.

"The courier did not know. He thought they were standing firm." Cooper sighed. "You can probably guess why I've come, Colonel. Sir Henry wishes you to take an urgent message to General Wheeler, if you are willing to make the attempt to get through. He instructed me to tell you that he personally fears you may encounter some difficulty, unless the mutineers *have* left for Delhi."

"I have a powerful incentive, Mr Cooper. My wife and child are in Cawnpore." Alex checked the Adams carefully and then slid it into his belt. "Tell Sir Henry, if you please, that I will gladly make the attempt to deliver his message to General Wheeler."

The secretary looked relieved. "Good. Then I'm instructed to tell you that you should take the minimum escort you deem necessary and that you should hand over responsibility for the Sitapur party to your second-in-command. He's capable, isn't he?"

"Perfectly," Alex assured him. "Is my despatch ready?"

"It will be by the time you've mounted your escort. I'll bring it to you myself." The secretary eyed him unsmilingly. "It consists of two lines, written in Greek, so if you should—that is, you need not worry unduly should it fall into the wrong hands. And I fear it will disappoint General Wheeler, because it informs him that the reinforcements he is expecting are held up in Benares by an outbreak of mutiny there. The message reached Sir Henry from Calcutta only an hour ago." George Cooper hesitated and then held out his hand. "Good luck, Colonel Sheridan. I trust we shall see you back here, with your family, very soon."

Alex accepted the proffered hand. Less than half an hour later, with Ghulam Rasul and Partap Singh riding behind him, he set his face in the direction of Cawnpore and scarcely drew rein until the red glow of burning buildings, shining through the darkness, told him that he had reached his destination.

The burning buildings were civil and cantonment bungalows, he saw, as he approached cautiously, and there were a number of other fires in the native lines—the pattern of Meerut repeated, he reflected bitterly. Although the fires were dying down and he could hear no sound of shooting, which suggested that the mutineers had left on their way to Delhi. There was a guard of the Nana's troops posted in front of the Bridge of Boats and, biding his escort wait under cover, Alex rode over to them alone, to find a score of men with muskets lining the bank.

"Halt!" their commander shouted. "Who comes?"

Alex gave his name. "I have business with General Wheeler," he said crisply, deciding to treat them as friendly troops, despite the fact that he could see their fingers were on the triggers of the muskets levelled at him.

"No one enters," the guard commander returned, his tone arrogant. He moved closer, covered by the muskets of his men, but he had taken only a half-dozen paces when he was thrust aside by a tall, white-robed figure in a green turban, whose signal to the guard to lower their muskets was obeyed instantly.

"So we meet again, Sheridan Sahib!" the newcomer observed, with apparent pleasure, and Alex found himself looking into the dark, enigmatically smiling face of the Moulvi of Fyzabad. "Is it your wish to return to Cawnpore?"

"I have said so, Moulvi Sahib." Taken momentarily by surprise at the Moulvi's unexpected appearance, Alex recovered himself quickly and his tone was crisp and authoritative. "Would you seek to prevent me?"

Ahmad Ullah shook his head. "Nay, not I, Sahib," he answered, with mock humility. "Although I cannot promise that you will find it so easy to leave, should you desire to, but . . ." He called sharply to the guards, "Permit this Sahib to pass and his escort with him!" and stood aside, still smiling, to wave Alex and his two men on their way.

They entered the entrenchment a little later, to find the garrison at prayer and, when the service was over, Alex delivered his cryptic message to General Wheeler and went in search of Emmy. She heard his voice asking for her and came running joyfully to meet him, the baby in her arms.

"Oh, Alex!" She looked up at him, her eyes filled with tears and the lips she raised to his curving into a tremulous smile. "You came! I . . . I wanted you so much and you came. I . . . I had begun to fear that it was too late, I . . ." she choked on a sob. "But you are here! Oh, thank God, you are here!"

"I've come to take you to Lucknow," Alex said, shaken by the depths of his own emotion. He held her to him, ignoring the burden she carried in his pleasure and relief at seeing her again. Then, remembering, he gently drew back the shawl in which the baby was wrapped and asked, controlling his voice with difficulty, "Is this our son, Emmy? What have you called him?"

"William Alexander," Emmy answered proudly. "William, after William Beatson. I thought you would want that."

"Yes," Alex confirmed, his throat stiff as he studied the tiny, wizened face of his son. "Yes, indeed, darling, I—" he took a deep, uneven breath, shocked by the small creature's frailty, yet anxious not to upset his wife by uttering any hint of criticism. "He's so small, I can't believe he's real."

"He was premature," Emmy reminded him. She bit her lip and then unhappily voiced the fear that was now uppermost in her mind. "Alex, I do not think he could stand the journey to Lucknow—not yet, not till he is stronger. Will you . . . *must* you go back?"

Alex's hesitation was brief. It was his duty to go back, he knew. He would lose his command if he did not. But he knew also, with clear, cold certainty, that he could not again leave the two people who meant more to him than life itself, whatever the cost might be. He had little faith in General Wheeler's mud-walled and already overcrowded entrenchment, still less in the Nana Sahib's professions of friendship, and yet . . . he smothered a sigh. He could resign his command. Partap Singh could take a message to Sir Henry, explaining the reason for his absence which, God willing, need only be temporary. He looked down into Emmy's pale, anxious face and smilingly shook his head.

"No," be answered firmly, his mind made up. "My place is with you, my love—with you and William, now and always. We can stay here until it's possible to take the child with us to Lucknow. We'll be together, Emmy, until this is over."

"That's all I've ever wanted, Alex," Emmy told him. Her eyes were sparkling now, bright with renewed hope, the tears gone. "To be with you, for as long as we both shall live. I can bear anything with you beside me, darling—even this place." She stood on tiptoe to kiss his check and Alex saw that she was smiling.

GLOSSARY OF INDIAN TERMS

Achkan: knee-length tunic

Aista: slow

A-jao: go on

Ayah: female servant, children's nurse

Baksheesh: tip (cash)

Bazaar: market

Bhisti: water-carrier

Brahmin: highest Hindu caste

Budmash: rogue, ruffian

Bunnia: merchant, grain-dealer, moneylender

Cantonment: European residences, usually bungalows

Chappatti: unleavened cake of wheat flour

Charpoy: string bed

Chit/Chitti: note or letter

Chokra: young boy

Chowkidar: nightwatchman

Chuddar: cloak

Dacoit: robber.

Daffadar (cavalry): sergeant

Dak/Dawk: post

Deen: faith

Doolie: covered litter

Durbar: reception, audience

Fakir: Hindu holy man, usually itinerant

Feringhi: foreigner

Gharry/Gharri: cart or carriage

Ghaut: river bank, edge. Also landing place, quay

Ghee: clarified butter

Ghusl-khana: bathroom

Goojur: inhabitant of so-called Goojur villages, robbers and
    thieves

Han: Yes

Havildar (infantry): Sergeant

Huhm/Hukum: order

Huzoor: Lord (literally "presence")

Id: end of Ramadan

Jeldi: hurry

Jemadar: native officer

Ji-han: yes

Khansama: cook

Khitmatgar: butler, table servant.

Khuda hafiz: Go with God

Kotwal: police

Lal-kote: British soldier (literally "red coat")

Lines: long row of huts, thatched and built of mud, for
    accommodation of native troops

Maidan: square, parade ground

Mali: gardener

Moulvi: Moslem teacher

Nahin: no

Paltan: Regiment

Pandy/Pandies: Mutineer(s)

Pie/Pice (plural): lowest coin in Indian currency

Poorbeah: inhabitant of Oudh

Punkah: ceiling fan, pulled from outside room by coolie, who
    had cord attached to his foot

Raj: rule

Ramadan: Moslem holy month marked by day-time fasting

Rissala: cavalry

Rissaldar: cavalry Sergeant-Major (*Rissaldar-Major:* R.S.M.)

Ryot: peasant cultivator, smallholder

Sepoy: infantry soldier

Sahib-log: European people

Sowar: cavalry trooper

Subadar: infantry Sergeant-Major (*Subadar-Major:* S.M.)

Syce: groom

Talukdar: landowner

Thug/Thuggee: Highway robber, follower of the killer cult of
    Hindu goddess Kali

Tiffin: lunch

Tulwar: sword or sabre

Zamindar: peasant landowner

HISTORICAL NOTES
➤➤➤ • ❈❈❈

IN HIS admirably researched book, *The Indian Mutiny in Perspective* (Bell, 1931) Lieutenant General Sir George MacMunn stated that: "The Indian Mutiny, even when it grew to rebellion, was not a war between British and Indian. Tens of thousands of Indian soldiers, from all parts of India, took part in its repression."

It was, in fact, the mutiny of a single Presidency Army——the Sepoy Army of Bengal—which broke out at Meerut on 10 May 1857 and brought to an end the long rule of the Honourable East India Company. On 1 November 1858, when all but the last smouldering embers of revolt had been extinguished, the government of British India was assumed by the Crown. An amnesty was granted to all who had been in rebellion against the Company "except those who have been or shall be convicted of having directly taken part in the murder of British subjects. With regard to such, the demands of justice forbid the exercise of mercy." The instigators of revolt were promised their lives but warned that they would not escape punishment and the amnesty was extended only until 1 January 1859.

In order to fully understand what caused a hitherto loyal and disciplined army of 150,000 men to break out in open mutiny, it is necessary to go back in history very briefly to the beginnings and subsequent expansion of the East India Company.

It was founded in the year 1600 by a group of merchant adventurers, to whom Queen Elizabeth I granted a fifteen-year charter (later renewed by James I) "for the purpose of trading into the East Indies." Holding an initial capital of £30,000, sub-scribed in shares, the aim of the governor and 24 directors was simply to reap a profit for themselves and their shareholders. They had no wish to acquire territory, to exercise military power or to govern an alien race; still less had they any thought of founding an empire.

Circumstances, however, compelled John Company*—as it later became known—to recruit and train a mercenary native army commanded by British officers. This was intended for the defense of its factories and agents and the protection of its trad-ing concessions, which were in constant danger from the treachery of native rulers and the rival territorial claims of the French who, all too frequently, were instigators of the treachery. The factories became forts and Robert Clive's victory over Surajah Dowla† at the Battle of Plassey, on 23 June 1757, established the Company as a military power and dictated its future policy. Under Clive's governorship, annual profits rose to £1,250,000, with dividends at 12 per cent.

As profits increased and more territory was acquired, by both conquest and treaty, the administration of British India became, in the view of the British Parliament, more than a commercial trading establishment could be permitted to undertake. The India Bill was introduced in 1794 in order to provide for a form of double government. To the Honourable Company's two Courts of Directors and Proprietors was added a Board of Control, presided over by a cabinet minister, its members chosen by the

---

*A humorous nickname, like that given to the Dutch East India Com-pany—*Jan Kompanie.*

†Perpetrator of the Black Hole of Calcutta outrage, in which 146 British captives were imprisoned in an eighteen-foot-square strong-room and only 23 survived.

British government but paid by the Company and with power to overrule the Directors on matters of political policy. These Courts were resident in London and represented in India by a governor-general, also appointed by Parliament, so that in effect the Company governed as an agent of the Crown.

British regiments were sent to serve with the Company's troops and fought side by side with them in the numerous Indian wars in which they were almost continuously engaged during the first half of the nineteenth century. The Company possessed three Presidency Armies, those of Bengal, Madras and Bombay, each under its own commander-in-chief. Apart from a limited number of European regiments raised by the Company for service in India and a few battalions of artillery, the three Presidency Armies were composed entirely of native troops, under the command of British officers, who were trained and commissioned by the Company and from whose ranks political officers were selected for civil administrative duties.

Known to the Indians themselves as *Shaitan ka hawa*—The Devil's Wind—the mutiny of the Bengal army was confined to that army. The mutineers received encouragement and active aid from a few chiefs and princes, who were driven to rebellion by a very real sense of grievance as a result of the Company's policy of annexing ("annexation by right of lapse") native states to which there was no direct heir. By means of this policy, implemented by Lord Dalhousie, governor-general from 1848 to 1856, 250,000 square miles were added to British Indian territory so that, by 1857, the Company held sway over some 838,000 square miles. Under the despotic Dalhousie, 21,000 plots of land, to which their owners could not prove documentary right of tenure, were confiscated; the States of Satara, Nagpur and Jhansi seized and the Punjab and Scinde conquered by force of arms. Finally the ancient kingdom of Oudh—from which the bulk of the sepoys of the Bengal army were recruited—was also annexed.

Added to the resentment, by princes and peasants, of the arbitrary seizure of their land, the root cause of the Mutiny was the fear—which rapidly became widespread among the sepoys—that their British commanders, on instructions from the Company, had embarked on a deliberate campaign aimed at destroying their caste system, with the ultimate intention of compelling the entire army to embrace the Christian religion. The issue of supposedly tainted cartridges, and the sepoys' refusal to accept them, was the excuse for the outbreak which, by the time Lord Canning succeeded Dalhousie as governor-general, had become inevitable.

And the time was well chosen. In 1857 Britain was still recovering from the ravages of the Crimean War, was fighting in China, and had recently been fighting in Burma and Persia. As a result, India had been drained of white troops, the British numbering only 40,000—exclusive of some 5,000 British officers of native regiments—while the sepoys in the three Presidency Armies numbered 311,000, with the bulk of the artillery in their hands. The territory for which the Bengal army was responsible included all northern India, from Calcutta to the Afghan frontier and the Punjab.

The Punjab had only lately been subdued and there was a constant threat of border raids by the Afghan tribes, so that most of the available British regiments* were stationed at these danger points and on the Burmese frontier, with 10,000 British and Indian troops in the Punjab alone. The 53rd Queen's Regiment of Foot was at Calcutta, the 10th at Dinapur—400 miles up the

---

* Also called HM's or Queen's regiments.

River Ganges—the 32nd Foot was at Lucknow and a newly raised regiment, the Company's 3rd Bengal Fusiliers, at Agra. Thirty-eight miles away there was a strong European garrison, consisting of the 60th Rifles—1,000 men—600 troopers of the 6th Dragoons, a troop of horse artillery, and details of various other regiments—2,200 men in all. Stationed with them were three native regiments, the 3rd Light Cavalry and the 11th and 20th Bengal Native Infantry, under the command of 75-year-old Major-General William Hewitt, whose division included Delhi.

On the face of it, Meerut seemed the most unlikely station in all India to become the scene of a revolt by native troops, and the outbreak, when it came, took everyone—not least the commanding general and his brigadier—so completely by surprise that they did virtually nothing to put it down, with the result that Delhi was lost.

There had, of course, been warnings but for the most part, these were ignored or treated with scorn and disbelief. The officers of the Bengal native regiments continued, until the last, to place the most implicit trust in the loyalty of the sepoys they commanded. But Sir Henry Lawrence, who was later to defend Lucknow against the insurgents, writing in the *Calcutta Review* in 1843, had pointed out how easily a hostile force could seize Delhi, adding: "And does any sane man doubt that 24 hours would swell the hundreds of rebels into thousands, and in a week every ploughshare in Delhi would be turned into a sword? . . ." These words were to prove prophetic, fourteen years afterwards, when Delhi and the last of the Moguls—82-year-old Shah Bahadur—became the focal point of the Great Mutiny.

The first tangible warning came early in 1857, with the incident of the greased cartridges. The new Enfield rifle, which had proved its superiority in the Crimea, was ordered to be issued to the army in place of the out-dated Brown Bess musket. Both were muzzle-loaders, but the cartridge of the new weapon included a greased patch at the top which—like the earlier, ungreased type—had to be torn off with the teeth. The greased patch was used to assist in ramming home the bullet, which was a tight fit in the rifle barrel. It had apparently not occurred to the Ordnance Committee in England or, indeed, to anyone in India, that the composition of the greased patch and the instruction to bite through it might offend against the religious scruples of high caste Hindu sepoys, of whom there were a great many in the Bengal army.

At the arsenal at Dum Dum, near Calcutta, a lascar of humble caste was abused by a Brahmin sepoy of the 34th Native Infantry. The man retaliated with the claim that the new Enfield cartridges were smeared with the fat of the cow (sacred to Hindus) and of the pig (considered unclean by Muslims). Biting it, the lascar jeered, would destroy the caste of the Hindu and the ceremonial purity of the Muslim. The story spread like wildfire throughout the native regiments. The men were assured that they could grease the cartridges with their own *ghee,* or tear them by hand, but the paper in which they were wrapped had a suspiciously greasy appearance and the sepoys refused to accept them.

Already fearful that it was the intention of their British rulers to destroy the caste system in order that the army might be unwillingly converted to Christianity, some sepoys who had been detailed for service in Burma, refused to go. To "cross salt water"— that is to say, to travel by sea—also entailed loss of caste, and a new form of the military oath, which made the sepoy liable for service overseas, added fuel to the flames of discontent and suspicion.

Religious leaders of both the Hindu and the Muslim faiths, conscious that their own power was waning under British rule, fanned the flames assiduously. Fakirs and holy men traveled from garrison to garrison; an ancient prophecy was revived and whispered among them. The Battle of Plassey had been fought in 1757 and John Company, the prediction ran, would last for exactly a hundred years, so that this year would see its fall. Small, unleavened cakes of wholemeal flour, called *chappaties,* were distributed throughout the country, from village to village with the cryptic message, "From the North to the South and from the East to the West," and each headman was told to keep two and make six more *chappaties,* which were to be sent on with the same message. Others were sent on with the still more cryptic message *"Sub lal hojaega."* ("Everything will become red"). It was predicted that a comet would be seen in the eastern sky when the moment for action had come.

The first serious sign of trouble came on February 24th, when the 19th Bengal Infantry, stationed at Berhampur, just over one hundred miles from Calcutta, refused an order to exercise with blank cartridges or to accept cartridges of the type they had used with the old Brown Bess musket for years. An ugly situation was averted by the commanding officer, Colonel Mitchell, and the men returned to duty, but Lord Canning, having sent for the 84th Queen's Regiment from Rangoon, decided to take the drastic step of disbanding the mutinous 19th, who were ordered to march to Barrackpore (near Calcutta) to hear their sentence.

Before they arrived, however, a still graver incident took place at Barrackpore itself, where the garrison consisted of the 34th, 43rd, and 70th Native Infantry and the 2nd Bengal Grenadiers, the only British regiment on the station being the 53rd Queen's, which had a wing at Dum Dum. On March 29th, in front of the quarter-guard of the 34th—a regiment composed mainly of high caste Brahmins—one of its sepoys, by name Mangal Pandy, armed with a loaded musket and drunk with *bhang* (hashish) and religious fervor, called upon his comrades to mutiny, declaring that he would shoot the first Englishman he came across.

The adjutant, Lieutenant Baugh, summoned by a runner, hastily donned his uniform, loaded his pistol and, accompanied by the British sergeant-major, rode at once to the quarter-guard. Mangal Pandy fired at him, bringing his horse down. Baugh scrambled up and advanced on the sepoy, pistol in hand, as the man drew his *tulwar,* but his shot missed and Pandy savagely cut him down. Sergeant-Major Hewson, stout and middle-aged, ran up breathlessly, calling on the guard—a *jemadar* (native officer) and twenty men—to place the mutineer under arrest before he murdered the unfortunate Baugh. The *jemadar* forbade the guard to move and Hewson attempted to seize Pandy unaided, only to be set on in his turn and fall to his knees under a rain of blows from the *tulwar.* His life and that of the adjutant were saved by the courageous intervention of the latter's Muslim orderly, Sheikh Pultoo, who held off the blood-crazed Pandy until both had dragged themselves to safety.

By this time most of the regiment had assembled in a state of considerable excitement and Mangal Pandy reloaded his musket, and marched up and down, reviling his comrades for their failure to join him to fight for their faith. The situation was getting out of hand when the district commander, Major-General Sir John Hearsey, rode on to the parade ground, flanked by his two sons, having been informed by a panic-stricken messenger that the whole regiment had mutinied. He rode straight for the quarter-guard and, when someone shouted a warning that Pandy's musket was loaded, was heard to retort contemptuously, "Damn his musket!"

Hearsey was seventy years old but, as a young officer, he had won a reputation for courage which did not desert him now. Aware that the eyes of close to a thousand wildly excited sepoys were on him and that this was a battle for their allegiance, he did not hesitate. They were wavering and the old man knew that if he faltered, they would break and it would be beyond the power of anyone on the parade ground to control them. He said urgently to his elder son, "If I fall, John, rush in and put him to death," and then, his pistol leveled at the *jemadar,* he called on the guard to do their duty or take the consequences.

Such was the respect they had for the fine old soldier that they obeyed him instantly, falling in behind him in response to his harsh command. The general, undeterred by his son's anxious cry, "Father, he's taking aim at you!" advanced on Mangal Pandy and, faced by the stern old veteran, the sepoy's nerve broke. He turned his musket on himself, a bare toe feeling for the trigger and, wounded, was dragged away by the now obedient guard. General Hearsey promoted the loyal Moslem orderly to *havildar* (sergeant) on the spot. Next day, the 19th Native Infantry reported, and the 84th Queen's and a wing of the 53rd marched in. The 19th were disbanded, in a curiously moving ceremony, in which Hearsey thanked them for their previous loyal service and the disgraced regiment cheered him as he rode off the parade ground.

A week later, Mangal Pandy and the *jemadar* commanding the guard were tried by court martial and both were sentenced to death. Pandy's sentence was carried out within two days. He was hanged in the presence of his regiment, and the *jemadar*—whose name, by coincidence, was also Pandy—suffered a similar fate on April 21st, soon after which the 34th were also disbanded. Both men achieved ironic fame, for to the British in India the word "Pandy" came to symbolize the Mutiny and henceforth all mutineers were referred to as "Pandies." They began what was to be a tragic and bloody chapter in British history, in which no quarter was given by either side and in which many innocents were to lose their lives in horrifying fashion, at the hands of bitter, vengeful men, both Indian and British.

The Mutiny fulfilled the prophecy, for it brought about the fall of the powerful John Company, but British India was saved by the fidelity of the Sikh chiefs in the Punjab, by those sepoys— even in the Bengal army—who remained true and fought against the mutineers, and by the fact that very few of India's 180,000,000 people gave active support to the uprising. Had they, in fact, done so, not a European would have remained alive.

Perhaps the greatest tragedy of the Sepoy Mutiny was that it could, so easily, have been averted. The sepoys' fears were very real but no official attempt was made to set them at rest and neither was justice done to those whom Lord Dalhousie had dispossessed. Even at the eleventh hour in Meerut, a Hearsey in the place of the inept Hewitt might well have prevented disaster . . . but so often it is by human error that history is made.